MADDOX

LANTERN BEACH BLACKOUT: DANGER RISING,
BOOK 3

CHRISTY BARRITT

CHAPTER
ONE

TARYN PARSONS GLANCED behind her at the winding maze of greenery. Her entire body tensed as she waited for another telltale sign.

Who was in here with her?

She'd seen the shadow moving. Had heard something jangling.

What had started as a peaceful walk through the labyrinth located behind her boss's house had turned into panic. But maybe—just maybe—she was misunderstanding something.

She paused and glanced behind her. "Hello?"

Again, no answer.

The manicured boxwood hedges were too high to see over, reaching at least a foot above her head.

She could walk toward the sound of the clinking,

but then she feared she'd be walking straight toward trouble.

If the shadow belonged to another of Mr. Whitlock's employees, they would have responded to her call.

Given everything that had happened around here lately, Taryn couldn't take any chances. She had to assume danger was near.

Her lungs tightened.

The clanking sounded again.

Coming her way.

Moving more quickly.

Her heart pounded harder.

For the past two weeks, she'd suspected something was awry at Mr. Whitlock's estate. She'd felt the impending sense of danger in the air. Feared that someone would not only get hurt—but that someone could die.

Someone like Mr. Whitlock.

Or what if *she* was the target? What if someone needed to get her out of the way in order to take advantage of the dying man?

As she heard the jangle again, Taryn took off into a run.

She knew her way around the half-acre labyrinth. But stress scrambled her thoughts, made everything feel unclear.

Made her second-guess herself.

The last thing she wanted was to run into a dead end. Several were in the elaborate, twisting maze.

If she took a wrong turn, she'd be trapped. The branches surrounding her were so tightly woven they might as well be brick walls. Bursting through them to escape wasn't an option.

Taryn continued to push herself down the pathway. Her muscles burned as adrenaline kicked in, propelling her to move faster than she thought was possible.

The steps behind her quickened also.

How had this once peaceful estate transformed into a nightmare?

And who would be chasing her right now? Why?

Taryn was simply a caregiver for a dying old man —a dying old man who happened to be one of the richest men in the country.

Did someone think that getting to her might somehow influence what happened to Mr. Whitlock's money after he passed?

Taryn would have to think about those things later.

Right now, she dodged corners. Headed down long, arched stretches. Followed the curves of the hedges.

The jangling footsteps following her remained steady, fast.

Persistent.

She pushed herself even harder. As her lungs tightened, she tried to force air into her windpipe. But the tension gripping her chest made the task feel impossible.

As Taryn glanced behind her again her foot hit something.

She stumbled, face-planting on the grass. Her palms hit the ground, and any remaining air left her lungs.

What . . . ?

She looked at the ground around her.

A large rock had been placed in the center of the walkway.

A large *painted* rock.

Had this been here before?

She didn't think so.

Leroy Matthews, the gardener, was usually so meticulous about this space.

Wincing, Taryn pulled herself back to her feet. She'd lost time, but otherwise she was okay.

She quickly glanced behind her again, expecting to see a figure.

There was no one.

Maybe the person behind her had run into a dead end.

She hoped.

The chain clanked again.

"Who's there?" she asked.

She had to believe if someone legitimate was following her that they'd call out. Instead, her cry went unanswered.

Whoever was here didn't want her to know who they were.

This person wanted her to feel fear.

It was working.

Picking up speed, Taryn rounded another corner. An exit waited for her straight ahead.

She would run from this place, dart into the house, and lock the doors.

Then she'd call 911. Or maybe she would find Leroy and have him look for this person.

Taryn didn't know.

All she knew was she wanted this to be over.

She kept her focus on the exit just ahead.

As she neared the break in the hedges, her shoulders softened with relief—but only for a moment.

She wasn't out of danger yet.

One last burst of energy shot through her as she sprinted toward safety.

Just as she emerged from the maze, she collided into a brick wall.

At least, she collided into something that *felt* like a brick wall.

As she glanced up, the blood drained from her face.

A man with brooding, narrowed eyes and an imposing build had planted himself in front of her.

As he stared at her, danger cracked through the air.

How had her pursuer gotten in front of her?

Had he found one of the other exits and cut her off?

Suddenly, Taryn's life flashed before her eyes.

Was this the moment she was going to die?

Maddox King stared at the woman in front of him.

Taryn Parsons.

Five foot four. Dark, wavy hair to her shoulders. Slim build.

Frightened blue eyes.

Frightened?

Why had the woman been running as if chased by fire? From his observation, she was the only one out here.

She stumbled back, something close to the start of a scream escaping her lips. The noise morphed into a cry, almost as if her vocal cords weren't working. As she wobbled unsteadily, Maddox grabbed her arm before she hit the ground.

"Whoa . . ." he muttered.

At his touch, the woman sprang to life. Her fists pounded his chest. Her eyes lit with fear.

"Let go of me!" she yelled through clenched teeth. "You're not going to get away with this!"

Maddox raised his hands in the air and stepped back, unsure how he'd given her such a wrong impression. But he needed to nip this misunderstanding in the bud before it turned any uglier.

"Whoa," he murmured again. "It's okay."

Taryn backed up and silently stared at him. Her breaths were raspy, and perspiration scattered over her skin. Quickly, she glanced behind her and rubbed her arms as a tremble overtook her.

Something was clearly wrong.

"I'm not here to hurt you," Maddox continued, making sure to keep his voice soft. "The woman who answered the door sent me out here to find you."

Taryn blinked as if confused.

Then she glanced behind her again.

He followed her gaze but saw only the hedged corridors of the labyrinth.

"What's going on?" Maddox's years of training and experience wanted to kick in. He wanted to take charge. To figure out what was wrong.

But he needed to be subtle, to not show his hand too quickly.

He was here trying to get a job as a maintenance worker.

On paper that was true, at least.

In reality, he was a former Navy SEAL sent here to find answers. If his mission wasn't successful, he feared more people might die.

"Were you just in the labyrinth?" Taryn stared at him with a scrutinizing expression as her question hung in the air.

Maddox shook his head and kept his hands raised. "No. I'd just walked up when you emerged. I'm supposed to have a job interview."

Taryn glanced back again, clearly still on edge.

Realization clicked in Maddox's mind. She feared for her life.

"Was someone in that labyrinth with you?" he asked softly.

"I . . . I thought I heard someone. Let's just get inside." She cast a glance behind her again before turning back to him. "Come with me."

Maddox followed her gaze, but he saw nothing. He heard nothing. That wasn't to say someone wasn't hiding behind those hedges, their footsteps muted by the grass.

The meandering maze appeared huge and majestic with its curved lines and neatly trimmed bushes. Based on the wide girth of the space, it would be an easy place for someone to hide.

But whatever had just happened, Taryn was clearly spooked.

Maddox pulled his gaze from the labyrinth and followed Taryn toward the regal, sweeping patio at the back of the estate. As he climbed the brick steps, he glanced back one more time.

From here, he had a better view of the labyrinth. But he still couldn't see all the passages inside it. Couldn't see if there were any signs of trouble.

Maybe from the third-floor balcony someone could.

In fact, Maddox had seen someone up on that very balcony just as he'd stepped outside to find Taryn. Maddox hadn't been able to get a good look at the person before the man had slipped back inside.

Whoever it was, he might have answers for Taryn —if that person felt free to offer them.

Or had the person been enjoying watching what happened, almost like a spectator watching gladiators fight?

A bad feeling twisted inside him.

This whole place already had Maddox on edge.

But, right now, he needed to focus on Taryn.

She was the most likely person who could provide the information he needed in this undercover operation.

Because she was the prime suspect in the crimes Blackout was investigating.

CHAPTER
TWO

STANDING ON THE PATIO, Taryn couldn't stop scanning everything around her. The bright blue midafternoon sky seemed to contradict the clouds crowding her thoughts.

Someone else had been in that labyrinth with her.

She was certain of it.

But the man standing in front of her did not appear to be that person.

He hadn't seemed winded when she'd collided with him, indicating that he hadn't been running. Nothing on him jangled when he walked. He wasn't carrying a chain or anything that could make the noise she'd heard.

Plus, he was already outside the labyrinth, and the person who'd been chasing her had been mere feet behind her.

But his timing seemed peculiar.

However, Taryn *had* arranged this interview. The appointment had simply slipped her mind, and now she was reading too much into things. Fear played with her thoughts and emotions. If she wasn't careful, those very things could destroy her.

She'd worked so hard to overcome the struggles in her life. She couldn't take steps backward now. Even one small setback could mean she'd be back out on the streets.

A block of ice formed in her chest at the thought.

Never again. She never wanted to face those kinds of uncertainties again.

That meant she had to compose herself and do her job.

The man in front of her had a dark beard, short hair, and a fit build. A tattoo peeked out from beneath one sleeve of his white T-shirt. His eyes were serious, almost brooding.

And he seemed to grunt a lot.

Something about the man . . . almost made him seem dangerous.

Another tremble raked through her at the thought.

"Are you sure you're okay?" The man's hands rested on his narrow hips as he observed her.

Taryn cleared her throat, trying to get her fear

under control. "I'm sorry—what was your name again?"

His expression softened, and he let out another grunt. "Maddox King. I'm here to interview for a maintenance position at the estate."

"That's right. I remember now." She shook her head. "My apologies. I'm Taryn Parsons."

"I'm sorry for the confusion. I feel like we've gotten off to the wrong start." He extended his arm.

She took his hand in hers and offered a firm hand-shake. "You have nothing to apologize for. I'm the one who's all out of sorts. I'm Mr. Whitlock's care-giver, and I manage the estate—including hiring new staff members."

"Nice to meet you, Ms. Parsons."

"Please, call me Taryn."

"Okay. Taryn, then. This is a beautiful estate." Maddox glanced at the labyrinth in the distance with its Celtic design, looking as if he were still curious about what he'd walked in on. "Not many people can say they have one of those."

Taryn shivered again. "It's actually a nice place to take long walks when you need to think. A lot of people use them for prayer, for that matter."

"Ever gotten lost?"

She remembered the panicky feeling that had gripped her the first time she'd walked through the maze-like structure. "Once or twice. It's easy to get turned around. Every direction you go looks the same after a while."

She'd learned the way through the maze early on so she wouldn't feel that fear again.

But she hadn't counted on being chased through the hedges.

Taryn shoved aside the thought of the person who'd been following her. She hadn't seen him. Hadn't heard his voice. She'd simply known he was there by the shadows and sounds closing in.

But now it seemed like the man had disappeared.

Could that whole experience have all been a figment of her imagination?

She knew it hadn't been.

Taryn turned back to Maddox, knowing she had to pull herself together. "So, you're looking for a job in maintenance?"

"That's right. I saw the ad in the paper and emailed you."

"I apologize again. With everything that's been going on around here lately, it slipped my mind." She dragged in a deep breath as she tried to pull herself together. "Why don't we go inside and sit down then so I can get started with the interview?"

With everything that's been going on around here lately . .
.

Taryn's words had sounded ominous, Maddox mused as he sat with Taryn at a massive dining room table with a glass of water resting on the thick wooden surface in front of him.

Maddox knew something was awry here at the estate. It was why he'd come.

Why he'd been *hired* to come.

Although, why he'd been chosen over other members of his team still perplexed him. It seemed Colton Locke, his leader at Blackout, might have picked someone a little more sociable than Maddox. Maddox often told his friends how he enjoyed his own company—and there was no shame in that.

Colton had insisted Maddox was perfect for this job. Maybe it was because he had a knack for fixing things and remaining low-key.

But Maddox hated being fake.

Nope. With him, what you saw was what you got.

Except in this case.

Finley Cooper, the CEO of Embolden Tech, had learned that a shipment of her proprietary technology had gone missing. Instead of being delivered to the legitimate buyer in Georgia, the shipment had disappeared.

The last known location of the package—

according to a tracker planted inside—had been here at Mr. Whitlock's estate.

Then the tracker had gone silent—probably smashed.

The delivery truck driver had been found dead, his body abandoned on the side of the road forty-five minutes away.

Had someone here stolen the products?

That's what Maddox needed to find out.

In the wrong hands, this tech could be dangerous.

Maddox needed to track down the missing items before they could be used for nefarious purposes. The best way to do so was by working undercover here at Whitlock's estate. He needed to find out if someone here had stolen those products and killed the driver.

Since no one would willingly admit to that, he needed to snoop around.

But first, he had to get his foot in the door.

"It looks like you have plenty of experience." Taryn glanced at his résumé and frowned. "You served in the military for fifteen years?"

Maddox nodded. "Now that I'm out, I'm looking for something a little simpler."

Taryn looked up at him and studied his face. "Are you from this area?"

Her confidence surprised him—as did her upscale clothing. Black dress slacks, flats, a light-blue blouse.

Her dark hair hung around her face—slightly disheveled after their earlier encounter—and understated earrings graced her ears.

Maddox knew much of Taryn's back story—knew how she'd come from nothing to working and living at this huge estate. Not only did her appearance here seem suspect, but she was also a known acquaintance of Grissom Smith. The man had a long rap sheet and seemed like the kind of guy who'd be up to no good.

Maddox didn't believe in coincidences.

Which was why Taryn was his main suspect.

"I'm from Upstate New York," he told her. "But I have friends in this area, and I fell in love with the mountains of Western North Carolina. So, I decided to see if I could stay."

His words were partly the truth. Maddox really was from New York. He really did have friends who'd done contract work in this area. He really did think the mountains were beautiful.

"And you're good with your hands?" Taryn narrowed her eyes as she continued to unapologetically study him, a stray strand of wavy dark hair creeping across her forehead. She carefully shoved it back. "You can fix small motors and appliances? You don't mind doing mundane tasks around the property?"

"I love nothing more than working with my hands." Maddox was a tactical kind of guy who preferred to stay busy, who liked doing tasks more than he liked socializing.

Taryn stared at Maddox another moment, clearly studying him to figure out if he was trustworthy or not.

Finally, she nodded and stood. "Well, Maddox King. I'd like to hire you on a trial basis. Let's give this a week and see how you work out before I make a final decision. Do you find those terms acceptable?"

Maddox rose to his feet also, relief washing through him. A week should be plenty of time.

First part of his mission? Check.

He was in.

He offered what he hoped was a winning grin. His colleagues had informed him that sometimes his "winning smile" looked more like an awkward cringe.

He averted his grin and settled on a nod instead. "I appreciate the opportunity, Ms. Parsons."

Taryn pushed a dark hair behind her ear. "Very well then. We have a full-time staff of five people here at the estate. You'll be staying in the east wing with us. The accommodations are nothing fancy, but I think you'll find them ample."

"I'm a simple guy, so I'm sure they'll be fine."

"Do you need to pick up your things?"

"I have everything I need in my SUV." He

shrugged. "What can I say? I was hopeful I'd get the job."

The most important thing was that Maddox was here and that he had access to what he hoped to find.

However, one look at Taryn's intelligent gaze and Maddox knew that this job might not be as straight-forward as he'd initially thought.

He would do whatever he needed to find answers.

Because the safety of innocent people depended on his success.

Before he could dwell on that thought any longer, a yell sounded outside.

Maddox and Taryn both turned and darted out the back door to find out what was wrong.

TARYN RUSHED TOWARD THE SOUND, Maddox right behind her.

Who'd let out that yell?

As far as she knew, Danielle—who worked at the stables—and Leroy were the only employees outside right now.

What if the man who'd chased Taryn through the labyrinth had somehow found one of them instead? Maybe she should have warned them.

Or called the police.

Or . . .

This was no time to think about the what-ifs.

Instead, she tore across the yard and headed toward the greenhouse. Leroy spent much of his time in the building located at the back of the property, and the yell sounded like it had come from that direction.

Maddox stayed on her heels as she threw the greenhouse door open and stepped inside. Muggy air surrounded them, the space much warmer than the temperate spring air outside.

As soon as they stepped into the space, Taryn spotted Leroy leaning over a bag of potting soil, one hand gripping the other as blood dripped onto the ground.

"Leroy . . ." Taryn grabbed a wad of paper towels from a workbench and rushed toward him. Moving quickly, she pressed the towels into his wound to try to stop the bleeding.

"Help is on the way." Maddox slid his phone back into his pocket before stepping closer.

Good. He'd called 911. Leroy would most likely need stitches. That was her best guess based on the amount of blood she'd seen.

Taryn studied Leroy, unable to mask her concern.

The man's wrinkled face was pale, and his arms trembled. His years outside had given his skin a weathered look with noticeable deep browlines. His salt-and-pepper hair fell into his face as he bent forward in pain.

"What happened?" Taryn asked.

"I reached into the bag of potting soil and felt

something slice into my skin." Leroy winced as if reliving the moment.

"What was it?" Maddox crowded closer, his jaw hard and his gaze even harder.

Leroy shook his head. "I'm not sure. Maybe razor blades or something."

"Who would put razors in your potting soil?" Taryn's heart thumped in her ears at the mere thought of it. If that was true . . . then this was no accident.

Someone had wanted to hurt Leroy.

Again.

Well . . . maybe not to specifically hurt Leroy. But to hurt another staff member.

A bad feeling churned in her gut.

"I have no idea. I just know they were in there." Leroy let out another moan as he glanced at his hand. "I never wear gloves because I like the feel of dirt on my skin. But . . ."

"Maybe you should sit down." Maddox helped the man to a paint-splattered wooden bench against the wall. "Hold your arm up to slow the blood flow. We can help."

At his words, Taryn raised Leroy's hand in the air, still pressing those paper towels into his wound.

Whatever had been in the bag—razors or not— had been sharp. The man's cuts looked deep.

There was no way that had been an accident.

Someone had planted something in that bag.

Taryn frowned.

Just one more accident to add to a growing list.

As paramedics treated Leroy, Maddox and Taryn stood outside the greenhouse to give them space.

What happened to Leroy had *not* been an accident, Maddox mused.

Someone had planned this.

There had definitely been razor blades in the bag of potting soil. Maddox had seen the police officer retrieve them.

Whatever was going on here . . . it was even more full-blown than Maddox had imagined.

He glanced at Taryn as she paced across the grass. The woman looked genuinely surprised and frightened.

But that didn't fit his assumptions about her.

Many people thought Taryn was out for Mr. Whitlock's fortune. That she was maybe even a gold digger trying to woo the man before his death.

However, if that was true, then this woman was a great actress.

Maddox didn't know Taryn yet. Until he did, he had to assume that was the case—that the fear, the surprise, the forgetfulness was just an act.

Someone cunning enough could pull that off.

Was Taryn that kind of person?

Only time would tell.

Thirty minutes later, paramedics left with Leroy, taking him to the hospital for stitches. Eleanor, the housekeeper, had accompanied him.

Once they were alone, Taryn turned toward Maddox and crossed her arms. "This is quite the start for you, huh?"

His initial impulse was to grunt in response. But he wasn't with the guys on the battlefield right now. He needed to show some decorum.

"Yes, quite the start," he finally said, mentally putting a mocking pinky in the air.

He *hated* putting on airs, and the way wealthy people acted above others usually struck him the wrong way.

Which was just another reason why he'd been surprised to be asked to take lead on this assignment.

Taryn released a long, almost labored breath. "I guess I need to show you to your room so you can get settled. In a couple of hours, it will be dinnertime already. This afternoon has certainly flown by."

"Emergencies have a way of doing that."

"I'm sure you probably want to unpack and become familiar with the estate." She sighed again and paused as if gathering her thoughts. "How about this? I'll show you to your room, and then I can give you the tour. By the time we finish, dinner will be ready. You'll have the chance then to meet Mr. Whitlock."

Maddox's blood spiked at that possibility. The more he could talk to Mr. Whitlock, the better. Though the man seemed too frail to be involved in the crime, it was still a good possibility—especially considering the fact the man was an inventor. Maybe, for some reason, he wanted this tech for himself.

"That sounds fantastic." He paused and stared at Taryn another minute as distress flitted through her gaze. "Are you sure there's nothing else I can do for you in the meantime?"

She offered what looked like a forced smile. "I'm fine. Thank you. Now, let me show you to your room."

CHAPTER
FOUR

AS TARYN CLOSED the door to Maddox's room, her heart raced.

Was this man's presence here a coincidence? Had he really seen the ad she'd placed for help?

Or was he a part of the cloak-and-dagger stunts happening around here?

She didn't know.

Part of her found a small measure of comfort in the fact that someone like Maddox would be in the house.

The man was tall and looked strong, like he could take care of himself and those around him.

Then again, that could be a disadvantage—if it turned out his motives for being here were less than honorable.

The rest of the household staff didn't give off the same protective vibes.

Chef Clara Mulligan was in her fifties, robust, and too persnickety for her own good.

Housekeeper Eleanor Hagedorn was in her late sixties and had been working here for thirty years.

Gardner Leroy Matthews was also in his fifties. His knees were already going bad, but he wanted to keep working for as long as he could.

Stable master Danielle Rodgers was in her early twenties and probably the most athletic of all the staff. She mainly kept to herself as she took care of the horses. On her time off, she liked to go into town —twenty minutes away—and enjoy the nightlife.

On occasion, Mr. Whitlock's only child, Phil, stopped by, sometimes staying for a day and sometimes for a month. The man was in his forties and loved to be waited on hand and foot, acting as if the staff were his personal servants. Today, Phil was gone, but he could reappear at any moment.

Taryn hurried down the hallway away from the staff quarters as she headed upstairs to check on Mr. Whitlock. The hospice nurse should be wrapping up by now, and Taryn wanted to make sure he didn't need anything.

She just didn't understand what was happening here lately—all the accidents haunting this place. A pot rack had fallen, nearly crushing Chef Mulligan.

An outlet had short-circuited when Eleanor plugged something in, starting a small fire on the wall of a guest bedroom. Danielle had been bucked from a horse and nearly broken her neck.

Not that Taryn believed a place could be haunted.

However, this estate was built nearly two hundred years ago and almost had an old castle vibe to it.

In fact, on her first day on the job, Taryn had gotten lost inside the fifteen thousand-square-foot house. The third floor had more than one hallway and a unique room layout, and she'd gotten turned around.

She still hadn't been brave enough to venture into the basement.

Taryn shoved those thoughts aside as she hurried to the west wing to check on Mr. Whitlock.

She did most of his caregiving, meaning that she helped him get ready for the day, ensured he ate as well as took his medication. A nurse still came twice a day—once either in the morning or afternoon, and another nurse stayed overnight—to make sure his health was holding up. While the nurse was there, Taryn usually took a break to do other things around the house.

The man had not only inherited his wealth from his family, but he'd been an inventor. He'd developed several products, but his most lucrative one had been a specialized clip that was used in almost every vehicle today. He was officially retired now, but he hadn't slowed down until diagnosed with congestive heart failure.

However, this wasn't what she considered a typical retirement.

Taryn had found letters in Mr. Whitlock's mailbox.

Letters threatening him.

Saying if he didn't pay up there would be consequences.

Indicating that people he cared about would be in danger if he didn't comply.

Taryn hadn't had the heart to share them with him. Mr. Whitlock could have a heart attack. The doctor had said he was getting weaker and needed to be cautious, to keep his stress level down.

Taryn had thought about telling the police about the letters. But the threats had said if he went to the authorities there would be consequences. She didn't know what to do, a realization that caused her to lose sleep at night.

As she stepped into Mr. Whitlock's room, she saw him snoozing in his bed.

A smile flitted across her lips at how peaceful he looked. His thin skin covering his long, lanky frame. A few wisps of hair remained on top of his head, which was dotted with age spots. Because of his heart failure, fluid often gathered in his legs and ankles, which made it harder for him to walk.

Taryn wouldn't disturb him.

Instead, she paced to the French doors leading to his balcony and glanced outside.

Mr. Whitlock had a bird's-eye view of the grounds from here. He told her it was why he'd picked this room. Not only was it grand with a high ceiling and amazing finishing work, but he was like a king looking over his domain when he stepped onto the balcony.

If it wasn't for the elevator, he wouldn't be able to stay in this room. The stairs would be too much for him.

Had he seen anything earlier? After all, he had a clear view of the labyrinth from his room. Should she ask him when he awoke?

Before she could think about it any longer, he let out a moan.

Taryn glanced back at him and saw he'd begun thrashing in bed. He must be having a nightmare.

Quickly, she walked toward him, contemplating whether to wake him.

Just as she reached his bed, Mr. Whitlock muttered, "I didn't mean to. I didn't mean to do it. You've got to believe me."

His words made Taryn's blood turn cold.

Someone as wealthy and successful as Mr. Whitlock . . . certainly had secrets. Didn't everyone?

But considering the amount of money he'd made, she had to wonder if the stakes were even higher with him.

Maddox finished unpacking the small bag he'd brought with him and then walked to the window. He had the perfect view of the backyard from here.

He opened the window and let fresh air float inside.

It was May, and the weather was getting warm. But here in the mountains, a nice chill remained in the air. Maddox had always preferred cold weather to warm anyway. His Upstate New York upbringing had been a part of that.

In the distance, dark clouds edged the sky. Was it supposed to storm here tonight?

That's how it appeared.

His gaze stopped on the labyrinth.

He was too low to see inside it, but the structure formed a striking image, almost giving the property a sense of royalty.

As he stared outside, someone stepped from the back hedges of the maze-like structure and walked toward the woods running alongside the property.

Maddox tried to take in details about the man, but the figure wore all black—including a hood.

He appeared to be average in height and overall size.

Maddox frowned.

Strange.

Something was definitely going on here.

Images of his initial meeting with Taryn filled his mind.

The woman had clearly been spooked.

Or had she been secretly meeting with someone? Was that why Maddox's appearance had surprised her so much?

Maybe she was even meeting with someone about whatever was going on here at the estate.

Who was that man who'd just disappeared into the woods? Could it be Grissom?

Even more so, what happened to that missing technology? Was it still somewhere on Mr. Whitlock's property?

Whatever was happening here, he didn't like it.

Maddox had thought this would be an easy job. That he'd simply come here, find the information, and report it to his superiors.

But, so far, the assignment was shaping up to be more involved than that.

Maddox glanced at his watch. In five minutes,

Taryn was supposed to return to give him a tour of this place.

Had she been planted here to keep an eye on Whitlock? Maybe she'd even been the one who'd arranged for that technology to be brought here. Had she done something with it?

If he had the chance, he'd need to search her room.

All the rooms here, really.

He hoped since he was working maintenance, he'd have plenty of opportunities.

He stepped away from the window.

This job would be far more interesting than Maddox had assumed.

Especially considering the fact that the last maintenance worker had been found dead of an apparent heart attack . . . at the age of thirty-five.

CHAPTER
FIVE

TARYN FOUGHT exhaustion as she headed down the dark, narrow hallway back to Maddox's room. Various paintings—probably valuable—lined either side of the walls. The scent of lemon Pledge filled the space, in part because of the stained wooden walls on either side of her—walls that often needed to be polished.

This whole house seemed to smell like the scent.

When she'd taken this job with Mr. Whitlock, she had no idea how taxing the schedule would be.

But now that she knew Mr. Whitlock, there was no way she'd leave him here without someone to watch his back.

It seemed like everyone wanted something from the man she'd come to think of as a father figure. Mostly, they wanted his money. Sometimes, just in small amounts—to pay for a trip or as a small loan or as a donation to a charity. Someone had even offered to buy this property about a month ago.

The thing was, Taryn didn't want anything from him. Certainly not his money or this house or any of the property he owned.

She'd felt an instant bond with the man. He'd taught her so much about life. He'd freely shared his wisdom. Since she'd grown up without a father, his relationship with her seemed to fill in some gaps.

Taryn had never expected to find the man's favor or to be offered this job.

She'd been at rock bottom when the two of them had met, and her life had been changed forever when he'd hired her.

But the grass wasn't always greener on the other side. The last couple of weeks had proven that. Taryn was now constantly on edge and unsure who to trust.

A quiver of nerves raked through her as she raised her hand to knock at Maddox's door. Before her hand connected with the wood, he pulled it open.

Taryn sucked in a breath when she saw Maddox standing so close.

Her reaction didn't make sense. Why would she feel a rush of attraction toward a man she'd just met?

It wasn't like her. Especially after Grissom.

She frowned.

She'd been hurt so many times that permanent walls had gone up around her heart.

Quickly, she stepped back before Maddox could see her reaction. She was officially his boss now, and she needed to act like it.

"Is it time for the tour?" Maddox's voice broke her from her thoughts.

She swallowed hard as she pulled herself together. "It is. Are you ready?"

He stepped from his room and nodded. "I look forward to seeing the place."

Taryn began showing him around the mansion Mr. Whitlock called home.

As she'd told him earlier, the east wing was primarily the staff quarters. But many unused bedrooms filled the space, dating back to when this place had a large workforce running daily operations.

At the center of the house was the main living area including a kitchen, a large living room, a banquet/dining room, and a library.

The west wing was Mr. Whitlock's personal living space. His massive bedroom was on the third floor. The other floors contained a private living room, office, and multiple suites for family.

"It looks like Mr. Whitlock has a perfect view of the labyrinth," Maddox muttered as they gazed out a window on the third story.

She glanced at him, surprised by the observation. "He does. It's one of his favorite features of the estate."

Had Mr. Whitlock seen her being chased earlier? If so, certainly he'd say something . . . right?

She shoved the question aside for now and continued through the extravagant house.

Taryn hadn't grown up with money. In fact, she'd lived most of her childhood in a nine hundred-square-foot apartment. The enormity of this place still overwhelmed her at times.

"This house is really incredible," Maddox told her as they paused in the foyer.

"It really is." Taryn glanced at the three-story-high ceiling and the stately iron chandelier hanging there. "When I first got here, the place reminded me of something I might see in a fairy tale, especially with the stone walls and massive columns out front."

"It almost does feel as if you've stepped back into a different time, doesn't it?" He glanced around as if in wonder.

"Yes, it does."

Maddox grunted before nodding toward the back of the property. "Does the tour include the outside portion of the estate also? I mean, I guess I already saw a lot of the grounds—but I wasn't properly intro-duced, if you know what I mean."

Taryn ran her sweaty palms down the sides of her black pants. "If you'd like to."

"I don't want to take up too much of your time if you have other things to do."

"No, you need to see this place, especially if you'll be working here. Besides, it's a beautiful day outside, and I could use some fresh air. A storm is coming in later."

As Taryn glanced at the backyard, she remembered the intruder in the labyrinth earlier.

Part of her dreaded going out there again.

But the thought was ridiculous, and she would have to get over it. Danger didn't await around every corner.

So why did she still hesitate before opening the back door?

Maddox walked beside Taryn as she gave him a tour of the greenhouse. Then they walked past the labyrinth toward the pool and the pool house.

No expense or luxury had been spared. In fact, the grounds almost seemed too extravagant and meticulously kept.

Maddox and Taryn made small talk as they walked, mostly sticking to details about the job,

Maddox's schedule, and what was expected of him in his new position.

He took mental notes of everything Taryn said while also keeping an eye on their surroundings.

As they reached the stables, movement in the distance caught his eye.

He paused, and his arm jutted out to stop Taryn from going any farther.

She followed his gaze and gasped.

A man darted across the lawn and into the nearby woods. Could that be the same guy Maddox had seen earlier?

"You recognize him?" Maddox muttered.

Taryn shook her head, and her voice trembled as she said, "No."

Without wasting any time, Maddox took off after the man.

He hadn't expected to jump in trying to find answers so quickly. But Taryn was obviously frightened, and this man was trespassing on the property. The fact he'd been running away only made him look more guilty.

Maddox raced through the woods, trying to track the man.

But the intruder was nowhere to be seen, almost as if he'd disappeared into thin air.

Maddox paused and sucked in a deep breath as

he surveyed the woods. The trees. The boulders. A small creek.

Where had the man gone?

He couldn't have disappeared this easily.

But he *could* be hiding.

Maddox bristled as he waited and listened.

All he needed was one telltale sign, and he could find this man and demand some answers.

But everything remained quiet except for some squirrels jumping from branch to branch in the distance.

Maddox took a step, still studying everything around him. His shoulders were tight and his body on guard as he braced himself for any surprises.

A bad feeling swirled in his gut.

He would wait here for as long as it took to find some answers.

Just as the thought rushed through his mind, a yell sounded in the distance.

Taryn.

That had been *Taryn*.

He shouldn't have left her alone.

Maddox needed to make sure she was okay.

He prayed he wasn't too late.

Taryn stared at the rocks in front of her.

After Maddox had run off, she'd trailed behind, not daring to go into the woods. But she'd paused at the edge of the trees and prayed that Maddox was okay.

She hadn't expected him to chase after the man who'd been trespassing.

Part of her admired him for his bravery. Another part feared he would get hurt.

She hadn't told him about everything happening here. Maybe she should have warned him.

Unless he was somehow involved.

She frowned and nibbled on her lip.

It was so hard to know who to trust.

But as she stared at the rocks in front of her, her heart thumped in her ears.

These were painted rocks—just like the one she'd stumbled over in the labyrinth.

Four of them lay in front of her, stashed behind a tree where she wouldn't have otherwise seen them. Someone had hidden them here.

But why?

Maddox burst from the woods and darted toward her. He stopped in front of her, his chest rising and falling with exertion.

"Are you okay?" he asked, studying her face.

Taryn's hand covered her mouth. She must have made a noise. Must have vocalized her surprise more than she'd realized.

"I'm . . . yes, I'm okay. I just . . ." She glanced at the rocks, unsure how to answer him.

He followed her gaze. "Aren't those the kind of rocks people usually hide around town for people to find?"

She nodded, hating the numb feeling inside her. "They are. It's just that . . . well, I found one earlier and tripped on it while in the labyrinth. I know this might sound like an exaggeration, but I'm nearly certain someone put it in my path in hopes that I'd fall. And now these . . ."

Maddox leaned down to examine them. Using a stick, he turned one over.

He was trying to preserve fingerprints, wasn't he? Was that something that normal people did?

Taryn wasn't sure.

"There's a letter on each of them," Maddox mumbled. "Almost like someone was trying to spell out a message."

She squatted beside him, curious now. "What letters?"

"E. T. A. H." Maddox glanced at her. "Was there a letter on the rock you stumbled on?"

She shrugged. "I . . . I don't know. I didn't take the time to look."

He gave her another glance, one that clearly indicated he knew there was more to her story.

Taryn let out a sigh. She'd been avoiding telling

him the truth. But now it only made sense to share some details now.

"When I was in the labyrinth earlier, someone was chasing me. I'm certain of it. Then I ran into you and . . . I didn't hear anything else."

His eyes narrowed. "And the person never emerged?"

"Not that I saw." Taryn tried to push away her fear before it gripped her any further.

"The man we saw running . . . could he have been the same person?" Maddox continued.

She shrugged, trying to hold herself together. She hadn't come this far only to be derailed by someone playing a few ill-timed pranks on the estate staff.

"Maybe," she answered. "I never saw the man. I only noticed his shadow and heard some type of chain clanking as he chased me."

Maddox stood, his shoulders appearing tighter now. He pulled out his phone and snapped a picture of the rocks, muttering, "Just in case."

Just in case what?

Part of Taryn didn't want to know.

Maddox shifted before nodding toward the labyrinth. "I think we should try to find this other rock—before the storm comes."

Taryn rose also. "Not a bad idea."

She should have gone back earlier, but she hadn't

been able to force herself to do so. Fear had kept her away.

Another part of her feared more surprises could be awaiting in that labyrinth.

She wasn't sure if she could handle any more brushes with danger.

CHAPTER
SIX

MADDOX DIDN'T LIKE what was going on here.

The fear on Taryn's face looked real.

Maybe she wasn't the one behind the missing technology.

Even though she made the most sense considering her ties with Grissom.

He'd have to think about that later. Right now, Maddox wanted to figure out what was going on with these rocks.

As he stared at them another moment, the wind swept over him. The storm was on its way and would probably be upon them by dinnertime. That didn't leave him much opportunity to figure things out.

He'd come back and get these rocks later. He just

needed to think of a good reason to do this, so Taryn didn't get suspicious of him.

Her skin looked pale as he glanced over at her.

Her fear was definitely real.

Part of him wanted to comfort her—something Maddox wasn't intrinsically good at doing. Ever since Lindsey had broken his heart, he hadn't gotten close to any other woman. In fact, he'd be quite content to remain single . . . forever. Women only complicated his life, and he liked things simple.

"I know you must think this is all strange."

Taryn's voice pulled Maddox from his thoughts.

He looked over at her as they started walking across the lawn. "Someone chasing you through that maze, razors being left in potting soil, and now some mysterious rocks? It's not exactly what I expected. Is this normal around here?"

She shrugged. "It's hard to say. I've only been here six months."

"When did this start? Or has this just been happening today?" *Since he arrived,* Maddox thought to himself.

He didn't like that timing. But it had to be a coincidence. No one knew he was coming here. No one except Blackout, the security operation he worked for.

Taryn nibbled on her bottom lip a moment in hesitation. "Today has definitely been a whirlwind.

But there have been a few other . . . incidents . . . here at the estate. I'm sure it's nothing to be worried about. Probably just someone who's up to some mischief."

She was trying to gloss it over. But why?

They stopped at the labyrinth, and Maddox saw Taryn draw back.

She was afraid to step between those hedges again, wasn't she?

I won't let anything happen to you.

Where had that thought come from? Maddox was supposed to be investigating here, not protecting Taryn.

But who said he couldn't do both?

***

Taryn's chest tightened as she stared at the labyrinth.

At once, memories of being chased through the passages filled her mind.

What if that man still waited behind these hedges?

No, that couldn't be the case.

Most likely, the man they'd seen run into the woods was the same person who'd chased her.

Still, she had no idea what was going on. She thought by coming here to Mr. Whitlock's estate she'd have some security in her life, a safety net. That was all she'd ever wanted after her tumultuous childhood.

Security.

Mr. Whitlock offered her that, as did this job.

But now everything felt up in the air again.

"Taryn?"

She looked up and saw Maddox staring at her.

She cleared her throat, trying to pull herself together. "I should be able to find the spot where that rock was left. But I wasn't exactly paying attention to where I was in the maze at the time."

He glanced through the greenery-lined passage. "That's understandable. Do you want me to go first?"

Her chest loosened at his words. "Actually, if you don't mind . . ."

Maddox nodded and stepped inside. Taryn stayed close behind him, listening for any signs that danger might be close. So far, she heard nothing.

"You from this area?" he asked her as they walked.

Was he just trying to distract her? Maybe.

But she was game for that.

"I grew up near Boone," she said. "So, about two hours from here."

"Nice area."

"I liked it."

"What did you do before working here?"

Her throat burned. The questions were just

casual, yet, at the same time, they somehow felt loaded. "I was a waitress, trying to save money to go back to college."

"What did you want to study?" He rounded a curve, heading toward the center of the hedges.

"Maybe administration. Maybe nursing. I'm not sure. When my mom got sick with pancreatic cancer, I took care of her. That's when I discovered I was pretty good at it."

A new emotion washed through his gaze. Surprise? Admiration?

She wasn't sure.

"So, it was a natural fit that you'd come here and help Mr. Whitlock . . ." he murmured.

"That's how it seems." Taryn kept her answer short.

By nature, she was guarded. But, given everything that had happened, being guarded seemed like a positive attribute.

Suddenly, Maddox stopped in front of her and pointed at something on the ground. "That the rock?"

She scooted around him and stared at the stone, which had been painted bright blue and yellow. "Yes, that's the one."

There it was. Left in the middle of the walkway, just waiting to trip an unsuspecting person.

Just waiting to trip *Taryn*.

She was the only person she knew who used this labyrinth on a regular basis.

She leaned down for a better look and saw a letter had been painted there also.

"It's a D," Maddox said. "So, we have an E, H, A, T, and D. Hated?"

Taryn felt the blood leave her face.

She straightened as her eyes met Maddox's. "Could be. Or it could spell *death*."

CHAPTER
SEVEN

TARYN TRIED NOT to stare at the rock, but how could she not? This only confirmed that someone had placed it there on purpose. Whoever had been chasing her through here had wanted her to find it. To possibly trip over it.

But why just the one rock? Had the person planned to plant the other rocks in a different location?

Were they trying to play some kind of game with her?

Because nothing that was happening here was accidental.

Nothing.

"Taryn?"

She glanced up and saw Maddox staring at her.

She drew in a deep breath as she tried to pull herself back together.

If she kept acting like this, Maddox would run from this place. Who in their right mind would want to work here if they knew about all the recent accidents? Besides, something about Maddox made her want to keep him around.

But . . . what if he was somehow involved in this whole mess?

A block of ice formed in her chest . . .

Mr. Whitlock was the only person she had any confidence in.

In fact, at times she'd been tempted to run from this new job. But not only did she have nowhere to go, Mr. Whitlock needed her.

She didn't trust anyone else to take care of him. Not the rest of the staff. Not his nurses. Not even Phil, the man's son. Any one of them could have a hidden agenda.

Taryn lifted her head, thankful for the gentle breeze sweeping over her face. The fresh air filled her lungs and grounded her a moment.

As a faint sound of thunder rumbled through the air, it reminded her that the storm would soon be upon them. They didn't have much time.

The thought caused her to shiver. Taryn had never liked thunderstorms. Not since she'd been left outside in an old shed during a bad storm when she was five so her mother could enjoy a date with a new boyfriend—a boyfriend who didn't want to date someone with kids.

Taryn could still remember how overpowering that storm had seemed—how alone she had felt. The thunder had muted her cries. The lightning had illuminated her tears.

She still hadn't gotten over it.

"Taryn . . . ?" Maddox said again.

She blinked, and Maddox came into view. She shook her head and pulled her thoughts back to the present. Dwelling on the past wouldn't help her move into the future.

"I guess we should head to the house." She snapped back to reality. "It's almost time for dinner, and I'd hate to keep Chef waiting. Tardiness makes her very cranky—and no one likes it when Chef is cranky."

"I'll bring this rock with us, and I'll get the rest later." Maddox picked up the stone and then followed behind her toward the house.

So far today, she had been chased, Leroy had been hurt, an intruder had run off, and they'd found these rocks.

Certainly, that was enough excitement for one day . . . wasn't it?

Maddox knew Taryn wasn't telling him something. But he also knew better than to ask her any questions. Not yet.

Right now, it was dinnertime.

He'd been seated with Taryn, Eleanor, Danielle, and Leroy at the massive dining room table. Shawn Edwards, Mr. Whitlock's financial manager, had been visiting so he also joined them.

Small talk sounded around the table as everyone waited for Mr. Whitlock to come down. Thunder rumbled overhead, and purple lightning lit the sky outside the windows. Wind smattered debris into the side of the house, and rain pelted the roof.

The storm seemed much more interesting than small talk. Maddox hated meaningless conversation almost as much as he hated lying.

He'd checked his weather app before he'd come down. The radar had indicated this system would stick around for a while.

That was fine by him. He'd always loved a good thunderstorm.

Right at six o'clock, Taryn left to help Mr. Whitlock down the elevator and settle him in his seat at the head of the table. The man—who was in his late seventies—looked much frailer than Maddox had anticipated. All the pictures he'd seen of Mr. Whitlock online had shown a strong, striking man.

The person before him looked so weak and shaky —a reminder of the fragility of life.

His gaze instantly went to Maddox.

"We have someone new with us," Mr. Whitlock murmured. "Welcome. You must be Maddox."

Maddox rose and extended his hand. "Nice to meet you, sir."

Whitlock stared at his hand before shaking it. Satisfaction crinkled in his eyes as if Maddox had just passed his first test.

"You have your work cut out for you here." Mr. Whitlock waved his linen napkin in the air before placing it in his lap.

This man had no idea. Maddox most certainly *did* have his work cut out for him.

The food was served. Prime rib, braised potatoes, and steamed green beans offered a nice distraction from Maddox's otherwise heavy thoughts. Not long ago, he'd been on the dusty streets of Iraq searching for insurgents and eating MREs.

Now here he was trying to relate to the equivalent of American royalty. His motto was that he'd do whatever the job demanded of him—though he did have limits. As a handyman, certainly no one expected him to be prim and proper.

He just needed to stay under the radar.

Mr. Whitlock seemed surprisingly pleasant considering his wealth. Maddox had expected the man to be stuck up or arrogant. But, so far, that hadn't been the case. Mr. Whitlock had been polite, had asked other people questions about their day, and he allowed his staff to eat with him.

But more than that revelation surprised Maddox. The banter between Mr. Whitlock and Taryn showed the two of them had a close bond. The affection in their voices proved a mutual respect.

Maddox stored that information away, adding it to his mental assessment of the situation.

This would be an interesting assignment. When Maddox got back to his room, he'd check in with his superiors. Right now, this seemed like a one-person job.

But he knew his team was working behind the scenes and would be here to help him if he asked. At least two members were staying close as they looked into other possibilities about what had happened to the missing shipment.

"So, you're a military veteran, huh?" Shawn practically turned his nose up at Maddox as he glanced over between bites of steak.

The forty-something man had shiny blond hair that fell in waves over his forehead. His features were thin and almost aristocratic—an observation that was accented by the man's cuff-linked sleeves and designer shoes.

Maddox was perfectly content in his navy-blue

work pants and the twenty-dollar polo shirt he'd picked up before coming.

He glanced at Shawn. "That's correct. Served for fifteen years."

"Admirable." Something about the way the man said the word made it sound as if that kind of job was beneath someone like him.

Chef Mulligan stepped from the kitchen and tapped a fork against her glass. "Dessert is ready. Baked Alaska, anyone?"

Just as she asked the question, the room went dark.

Blackness filled the house.

Then a crash sounded.

CHAPTER
EIGHT

TARYN FELT HER CHEST TIGHTEN.

Had the storm knocked the power out?

Or was something else going on?

Her heart thrummed in her ears as she jumped to her feet. She needed to take charge. That was her role as estate manager.

"Let me find some candles," she rushed, stepping toward the buffet behind her. She thought she'd seen some in one of its drawers.

Before she could reach it, a small beam of light filled the room.

From Maddox's phone, she realized.

"Everyone okay?" Maddox shone the light on each person.

A murmuring of yeses went around the table.

Relief filled Taryn.

Good.

What had Taryn expected? To discover someone had been stabbed in the brief moment of pitch darkness?

Maybe she'd been reading too many Agatha Christie novels lately.

"Why don't you all stay here, and I'll see if I can figure out what happened?" Maddox glanced around the table. "It's probably just a breaker. Does anyone else have a phone you can use for light while I'm gone?"

Taryn grabbed her phone from her pocket and found the flashlight app. Relief filled her as the beam cast illumination over the table.

Just then, lightning lit the sky followed by the low rumble of thunder.

Another shiver went through her.

She was paranoid.

That was all.

There was no reason to be scared. It wasn't unusual for a storm like this to cause power outages.

But something was undoubtedly going on here at the estate.

After everything that had happened today, Taryn could no longer deny it.

Just how far would someone go to send these messages—messages that Mr. Whitlock was in danger if he didn't comply?

However, Taryn had no idea what he was supposed to comply with.

———

Something was definitely going on here.

Whatever it was, the situation was escalating quickly.

Maddox's muscles tightened as he walked toward the garage where the breaker box was located. Taryn had pointed it out during their tour.

Had the storm done this?

Or was someone planning something and trying to use a cover of darkness?

He paused in the hallway and shined his light on the floor.

A vase lay shattered on the wooden floor.

An open window stretched above the space, the curtains fluttering in the wind and rain pelting inside.

Strange. He wondered if people usually left windows open around here.

At least, this explained the crash.

At once, Maddox felt as if he were a live actor in the game of Clue.

Only the stakes were deadly now, and they were real life.

Someone in this house was pulling the strings.

Someone knew what was happening on this property Mr. Whitlock owned.

Sometimes, war felt easier than these kinds of assignments.

At least, during war, there was a clear bad guy.

In missions like this one, it was anyone's guess.

Maddox needed to find those answers.

Mr. Whitlock was so weak that Maddox had trouble imagining him doing much to protect himself. The man looked as if he lifted a fifty-pound weight every time he raised his fork to his mouth at dinner.

If he was behind the missing tech, he wasn't doing the footwork himself. It wasn't physically possible.

Maddox wondered how much time the man had left. Mere months, if he had to guess.

With the amount of money on the line . . . Maddox could only imagine what the stakes were.

He shut and locked the open window before moving on. He reached the garage and pushed the door open.

More darkness waited for him on the other side.

His light skimmed the interior as he looked for any sign of intruders.

All he saw were four cars with covers, a well-organized wall of tools, and a workbench with several stacks of drawers.

Carefully, Maddox walked down six steps until he reached the shiny, epoxy floor of the upscale garage.

He sniffed.

What kind of garage didn't smell like oil?

None where he'd grown up.

This place smelled clean, almost like a museum. It didn't even seem right.

He strode across the garage, still on guard, until he reached the breaker box.

Quickly, he opened it and looked for a tripped circuit breaker.

He didn't see anything that had switched off. He flipped all the circuits off and then back on to be sure.

Nothing happened.

The bad feeling in his gut continued to grow.

Had someone cut the power outside?

It was a possibility.

Maddox glanced around the garage one more time before heading back up the stairs and finding everyone still in the dining room. He hadn't wanted to leave them, but he figured if they were all together, they'd be okay.

Using his flashlight, he glanced around the room.

"Maddox?" Taryn's voice sounded fragile.

"It's me." He paused at the head of the table. "The breakers are fine. I wonder if something happened to a powerline outside. We should call the power company."

"Shawn, you get on that." Mr. Whitlock turned toward his financial planner and snapped his fingers.

The man blinked, as if surprised by the order, before grabbing his cell phone. "Of course."

"Do you have a generator?" A house of this size—and one this expensive—was bound to have a backup system. Maddox was surprised it hadn't kicked on.

"I do." Mr. Whitlock's wrinkled face creased into a frown.

"I can go check it out if you'll tell me where it is."

"Taryn, why don't you show him?" Whitlock glanced at her.

Alarm spread across her face, and she swallowed hard enough that Maddox saw her throat tighten.

"But . . . I don't want to leave you." Her voice quivered as she said the words.

"I'll be fine." Mr. Whitlock's firm voice drove away any doubts. "I'm not afraid of the dark."

Taryn stared at him another moment as if she wanted to refuse.

Why did she look so frightened? Was she afraid to be alone with him in the dark? Or did she know something Maddox didn't?

"If it makes you feel better, I'll make everyone

else stay with me." Mr. Whitlock glanced at everyone around the table before nodding reassuringly.

Taryn finally nodded, though the tautness in her shoulders was still visible. "Of course. Let me grab my raincoat."

Why was she so nervous?

Maddox needed to be wise—to get to know this woman without getting too close.

Because she just might have the answers he needed.

TARYN COULDN'T SHAKE her jitters. Every time the wind blew against the house, she jumped. Each time thunder crashed overhead, she flinched. Every time lightning flashed, she wanted to hide.

She walked to the closet near the front of the house and grabbed a raincoat for herself and an extra one for Maddox.

She handed the navy-blue slicker to him. "You'll need this."

"Thanks."

They started back through the dining room toward the back of the house.

Taryn slowed her steps, in no hurry to go outside. But she had no good excuse not to go—not unless she wanted to appear childish by admitting that, at twenty-eight years old, she was still afraid of thunderstorms. What kind of self-respecting adult feared storms?

Maddox seemed to sense her hesitation and touched her back.

Taryn flinched, already on edge.

Instantly, he dropped his hand to his side. "Sorry. Didn't mean to frighten you."

Taryn opened her mouth, feeling as if she should apologize.

But she didn't. The words wouldn't leave her lips.

Maddox paused and leveled his gaze with her. "You don't have to go with me, you know."

She swallowed hard when she saw how close he was. When she heard the low, rumbling tone of his voice.

Why did she feel like this man could see through her?

She pulled herself together and cleared her throat. "Thank you, but . . . it's no big deal."

But it *was* a big deal. A *very* big deal.

Feeling the urge to flee from him, her gaze wandered the darkness, almost as if she expected some type of figure to emerge from the shadows.

Which was ridiculous.

Or was it?

Taryn liked to keep the house locked up tight. But so many people came and went throughout the day that it was difficult to be certain all the doors were secure. Plus, she'd counted the number of outside doors once.

There were more than twenty.

She glanced at Mr. Whitlock as she passed.

Taryn hadn't known the man back when he was powerful and arrogant. That's what people had told her he'd been like, at least. Facing death had humbled him and made him into a different person —a person she liked and enjoyed being around.

For some reason, Taryn was the one he trusted the most even though they'd only known each other for six months.

"Are you doing okay, Mr. Whitlock?" She paused beside him before heading toward the door. She remained concerned about his heart and the stress he could be under.

He nodded before waving her off. "Oh, I'm fine. You don't worry about me."

Yet she did. Everyone in this house had been targeted at some point or another over the last couple of weeks. What if someone went after Mr. Whitlock while Taryn wasn't here to protect him?

She had to believe that no one would strike while so many people were nearby.

She prayed that was the case.

As she stepped away, she heard Shawn say, "The electric company thinks a powerline is down near the estate. They are going to send a crew out here, but it could still be a few hours until the power is back on."

"Then you might as well stay here for the night, Shawn," Mr. Whitlock said. "These are no conditions to be driving in. I'm sure we can make up one of the rooms in the guest wing. If you need to, you can work here tomorrow and maybe take one of the horses out for a ride. I know how much you like doing that."

Taryn glanced at Maddox, wondering why she felt even more anxious.

Since when had Taryn been this nervous? This hadn't always been how she operated. But after the incident earlier today in the labyrinth and what happened to Leroy, she was definitely on edge.

For now, her main priority was to make sure Mr. Whitlock was safe and comfortable. She needed to keep *his* anxiety down. He was already going through so much.

Taryn only hoped they had no more problems today.

But for now, she and Maddox needed to check on that generator.

Maddox pulled the hood up higher on his raincoat.

The rain poured down in unrelenting sheets. He lowered his head as moisture pelted him.

Taryn really didn't have to come out here with him. Since Mr. Whitlock had insisted, Maddox didn't want to raise any eyebrows by going against him. But they were both going to be soaked by the end of this.

He shone his flashlight on the grass as he strode along the edge of the house toward the generator.

As thunder shook the air, Taryn gasped beside him.

Again, Maddox's protective instincts wanted to kick in. He wanted to put his arm around her and tell her everything would be okay.

But that wasn't his place.

Besides, someone at this house was most likely responsible for the missing technology from Embolden Tech.

Maddox had come here for answers.

He hadn't exactly expected this danger.

Taryn pointed behind the garage. "It's right over there!"

Still walking against the pounding rain, they trudged toward the area. The soggy ground sloshed at their feet, and lightning filled the sky just long enough that Maddox caught a glimpse of the fear on Taryn's face.

"I've got it from here." He raised his voice to be heard over the wind and rain.

She shook her head as she pulled her jacket closer. "I'll wait."

Maddox had a feeling Taryn didn't want to walk back by herself.

Maybe that was a wise move, considering everything that had happened.

He popped open the generator hood and glanced inside.

Right away, he spotted what was wrong.

Two wires had been cut.

"Maddox?" Taryn leaned closer.

He pointed to the wires and explained what was wrong.

"Why would someone do that?" she shouted above the storm.

Maddox didn't want to answer that question.

He guessed that someone did this as a power play.

They probably wanted everyone inside the house to feel uneasy.

Or maybe there was even more to it.

As lightning filled the sky, Maddox spotted a figure running across the field in the distance.

Most likely, the person who'd done this.

And maybe the person he'd seen earlier also.

CHAPTER
TEN

TARYN FOLLOWED Maddox's gaze and saw the man in the distance.

She gasped.

Was that the person who'd done this?

It had to be.

"We won't catch him." Maddox's voice cut into her thoughts. "He's too far away."

That was fine with Taryn. She certainly didn't want Maddox to chase him and leave her here by herself. But still . . . they needed to figure out who was behind these crimes.

They?

She'd meant *she*. *Taryn* needed to figure out who was behind these crimes.

Maddox . . . well, he could very well be another suspect here. Sure, some strange man was running across the lawn. But who was to say that man wasn't working with someone?

She needed to be careful.

Maddox nodded toward the house. "Let's get you back inside. I'm going to need to grab some tools and supplies before I can fix this."

She didn't argue.

He placed his hand on her arm as he directed her back inside, where they stripped off their raincoats and hung them on hooks by the back door. Though the jackets had helped some, they were both still soaking wet.

Taryn glanced through the doorway at the dining room as she removed her wet shoes.

Everyone seemed okay, and no one seemed to notice they were back inside.

Maddox also took off his wet shoes and set them by the door as he asked, "Taryn, what entrances are on this side of the house?"

Her eyes widened in surprise at his question. Where was he going with this? "There are several. But the closest one opens to a hallway leading to the west wing."

"Could you show me where that door is?"

She stared at him another moment, questions rushing through her head, before nodding. "Of course."

He followed her toward the west wing.

As they reached the patio doors there, Taryn paused.

Maddox shone his light on the floor.

Wet footprints tracked in from outside.

Taryn gasped at the sight of them. "Who could have left those?"

Maddox didn't respond. Instead, he followed the tracks.

Taryn remained behind him, wondering what might be waiting for them in the dark.

Was someone poised to pounce? Had a trap been set?

Nothing seemed certain.

The prints stopped outside a large wooden door.

"Mr. Whitlock's office," Taryn muttered.

Maddox glanced back at her. "Can you get inside?"

She shook her head. "I don't have a key with me."

Maddox reached for the door anyway. When he twisted the handle, it opened.

He glanced at Taryn. "Should we tell Mr. Whitlock first?"

She thought about it before shaking her head again. "Not yet. We should check it out first. I don't want to upset him if there's no reason for it."

Maddox hesitated only a moment before stepping inside.

Taryn followed behind him, anxious to see what might await.

———

Taryn's nerves consumed her until her limbs trembled uncontrollably, and her throat tightened until she felt as if she couldn't breathe.

"Stay behind me," Maddox whispered as he crept forward into the dark space with only his flashlight to light the way.

Oh, Taryn would have no problem doing that.

This had already been one rotten day.

And now this?

Why would someone want to get into Mr. Whitlock's office?

Taryn had only been in here once, but she couldn't imagine he kept very many valuables inside.

Unless . . .

Was this where his safe was?

She didn't even know. She'd never really thought about it.

She remained in Maddox's shadow as he searched the space.

It was clear.

Whoever had been inside was now gone.

It was probably the same person they'd seen running across the backyard.

"Let me know if you see anything out of place," Maddox said quietly.

But everything appeared in perfect order.

After Maddox examined the room, he turned toward her, his shoulders relaxing slightly. "I don't know why someone would have been in here."

"Me neither." Taryn rubbed her arms, another chill washing over her. "But I don't like this."

Maddox frowned. "I don't either. We should tell Mr. Whitlock."

She grabbed Maddox's arm before he could step toward the door and do just that. "I don't think that's a good idea."

He narrowed his eyes as he studied her face. "Why not?"

"With his heart troubles . . ."

He slowly nodded as if understanding had dawned on him. "You're afraid something will send him over the edge?"

Taryn nodded. "I don't want to treat him as if he's fragile . . . but he is, whether he wants to admit it or not."

Maddox rubbed his beard as if in thought. "Does he know anything about the other incidents that have happened around here? Did you tell him you were chased through the maze? About Leroy? About the rocks?"

"I haven't had the heart to tell him about what

happened to me. Leroy . . . Mr. Whitlock heard the ambulance when it came, but he thinks it was just an accident. I didn't correct him."

"I can respect that . . . but he probably needs to know, Taryn." His voice didn't sound pushy or judgmental—more like a counselor encouraging someone to do the right thing.

And something about the way Maddox said her name made fire race through Taryn's blood.

That was bad. *Very* bad.

The last time she'd fallen for a guy, he'd turned her life upside down—in a devastating way. Taryn had to protect herself—and her heart. This was no time to feel tingles around a guy.

Especially not one who grunted, who had tattoos, and whose eyes were brooding.

Yet, another part of her felt like she could see beyond that, see beyond the physical to who this guy really was: a gentle spirit clothed with a rough past.

Maybe Taryn could see those qualities because she could relate so well.

"For now, we'll keep this quiet," Maddox said. "But we really need to give this some thought. Until then, let's set up some extra security measures here at the estate. I can help you with that if you'd like."

Taryn nodded as relief flushed through her. "Good idea."

That might hold off more trouble for a while.

But as soon as Mr. Whitlock found out about these incidents, Taryn would have no choice but to also tell him about the threats he'd been receiving in the mail.

Once she unleashed that information, she had no idea what the outcome might be.

Then she remembered the word those rocks had spelled out.

Death.

That's how this would end, wasn't it?

She swallowed back a cry at the thought.

The question was: whose death?

CHAPTER
ELEVEN

TARYN HADN'T BEEN able to sleep all night.

Every time she closed her eyes, she remembered seeing that figure running across the lawn as lightning illuminated the sky.

She remembered being chased through the labyrinth.

She remembered finding Leroy with blood dripping from his hand.

She remembered those rocks spelling DEATH.

What was going on here? Was someone trying to scare everyone off so they could get Mr. Whitlock's money?

It was a possibility.

If that was the case, then Phil was her top suspect.

Mr. Whitlock's son was clearly money hungry. In fact, every time he came by, he asked for more cash from his father—even though he already had full access to his trust fund.

Did he want his father's fortune enough to scare others for it? It seemed so . . . extreme.

But all the staff had been at the dinner table last night.

So, whoever was behind this . . . it wasn't someone who worked here.

Which again brought Taryn back to Phil.

Where had he been last night?

The man gave her bad vibes for other reasons than being a spoiled brat.

He'd actually hit on her a couple of times. Taryn had made it clear she wasn't interested, but she wasn't sure Phil had taken the hint. He was the type who got whatever he wanted and didn't like hearing no.

She sighed as she stepped out of her room to begin her day.

The first thing she did was go through the mail from yesterday. Eleanor had left it on a table in the foyer.

Taryn's gaze stopped on one of the envelopes.

The address on the front was written in the same handwriting as the other letters—the ones with the threats inside.

Cautiously, she opened the envelope.

Just as she thought.

Another warning.

Leave now or something bad is going to happen. Go to a home for people who are dying. And leave this place be.

Taryn's heart pounded in her chest.

Who would send a dying man something like this?

Someone heartless, that was who.

———

Maddox awoke before the sun rose. He hadn't gotten much sleep last night.

As he'd pondered everything that had happened, he'd gone to his window to look outside.

He'd seen lights in the distance last night.

Faint lights behind the stables.

He'd started to go outside to check on them when he'd spotted Shawn on the patio. The man had been on the phone, talking to someone about an investment.

Who talked to people about investments in the middle of the night?

The whole thing was suspect.

He really hadn't been able to sleep after that. Instead, he'd sat in a chair in the corner of his room and done the one thing that always helped him relax.

Yes, crocheting. Something about the hobby kept his thoughts focused and even. The consistency of the motion was the crutch he needed to calm down or sort through his thoughts.

But now it was morning, and he needed to get to work—despite his tired mind and body.

As soon as possible, Maddox wanted to head out to the stables to see if there was anything behind those lights.

He headed toward the bathroom when he spotted a paper on the floor by his door.

His muscles tightened.

Could this be a threat?

Carefully—using the edge of his T-shirt—he lifted it.

As he opened the paper, a list appeared.

From Taryn.

He let out an airy chuckle as his muscles relaxed.

He scanned the words there.

She'd typed up everything Maddox needed to do today, including fixing a leaky toilet, replacing an old light fixture in a guest bathroom, and repainting the columns on the porch.

It looked like he'd be busy.

He hadn't gotten to bed until after midnight last night, mostly because he'd been thinking too much.

The happenings here at this estate were no acci-dent. Maddox was determined to get to the bottom of things—to find answers and report back to his team.

The danger here seemed to be quickly escalating, and he feared time was running out.

That meant he didn't have time to ease into this assignment.

As he got out of the shower and dressed, he thought about his suspects.

He'd been observing everyone at the estate since he arrived. He had reason to suspect each one.

Shawn was a numbers guy, so clearly the man realized how a windfall like Mr. Whitlock's estate could benefit someone—probably himself.

Danielle, the stable master, had quite a bit of debt thanks to a shopping addiction.

Chef Mulligan had once gone to prison for insurance fraud. She'd served only three months, but that proved she was capable of committing crimes.

Then there was Taryn . . . a woman who'd grown up with nothing, who had no professional management experience, who had no formal caregiving education, yet she'd landed a job here as Mr. Whitlock's personal assistant.

Worst of all, at one time she'd dated Grissom Smith.

Maddox was curious about the history between the two of them.

From what he could tell, Taryn didn't seem the type to date someone like Grissom. Then again, she could be acting her way through all this. Either way, last night it had become clear that, more than anything, she wanted to protect Mr. Whitlock. She was bending over backwards to prevent him from experiencing any more stress than necessary.

Maddox frowned as he looked in the mirror and combed his hair. He didn't get the impression that Mr. Whitlock was interested in Taryn romantically. Maddox had heard stories about wealthy, older men who liked younger women. Taryn was certainly pretty enough that Mr. Whitlock might be interested —if he was that type.

But Maddox didn't think that was the case. He hadn't witnessed Taryn flirting with Whitlock or any outward signs she'd do something like that.

Still, Maddox needed to be open to all the possibilities here.

With one last glance in the mirror, he started toward the door. He needed to get to work.

But, first, he needed to grab those painted rocks.

He wished he could have obtained them before it rained. Evidence could have been left on them. Besides, if they ever reported the incident to the police, the cops might want to see them.

Did they somehow tie in with the missing tech?

He didn't know.

But Maddox needed to put the puzzle pieces together . . . quickly.

CHAPTER
TWELVE

"READ ME JUST ONE MORE CHAPTER." Mr. Whitlock stared at Taryn as he sat in his recliner across from her. Sunlight from the window lit his face, and a blanket was pulled across his lap. Overall, he looked comfortable and content.

Taryn glanced at the book in her hands and nodded. *The Great Gatsby* by F. Scott Fitzgerald was a fascinating read.

Reading was one of her favorite activities the two of them did together. Taryn loved books, and Mr. Whitlock had introduced her to several new authors she'd never read before. She'd never really enjoyed the classics until she started working here.

Now she loved the tales written by Tolkien and Harper Lee and Jane Austen. She didn't realize how much she'd been missing out on until now.

Mr. Whitlock's hand covered hers as she finished the chapter. "Have I told you that I believe God sent you to me?"

Taryn smiled at the sincerity in his voice. "You have mentioned that."

"You're the only person here that I truly trust, Taryn."

Her heart pounded harder at his words.

Did Mr. Whitlock suspect something was going on?

Part of her wanted to tell him about the letters. Wanted to ask about the nightmare he'd been having yesterday. Wanted to know if he suspected anyone who worked for him could be involved in something sinister.

That wasn't even to mention the break-in in his office and all the questions arising from that.

But she kept those questions silent.

Instead, she forced a smile, trying to not let Mr. Whitlock know she was worried. "I'm so appreciative you feel that way about me. But you have other people here who love you also."

He grunted and looked away, his thin skin making him seem even more frail today. "These people . . . they either want money from me when I die, or they like me because I'm the one currently paying them."

Taryn waited for him to continue, sensing he had more to say and anxious to hear what it might be.

"I always thought I had all these people in my life who cared about me." Mr. Whitlock stared into the distance as if his mind had traveled to another time and place. "But it was all just some game. We were just running in the same circles, but none of them were truly my friends."

She squeezed his hand, unsure what to say. But she knew where he was coming from even though she didn't agree with him out loud.

She didn't trust most of the people here either.

"True friends can be hard to find," she murmured. "No matter what your financial situation is."

"Yes, that is true."

She licked her lips, hesitant to ask her next question. But she had to.

She shifted. "Mr. Whitlock . . . you didn't see anyone strange in the labyrinth yesterday, did you?"

"Yesterday?" He scratched his head. "No, I can't say I did. I stepped out for a minute, but my phone rang so I came back inside. Why?"

"Just curious. No reason."

His neutral expression faded in favor of a frown. "Taryn, there's something I need to tell you—"

Before he could finish, the doorbell rang.

Taryn knew Eleanor had gone to a dentist

appointment this morning, so Taryn would need to answer.

But she wanted to hear what he had to say also. It had sounded important.

"We'll finish talking later," Mr. Whitlock said.

She tried not to show her disappointment.

Hopefully, he'd tell her later.

For now, Taryn hurried down the stairs.

She wasn't expecting anyone here at the house today. Normally, answering the front door didn't make her cautious. But, given everything that had happened recently, it would be prudent to be on guard.

Taryn opened the door. A sixty-something woman with stark black hair, a model-thin build, and skintight leather pants lowered her sunglasses to observe Taryn over the top.

Without an invitation, the woman strode inside. "Who are you? Seymore's new girlfriend?"

"Excuse me?" Taryn's lungs filled with outrage at this woman's audacity. "You can't just barge in here. Who do you think you are? And, no, I'm not his girl-friend, thank you."

"Of course, I can barge in here. This house is part mine."

Taryn froze. "What do you mean?"

The woman observed her through narrowed eyes and an upturned nose.

"I'm Seymore's wife, Alana Whitlock. I'd say nice to meet you but . . ." She shrugged as if the words wouldn't be true. "Now, where's my husband?"

Maddox fixed the lock on the door leading to the patio as part of his upgraded security measures.

As he did, he replayed his morning so far—starting with the fact that when he'd gone to get the rocks, they were gone.

Someone had clearly been watching and waiting for the opportunity to take them.

Was it someone on staff? Or could someone from the outside be sneaking onto the property to wreak havoc?

He wasn't sure.

He glanced across the room to observe Alana Whitlock. Taryn stood beside him, also watching as Alana fanned herself while sitting in a chair. Mr. Whitlock had wanted to rest more before he came downstairs.

Apparently, the woman was Mr. Whitlock's *ex*-wife, but she liked to introduce herself as his *current* wife.

The man *had* been married three times. He had only one child, a fact that surprised Maddox.

"I don't like her," Taryn said quietly.

He glanced up at her before testing the door lock. "Why is that?"

"She shows up here now when Mr. Whitlock is dying? Certainly, you know how that looks." Taryn crossed her arms.

"I do. From what I've heard, she's a gold digger."

Taryn's eyes widened. "You've heard of her?"

Maddox raised his eyebrows in surprise. "You haven't?"

She shrugged. "I've never really been one to keep up with the lifestyles of the rich and famous."

"That's probably a good thing. Not much positive comes out of it. But she was an actress in a few B grade movies. Their relationship always seemed to make the tabloids."

"I would rather be poor and happy than have all this money and feel like I don't have anyone to trust."

Maddox glanced up and gave Taryn a nod. He understood. But he was surprised Taryn had opened up so easily.

She seemed to be equally surprised by the fact, and she straightened, pressing her lips together as if she hadn't meant to say those words.

She cleared her throat. "Anyway . . . good job here."

"Thanks."

She nodded at the hat on his head. "Nice beanie, by the way."

He touched the crocheted blue cap he'd pulled down to his ears. "This old thing? Thanks. It was a little chilly outside this morning."

"One day I'm going to learn how to knit those myself."

"Crochet," he said.

She squinted. "What?"

"This beanie is actually crocheted."

She nodded slowly. "Good to know."

As much as he'd love to continue this conversation, there were other things he needed to talk to her about—other more important things.

"Taryn . . ." he started.

"Yes?"

"You know how we've been talking about upping security measures?"

"I do."

"There's more to it than just fixing door locks. I feel like I need to get into Mr. Whitlock's office again. I want to see why someone might have broken in."

Her eyes widened, and she shook her head. "I'm not sure that's a good idea."

"I'm just concerned about whatever is going on here. I'm afraid someone might have left something in there. It's all I've been able to think about."

She nibbled on her bottom lip. "How do you suggest you get permission to go inside?"

"Tell Mr. Whitlock I need to check all the windows in this place to make sure they're secure. That would include his office."

Taryn stared at him another moment. "I don't know . . ."

"I promise—I won't get you in trouble."

She still seemed unconvinced.

"This is for Mr. Whitlock's sake," Maddox said. "I don't want anything to happen again."

Those seemed to be the magic words.

Taryn nodded—although still appearing hesitant. "I'll see what I can do. But no promises."

Maddox watched as she hurried back toward Alana.

This assignment was getting more interesting all the time.

Taryn seemed innocent.

But Maddox really needed to keep an eye on her.

And he needed to figure out what was in Mr. Whitlock's office.

What if it was the missing tech?

TARYN FELT a headache beginning to pound at her temples as she waited for Maddox in the breezeway leading into the west wing.

The headache had been simmering there all day. But now that the evening was coming to an end, the throbbing ache had unleashed itself at full force.

Alana had been demanding, to say the least.

The woman had asked for a salad at lunch with no stalks on her lettuce and with ranch dressing diluted 50 percent. She wanted one lemon slice in her filtered water—a lemon slice without any seeds. And, as the final straw, she'd demanded to eat outside on the patio with a mister to spritz her face.

Taryn straightened when she saw Maddox coming toward her. Another round of quivers raced through her.

She was incredibly uncomfortable with what Maddox was doing. Yet another part of her understood his reasoning.

Now, she just wanted to get this over with.

"I told Mr. Whitlock that you needed to get in here to check the windows for security purposes," Taryn told Maddox as they began walking toward the office. "So, you won't have much time. You really think you're going to find something?"

"I don't know, but I'd feel better looking, at least."

"You're not here to cause any trouble, right?" She hated to question him, but after everything that happened, how could she not? It was only wise to ask more questions, to be prudent.

He squinted, almost appearing injured by the question. "Taryn, I'm not here to start trouble. I promise you that. I don't want you or anyone else getting hurt."

Something about the way Maddox said the words caused another shiver to go down her spine. He sounded like he meant what he said, like he'd never want anything bad to happen to her.

Taryn hadn't realized how much she craved that security. She wanted a stable life and, so far, she'd never experienced anything like that.

Not until she came here.

But now this new position seemed so uncertain also.

With one more glance at him, Taryn unlocked the office door and pushed it open. "Good luck."

Maddox glanced at her a lingering moment before nodding. "Thank you for trusting me, Taryn."

She hoped she didn't regret it—especially when Chef texted and said she needed Taryn in the kitchen.

That meant she would have to leave Maddox here.

Alone.

Taryn frowned.

This had bad idea written all over it.

Maddox didn't know where to start in Mr. Whitlock's office. But this was his best chance of finding out more information—and looking for that missing tech.

Was Mr. Whitlock somehow involved in the theft?

Maddox couldn't rule anything out.

Not yet.

Someone could simply be taking advantage of the man, however.

Maddox had a lot of questions still.

He sat down at Mr. Whitlock's desk. Maddox had already checked the room to make sure no cameras were hidden.

From what Taryn had told him, most of the security cameras were located at the outside doors. But when the power had gone off last night, so had the cameras. Whoever their intruder had been, his images hadn't been caught on video.

No doubt this person had planned it that way. He'd most likely known about the security measures at the house and had knocked the power out because of that.

Maddox opened Mr. Whitlock's drawers, looking for something. Anything.

But nothing caught his eye.

Quickly, he moved to the filing cabinet and went through the papers stored there.

He stopped at a folder labeled "land deeds."

This could be useful.

He opened the folder and set it on the desk. He didn't have time to look at everything now, so instead he pulled out his phone and snapped some pictures. He could refer back to some of these later if they proved to be relevant.

Just as quickly as he'd pulled the folder out, he closed it again and shoved the papers back into the filing cabinet. Then he continued looking through things.

Nothing else caught his eye.

Next, Maddox moved to the bookshelf.

He paused by one set of books, noticing they looked odd. The hardback spines were all different colors and the row of books appeared shoved close together without as much as a sliver of space.

He pressed one of them. At once, eight books slid back as if spring-loaded.

A safe appeared on the other side.

Maddox stared at it for a moment, wondering exactly what was inside.

Money?

Or was it something else equally as valuable?

Even more: was this what the intruder last night had been looking for?

TARYN TRIED NOT to show her nerves, but it was difficult. Especially since Alana kept watching her.

Chef had called Taryn because she needed help serving food and drinks to Alana, who was driving her crazy and had her on the verge of quitting.

Even now that Alana had her sparkling water with grenadine and three cherries and her gluten-free charcuterie board, the woman still seemed terse as she sat in the living room with Mr. Whitlock.

Taryn wished she could lead the woman to the door and show her out. But that wasn't Taryn's call to make. Mr. Whitlock was capable of making that decision for himself.

Ten minutes into Alana's whiny soliloquy about alimony, the doorbell rang.

Great. Who now?

Taryn excused herself to answer—anxious for an excuse to get away. But when she pulled the door open, she was surprised to see Gerald Macintosh on the other side.

Mr. Whitlock's lawyer.

Glancing behind him, Taryn also spotted Phil. Mr. Whitlock's son shuffled back and forth from leg to leg as if impatient.

"Excuse me," Phil muttered. "But I had a long night, and I need to lie down."

A long night? Was that because he was involved in some of the mayhem here at the house?

Taryn shoved the thought aside—for now, at least.

He flashed a quick smile at Taryn as he breezed past. "Good to see you, Taryn."

She nodded, surprised by the warmth in his voice. "You too."

Taryn and Gerald watched as the man hurried up the stairs without attempting any more conversation.

That was typical of Phil. He defined spoiled brat.

Taryn turned back to Gerald. She recalled he was supposed to come by sometime today for a meeting with Mr. Whitlock. He hadn't set an exact time, but just said that he'd come after one of his meetings.

The appointment had nearly slipped her mind.

How was she forgetting so many things lately?

The stress of everything that had happened must be getting to her.

"Gerald, come on in." Taryn extended her hand behind her.

"Hello, Taryn." He paused, a short man with a full head of blond hair peppered with gray.

The man was nice enough, though very direct with little time for chitchat. Apparently, he was one of Mr. Whitlock's oldest friends.

Gerald pivoted toward her. "Is Seymore nearby?"

Taryn considered sharing with him that Alana was here, but she decided against it. Gerald would see that for himself soon enough.

"He is." Taryn showed him into the living room.

Mr. Whitlock rose when he saw his friend step into the room. "Gerald. I'm glad you made it by. I've been wanting to talk to you."

But Gerald's eyes went to Alana, and his gaze hardened. "Alana . . . I wasn't expecting to see you here."

"The pleasure is all mine," she purred despite the scowl on her face.

Clearly, no love was lost between the two.

"Gerald, how about if the two of us talk in my office." Mr. Whitlock glanced back at Alana. "But no one else."

Alarm rushed through Taryn.

What if Mr. Whitlock walked in and found

Maddox searching his things? No, not *searching* his things. But looking for a sign that anything had been tampered with.

Was Maddox still in there? How could Taryn warn him without giving away the fact she'd been the one who left him inside?

If he was caught, Taryn was the one who'd be fired.

She didn't want to lose the trust of the one person who'd believed in her.

Panic raced through her at the thought.

Taryn needed to figure out something, and she needed to do it soon.

Maddox closed the fake books, concealing the safe again. He'd taken a picture of it. The door needed a handprint to be opened, so getting inside wasn't a possibility. Not easily, at least.

As he stepped away, his phone rang. He glanced at the screen, wondering if it might be Taryn.

Instead, it was Colton.

If Colton was calling, there was probably a good reason.

"There's something I thought you might need to know about," Colton started.

"What's that?" Maddox paced to the window and

glanced outside, looking for any additional signs of trouble.

He didn't see anything suspicious.

"We interviewed a man named Abe Billings," Colton said. "He's the Embolden Tech employee who put the tracker in the package of cameras and listening devices before giving it to the delivery driver who was killed."

"Before you go on—do they always place trackers in their packages?"

"They only started after the incident we investigated there a couple of months ago."

"Good to know."

"Anyway, we just wanted to figure out if there was anything suspicious about the driver," Colton continued. "As we talked to Abe, it became clear he knew more than he was letting on. The police took him in, but he isn't talking."

Maddox's entire body hardened. "What?"

"Whoever wanted those products was willing to kill for them—and more than one person was obviously involved. We have to find some answers, and we need to find them soon."

"I agree. I'm doing the best I can here."

"I know you are. I just wanted to give you the heads-up."

"I appreciate that. I'll keep you updated." Just as

Maddox said the words, the door handle twisted. Deep voices sounded in the hall.

Someone was here, he realized.

Maddox had to act quickly, or he would be discovered . . . and his whole mission would be compromised.

"LET ME WALK WITH YOU," Taryn insisted, quickly moving to stand in place beside Mr. Whitlock.

He didn't argue—or miss a word in his conversation with Gerald as the two of them talked about golfing.

As they approached the office, Taryn laughed at a corny joke Gerald made. She laughed *especially* loud.

She needed to give Maddox a clue they were coming inside the office just in case he was still in there.

But a sick feeling churned in her stomach.

If she lost her job, she might have to go back to her old life. She had no real qualifications to get a better job. No one else around here would hire her.

She was sure of that fact—especially since Grissom had raked her name through the mud.

The thought of going back to living with that kind of uncertainty made her sick to her stomach.

She couldn't let that happen.

Taryn should have told Maddox he couldn't come in here. What had she been thinking? The man had been so convincing.

Mr. Whitlock unlocked the door and pushed it open.

She held her breath as she waited to see the office on the other side.

"Maddox . . ." Mr. Whitlock muttered, his brow wrinkling.

Taryn peered inside and saw Maddox near the window.

"I'm just about done here." Maddox shoved the window down before locking it. "The hardware was loose, and I didn't want to take any chances. I'm working on tightening all the window locks in an effort to make the house more secure."

"Glad that's taken care of." Mr. Whitlock's laser-like gaze remained on Maddox, watching his every move.

"I'll be out of your way now." Maddox slipped his screwdriver back into his toolbelt before striding past them, acting as if nothing was out of the ordinary.

But Taryn didn't miss the scrutinizing look Mr. Whitlock gave him.

When Maddox was out of sight, Mr. Whitlock turned to her. "We did do a background check on that man, didn't we?"

"Yes, sir," Taryn said. "He's clean."

"That's good. I didn't know he was in the office unattended." Disappointment stretched through his voice.

"I'm sorry. I was going to stay in here with him, but Chef texted me. She needed me in the kitchen. Then Gerald arrived and . . ."

He waved her off as he staggered forward. The man refused to use a cane or walker, even though he looked like he could fall over at any moment.

"No need to explain anymore," Mr. Whitlock said. "But, in the future, no one stays in here alone. Understand?"

Taryn nodded, her lungs loosening. "Understood."

"Now, if you'll close the door behind you as you leave . . ."

Taryn stepped into the hallway and released a long breath.

That had been close.

She started to step away when she heard the conversation drifting from inside the office.

"Shawn and I chatted earlier," Gerald started. "I

need to talk to you about several things—including your electric bills over the past few months . . ."

"Why isn't Shawn here?"

"My understanding is that he stayed here overnight. But, he had a couple of calls to make to his other clients—prearranged appointments—so I told him I'd handle it since I'd be here anyway."

"I shouldn't be using any more electricity than usual," Mr. Whitlock said.

"That's what concerns me . . ."

High electricity bills? Taryn mused. What sense did that make? Nothing had happened here that would explain the increase.

Unless something was going on that Taryn didn't know about.

That seemed more and more of a possibility all the time.

Now she needed to find Maddox.

Maddox returned to the garage to gather some tools.

He was grateful when he saw Taryn step inside a moment later. He wanted to talk to her and find out if Mr. Whitlock was suspicious.

And he needed to make sure she was okay. He'd put her in a tough spot, and he regretted that.

Her features seemed stiffer than before, like she was still reeling from the earlier events.

She paused beside him at the workbench and lowered her voice. "That was close."

"I know." Maddox picked out a few nails he needed to fix a railing outside.

"Did you find anything?"

He contemplated how much to say before deciding to ask, "Did you know Mr. Whitlock has a safe hidden behind some books in his office?"

Taryn's eyes widened. "No. I had no idea. Then again, I don't usually go snooping around, and I *definitely* don't go looking for safes."

Maddox studied her face, looking for any sign of deception. "So, you have no idea what's inside?"

"No, no idea. Probably valuables, right? Money, passports, jewelry. Aren't they what people usually keep in safes? I didn't exactly grow up having one. We didn't own anything worth stealing, for that matter. I suppose his patents could be there also."

So far, Taryn sounded and acted like she was telling the truth.

"Yes, valuables are kept in them," Maddox said. "It could definitely be those things you mentioned. Or it could be other information or objects Mr. Whitlock doesn't want people to get their hands on."

"He was an inventor. Maybe more than patents

could be inside. Could Mr. Whitlock have locked away some prototypes or something?"

"It's a good possibility." Maddox gave up on collecting his supplies and shifted toward Taryn. "Look, I'm not saying anything. I'm just a handyman. But if someone went through all that trouble to break into the house and if they're risky enough to threaten the people working here, then they're clearly after something that's of value to them."

Taryn frowned. "That makes sense . . ."

"Maybe it's money. That's the most logical conclusion, considering Mr. Whitlock's wealth. I don't really care what it is. I just don't like what's going on around here."

Taryn crossed her arms and shoved her hip up against the workbench. "Why do you even care so much?"

Maddox needed to back off. Maybe he'd come across as too eager. "I suppose I could ask the same of you."

She frowned and nibbled on her bottom lip. "He took a chance on me, he trusts me, and I don't want to let him down. Besides, if I fail here . . ."

Maddox paused, anxious to hear where Taryn was going with that statement.

She shrugged, seeming to think better of finishing her sentence. "Anyway, it's just that I need this job, okay? I don't want to do anything to mess it up."

Before Taryn could say more, her phone rang. She glanced down at it and excused herself to answer.

But when she turned back, her face again looked pale.

"What is it?" Maddox asked.

"That was Eleanor. She said Chef was looking for Leroy. She wanted him to bring some fresh basil from the greenhouse to her. Anyway, she can't find him. He's not answering his phone, and she didn't see him outside."

Concern pulsed through Maddox. Considering everything that had happened around here . . . they needed to take this seriously.

He nodded toward the door. "Come on. I'll help you look for him. Hopefully, Leroy just got distracted and didn't hear his phone ring."

But Maddox knew that the chances of that being true were slim to none.

CHAPTER
SIXTEEN

TARYN'S SHOULDERS knotted together as she walked with Maddox outside. Something close to an impending feeling of doom swept through her.

What was going on here?

She wanted to trust Maddox. She really did. Something about him just seemed so trustworthy.

But she'd be foolish to put her total trust in anyone right now—especially considering everything that was going on.

She'd partly hoped that yesterday had just been a fluke. She'd hoped that all the trouble was done with, and that life would go back to normal. Maybe the person behind these acts had given up and moved on.

But that didn't seem to be the case. Not even close.

She strode across the grassy lawn with Maddox, grateful it was sunny today and that yesterday's storm had passed. But it was springtime, and she was sure they'd get more.

Maddox had already repaired the generator, so hopefully there wouldn't be another power outage if the electricity went off again.

"What's Leroy like?" Maddox glanced at her, the sinking sun catching his hair and beard and almost giving his profile a glow.

Taryn slowed her steps as she pondered how to respond. "He's quiet. Keeps to himself. Prefers to be outside with nature rather than to be with people, I think."

"I can understand that."

She stole a glance at him. "Not much of a people person?"

"I like people—in small doses. But I'd rather have a small circle of close friends than a wide circle of people I only halfway know."

"I can understand that."

"How about you?" He looked over at her before scanning the back lawn again.

"It's hard to say. By the time I was old enough to work, I was getting jobs to try to help support my mom. She was sickly for a very long time. So, I'd go to school and then go to work then come home to do my homework and sleep. It didn't really give me much of a chance for a social life."

"I'm sorry to hear that."

Taryn shrugged. "That's just life. It doesn't do much good to feel sorry for yourself. You just have to keep going."

Maddox wondered again about Taryn. Wondered again about her past and what had made her into who she was today.

Wondered about her relationship with Grissom.

The more he got to know her, the less he saw Taryn as the type to be affiliated with a man like Grissom. Just what had happened between them?

He wanted to know—and not just for professional reasons.

They reached the greenhouse, and Maddox put up a hand to stop Taryn.

He would go inside first.

Just in case.

Maddox had seen more than his fair share of dead bodies in his lifetime.

Seeing a dead body could change a person.

He didn't want that to happen to Taryn.

And he didn't want Leroy to be dead.

Why was Maddox so easy to open up to? Taryn found herself sharing things with him that she normally didn't talk about. But instinctively, she wanted to trust him.

She hoped that impulse didn't get her in trouble.

She also hoped that the man's appearance here wasn't the reason so many bad things had been happening.

But what if while Maddox was working in Mr. Whitlock's office, he'd done something? What if he'd left a listening device? Was Maddox that sophisticated?

Taryn didn't know.

But things had certainly escalated since he'd come here.

She'd be wise to remember that.

She peered through the greenhouse door. More than anything, she wanted to go inside and check out things for herself. But Maddox had seemed adamant that she stay out here.

Was that because he wanted to protect her?

Or because he wanted to cover up something?

At the thought, Taryn peered through a crack in the door.

As she did, she spotted Maddox . . . slipping something into his pocket.

Alarm rushed through her.

What if she was right? What if, just as always, she

was a bad judge of character? Her gut told her she could trust Maddox. But what if, in reality, he was one of the bad guys?

Otherwise, why would he have slipped something into his pocket?

The door creaked, and Maddox jerked his head toward the sound. When he spotted her, his expression went from stiff to concerned.

Was there guilt in his gaze also?

Taryn wasn't sure.

He motioned for her to come inside. "Leroy's not in here."

She glanced around, trying to get a glimpse of things for herself. "Is there any evidence of foul play?"

"I don't see anything. You said this is where he usually likes to work, right?"

"Yes, but he takes care of this entire property."

"Maybe we should check out the stable area?"

Taryn considered it before nodding. "Probably a good idea—just so we can be certain."

But she couldn't get the image of Maddox slipping something into his pocket out of her mind.

What if Maddox's motives weren't what she'd assumed?

CHAPTER
SEVENTEEN

AS MADDOX and Taryn walked toward the stables, he thought about the paper he'd found.

Had Taryn seen him slip it into his pocket?

He hoped not.

A piece of paper had been on the ground. It might be nothing. There were no words on the torn slip, but a circular symbol had been stamped in the corner.

It only made sense that the paper had fallen out of Leroy's pocket.

Maddox wanted to look into what that symbol might mean.

But right now, they needed to find Leroy, and the stables seemed like the next logical place to look.

However, there was another reason he wanted to check around the stables.

He'd seen lights back there last night.

He wanted to see if there were any tire tracks that had been left. With everything going on, he didn't want any detail to slip by.

He glanced behind the stables.

A UTV was parked there, the kind used to carry equipment across large properties such as this one.

Was that what he'd seen?

The vehicle was pointed toward the woods.

As Maddox glanced that way, he wasn't sure if the trees were far enough apart for a vehicle to fit between them.

He'd have to explore the property in order to find that out.

"I don't see Leroy anywhere," Taryn muttered with a frown.

"Me neither. Maybe Danielle has seen him." He cupped his hands around his mouth. "Danielle?"

There was no answer.

"Let's check inside the stables, just in case," Taryn suggested.

As they stepped inside, Maddox looked at the ground.

He froze at what he saw there.

Those painted rocks they'd stumbled across.

The missing four were here.

In the stables.

Along with a bucket full of painting supplies.

As soon as Maddox spotted them, a shadow fell over the doorway.

He glanced back and spotted Danielle standing behind them.

———

"Why do you look like that?" Danielle's eyebrows shoved together.

Taryn took a step back, wondering just how trustworthy Danielle really was.

Had Danielle been the person in the labyrinth with Taryn yesterday?

Maddox crossed his arms as he glared at the woman. "Did you paint those rocks?"

"I did," Danielle said. "My friends and I are going to have a scavenger hunt. It's a bit macabre, but the letters were supposed to spell *death*. Not because we wanted to hurt anyone. But we've been playing this crime scene game online, and this was one of the puzzle pieces and—"

"Were you the one who chased Taryn yesterday?" Maddox interrupted, his shoulders seemed to broaden as he addressed Danielle.

Danielle's eyebrows shoved together. "Chased Taryn? No."

"You do realize one of these rocks was deliberately placed in her path, in an area where she didn't see it until she was right upon it. It made her stumble and—"

"I didn't do it," Danielle shook her head, her gaze filling with what appeared to be panic. "I promise. My rocks disappeared yesterday, and I only found them last night. Except one of them is still missing."

Taryn wanted to believe Danielle, but her story seemed shaky at best. "Who else knew about these rocks?"

"No one yet. Not even my friends. This was my mission on this game." She let out a sigh and rolled her eyes. "It seems silly to say it out loud. But you've got to know I would never try to hurt you, Taryn. I wouldn't. I'll send you the link for the game and everything if that's what it takes to prove it."

"I'd like to see that link," Maddox muttered before pressing his lips together in a tight line.

Danielle nodded and pulled out her phone. "Give me your number. I'll text it to you."

Maddox rattled off the information. A moment later, he grunted as he stared at his phone. "You're right. Those rocks are part of a live-action game."

Danielle's shoulders slumped as if she were relieved.

"What about Leroy?" Taryn didn't feel relaxed yet. There were still too many unknowns. "Have you seen him?"

Danielle stepped closer to one of her horses and rubbed the mare's head. "No, I haven't. Why?"

"He's not answering his phone, and he seems to have disappeared."

"I'll help you look," Danielle said. "I'll check out behind the pasture."

"Sounds good."

As she disappeared from sight, Taryn turned toward Maddox. "There's only one other place I can think to check."

Maddox glanced at her as if waiting for her to finish.

She swallowed hard. "The labyrinth."

For some reason, the thought of going back inside again sent a flash of terror down her spine.

"LEROY?" Maddox called as he stood at the start of the labyrinth.

He waited, but there was no answer.

He swallowed hard, a surge of caution shooting through him as he stepped between the hedges.

Something about this place made a chill wash through him.

He'd been in war zones. Had navigated minefields. Had invaded terrorist compounds.

But for some reason this circular maze made him feel uneasy. Something about it . . . about the uncertainty of being able to see only a few steps ahead. Of not knowing where the end was. Of not knowing if he could get out or if he'd walk in circles while the exit was only a few feet away but tucked out of sight.

"I think I told you before that a lot of people view

labyrinths as a place of prayer." Taryn's voice pulled him from his thoughts. "Walking it can be a spiritual practice when you focus your mind and simply talk to God as you move. Something about the quiet, about the movement makes me feel at peace."

Prayer? That shouldn't surprise Maddox. He'd noticed something different about Taryn.

She was a person of faith, wasn't she?

"Is that why you like to come and walk this area so much?" Maddox glanced at the shrubs around him, caution tightening each of his muscles.

"I suppose." She shrugged. "Something about being between those hedges just helps me to put life in focus. *Usually.*"

The woman continued to surprise him.

Maddox had expected someone shallow or selfish. But Taryn seemed neither of those things.

She seemed truly concerned about Mr. Whitlock. Intent on becoming a better person. Unafraid to talk about the struggles of her past.

Yet she was still Maddox's best suspect.

He had a long list of questions he wanted to ask her. If Taryn knew the truth about why he was here, he could dive into those inquiries. But Maddox couldn't risk blowing his cover yet—not until he knew with certainty he could trust her.

He wound around the edges of the labyrinth. The only other experience he'd had that was similar to being in these passages was when he'd gone to corn mazes as a child. He never really liked those either. He didn't like feeling unsure of himself.

That was exactly how he felt right now—like he could take one wrong turn and end up wandering these paths all day without finding a way out.

"Who designed it?" Maddox asked.

"Mr. Whitlock's grandfather."

Maddox stored that information away. That fact seemed like something he would have come across as he'd researched the man. But maybe not.

"We're getting closer to the center now." He could tell because the passageways were shorter, tighter.

"The circles are patterned, and if you want to, you can memorize them. It depends if you like uncertainty or not. The unknown versus the planned."

Taryn's words caused his heart to squeeze. Living in fear was no way to live. Maddox knew that first-hand. It wasn't necessarily fear he lived with but regret. Hurt.

Both of those things could transform into fear if he wasn't careful.

Just as he rounded another corner, Maddox stopped in his tracks.

Two legs protruded from the path in front of him.

Legs with feet wearing gardening clogs.

TARYN TRIED to see around Maddox, but he blocked her path.

"Is it Leroy?" Her voice came out breathless and tight.

Maddox turned back to her and nodded, compassion staining his gaze. "I'm sorry, Taryn. But it is."

A cry escaped from her, and her knees went weak. Maddox caught her and steadied her before she hit the ground.

Not Leroy . . .

Her hand covered her mouth as she processed the information.

She pulled herself together enough to ask, "What . . . what happened to him?"

"I need to take a better look. Can you call 911 for me?"

Taryn nodded and pulled out her phone, grateful for something to do—something to distract her from the horror mere feet away. Despite her quivering hands, she managed to dial the number and talk to the operator.

As she ended the call, she looked back at Maddox, who'd stood after examining Leroy.

"What happened?" she rushed.

"Honestly? It looks like he fell on his gardening shears . . ."

Maddox didn't have to finish. Taryn buried her face in her hands as an image formed in her mind.

Maddox placed an arm around her waist. "I'm sorry, Taryn."

She knew she probably shouldn't, but she fell into Maddox's embrace.

His strong arms felt safe. His strength—and ability to hold her up—felt reassuring.

Probably because for most of her life Taryn had been alone. She'd had to learn to hold herself up or fall. And she'd done plenty of falling . . .

"It's going to be okay," Maddox murmured. "The police will do their thing. How about if I get you back to the house?"

A gasp escaped as another thought filled her mind. "I'll have to tell Mr. Whitlock . . . he's still upset about Gary. He was our maintenance guy before you came, but he had a heart attack . . ."

"Mr. Whitlock is stronger than you think he is." Maddox locked gazes with her. "I know you're trying to protect him. But that doesn't mean you need to hold details back from him. Just from what I've seen of the man, I don't think that's what he would want."

Taryn raised her head and sniffled. "You're probably right. I just worry about him . . ."

"I'm glad he has someone looking out for him. I really am. How about if we get you back to the house now? It's not going to do you any good to stand right here."

"We shouldn't leave the body . . ." She glanced at Leroy's legs again and shivered.

"We'll stay close enough to keep an eye on the labyrinth," Maddox reassured her. "When the police arrive, I'll show them where the body is."

She nodded, grateful she didn't have to stand here and stare at those legs in the background any longer.

But poor Leroy . . . even though he didn't have kids or a wife, he was still important to the people here. He was important to Mr. Whitlock.

Taryn didn't say anything else as Maddox led her away. Instead, she tried to figure out what she would tell her boss—because she definitely couldn't keep Leroy's death from him.

Maddox turned his thoughts from the paper as he kept an eye on both the labyrinth and Taryn. He'd escorted her inside, where she'd found Mr. Whitlock sitting in his favorite chair by the fireplace.

She sat beside him and quietly said something.

Maddox couldn't hear the words exactly, but he knew what they were.

Leroy is dead.

Mr. Whitlock gasped, and his eyes widened. "What?"

Taryn grabbed his hand and squeezed it. "I'm so sorry."

She certainly didn't seem like a gold digger.

She seemed like the opposite, actually.

Were there really people in this world who had pure hearts?

Maddox wasn't sure. But the thought seemed refreshing.

His gaze went to the lawyer standing in the background. Gerald Macintosh. Maddox had researched the man earlier, right after he'd shown up.

He would keep his eye on the guy. From what he'd discovered, when Gerald Macintosh was in college, he'd been involved with some activists who had shady practices. The man hadn't gone to jail himself, but some of his associates had.

Maddox would need to keep an eye on him. As

far as Maddox was concerned, nobody was off the table right now.

Even Taryn.

The body count was now up to three—the delivery driver, Gary, and Leroy. Plus, someone had stolen that tech—listening devices and security cameras that were practically undetectable.

Just what did they want to use those for? Maddox wasn't naive enough to think the person who'd taken them had small-scale motives. Tech like that could be planted anywhere—anywhere highly guarded secrets could be shared.

If people knew how many dangerous things were going on in this world, they wouldn't sleep at night. Not everyone was cut out for this line of work. Not everyone could handle knowing about the amount of pure evil lurking around them.

Sometimes, Maddox was unsure he could even deal with it. After he'd returned from his last SEAL mission with PTSD, he knew he needed to find better ways to cope—ways other than drinking and partying. He'd started therapy and gone back to church. That's also when he'd started crocheting.

The stitches . . . they just made sense—unlike life.

He found joy in the predictability, in the consistency, in the control of looping together those chains of yarn.

His coworkers had all looked at him funny when he'd first started—a big, burly, tatted up guy whose hobby fell in line with that of an older generation. Now, they'd come to respect it.

They'd seen what a mess he was when he'd returned from his last mission as a SEAL.

Everyone said it wasn't his fault that a member of their support team had died. But Maddox couldn't help but think it was.

If only Maddox had been a little faster. Had thought a little more quickly. Had been more cautious.

But Stephen was dead, and Maddox had to live with that fact every day.

Maddox snapped his attention back to Taryn as she approached him. "The police are here. I'm going to go talk to them and then you can take them to the body."

"Of course." He cast a glance back at Mr. Whitlock and saw the man studying him again.

Was he suspicious of Maddox's appearance here?

Possibly—especially after Maddox had been caught in his office.

Now Leroy was dead.

Maddox would have to play it cool. Otherwise, he'd begin stirring too many questions.

The moment Mr. Whitlock was truly suspicious of

him, Maddox would either be fired . . . or he'd be added to the list of dead bodies already accumulating.

CHAPTER
TWENTY

AS MADDOX SHOWED the police where Leroy's body had been left, Taryn managed things inside the house.

A nurse had arrived and taken Mr. Whitlock upstairs, and Taryn had informed everyone else that the police would need to speak with them and they shouldn't go anywhere.

Alana had seemed perturbed, especially since she'd scheduled a massage at a spa in town. After complaining, she'd settled into a chair in the other room and texted someone on her cell phone.

Danielle, Eleanor, and Chef were outside.

Phil had gone somewhere a few hours ago.

That left Taryn standing in the living room with Gerald. He had a pensive expression on his face as he stared outside.

She'd met Mr. Whitlock's lawyer before on several occasions, and the man seemed reliable and trustworthy. Mr. Whitlock certainly seemed to trust him.

Did that mean she could also?

Since only the two of them were in the room right now, Taryn knew this was her opportunity to talk.

"Gerald . . ." She stepped closer to him and the window where he stood. "There's something I need to talk to you about."

He narrowed his eyes as he glanced at her. "What is it?"

She proceeded to tell him about the threatening letters she'd found as well as what had happened here at the estate over the past few weeks.

Gerald was the only person Taryn had poured all this out to. She'd told Maddox part of it but not everything.

It was so hard not knowing who to trust.

Gerald listened intently as Taryn talked, not asking any questions until she finished.

"You haven't told Mr. Whitlock any of this?" Gerald pushed his glasses up higher and crossed his arms. "Not even about the demands or the threats?"

"I'm afraid of what that might do to his heart." Taryn placed her hand over her own heart in an almost protective measure. She felt her pulse racing beneath her palm.

Gerald let out a long breath before frowning. "I guess I can understand that. But it still seems as if he should know—especially if the sender intends to carry through with those threats."

"I know. I've struggled with what to do, whether or not I should get the police involved."

"Do you trust everybody here?" He looked through the window and scanned the scene outside.

Maddox spoke with the detective. Police officers went in and out of the labyrinth as they collected evidence. Danielle stood in the distance, Eleanor with her, as they watched the scene through tear-bleary eyes.

"I . . . I think so." But even as Taryn said the words, she wasn't sure. She'd questioned everyone's motives at some point.

"What about that new maintenance guy?" Gerald nodded toward Maddox. "Something about him seems shady."

Her gaze traveled to Maddox as he continued speaking with the detective, his disposition tough and unwavering. The man seemed so solid, so trustworthy.

But was he?

A frown tugged at her lips before she finally asked, "You think so?"

"I don't know. But his timing here is suspicious,

wouldn't you say?" Gerald observed her as he waited for her response.

Taryn squirmed, not liking the scrutiny. Not liking how she felt loyal to Maddox even though she hardly knew him. "I did place an ad for the job . . ."

She wasn't ready to throw the man under the bus. Not yet. Maybe not ever.

She could sense people who'd been broken and then restored—probably because she was one of those people also.

"I'd keep an eye on him," Gerald said. "But if you don't feel safe staying here . . ."

Taryn drew in a sharp breath. "There's no way I could leave Mr. Whitlock. I promised I'd be here to help him. I can't break that promise."

Gerald nodded slowly again. "That's very noble of you. And loyal. But you need to be careful, Taryn. As a lawyer, I've got to advise you that you may need to go to the police about these threats."

"I'm considering it . . . I just don't know what to do." She raked a hand through her hair. "That's why I'm talking to you."

"You want my advice? Be very careful who you trust. When money gets involved, Taryn, you see sides of people you never expected. I could tell you about some of the clients I've worked for. Fistfights have literally broken out after I've read wills. Money brings out the best in people and the worst."

"I can imagine."

"Everyone knows Mr. Whitlock is practically at death's door. It's just a matter of time until . . ." He cleared his throat as if unable to finish his statement. "It could be a week. It could be six months. But it's coming soon."

His words caused a cry to catch in her throat.

"I know you're right. But it's not something I like to think about." Taryn rubbed her neck, wishing she didn't have to face that certainty.

Gerald's gaze locked on hers. "I just want you to be careful."

She drew in a deep breath and tried to pull herself together. Giving into her fears right now would only make her more vulnerable.

And, by default, would only make Mr. Whitlock more vulnerable also.

She couldn't let that happen.

Maddox watched as Detective Conners snapped his notepad shut.

The man was in his late thirties, and Maddox guessed, based on the way he carried himself, he used to be military. A marine most likely. He still sported the crewcut hair and upright posture.

Two people from the coroner's office wheeled

Leroy away on a gurney, his body covered with a sheet.

Conners turned toward Maddox and nodded. "Thank you for your help."

Maddox slowly nodded at the man as they stood on the lawn. "No problem. What happens next?"

Conners stared in the distance, his expression remaining stoic and professional. "My understanding is that Leroy was single with no kids, so we will need to track down next of kin and notify them. We'll also conduct an autopsy, just to be certain. But, by all appearances, this was a tragic accident."

Maddox hesitated, unsure what to say. He wanted to make it clear this wasn't an accident. But that *was* how it seemed.

And Maddox was supposed to keep a low profile. If he acted too comfortable or knowledgeable with the investigation, he'd surely raise red flags.

"You don't look convinced. Do you know something we don't know?" Detective Conners stared at him in expectation.

Maddox pulled himself from his thoughts and shrugged. "I'm just getting acclimated. I only started working here yesterday."

Maddox rubbed his fingers, wishing more than anything that he had his crochet hook and some yarn right now. He could use something to ease the tension between his shoulders. He'd even played with the idea of teaching Taryn how to make her very own beanie.

Or maybe he'd make one for her.

Burgundy would look nice against her alabaster skin.

Conners narrowed his gaze, his mind clearly racing through the possibilities of what might be going on. "I'd like to talk to Mr. Whitlock if possible."

Maddox snapped his thoughts back to the present. "I understand. However, you'll need to speak with his assistant or his attorney first. He's not well."

"That's what I've heard."

Apparently, everyone in town knew about Mr. Whitlock's health problems. Maddox stored that information away. That could potentially make him a target for a lot of people.

"How about if I show you inside?" Maddox offered. "Mr. Whitlock's assistant and attorney are already there."

"I'd appreciate that."

Maddox led him toward the patio. As he did, his thoughts continued to drift.

What was going on here at this estate?

Before he could ponder the question for too long, movement in the distance caught his eye.

Phil Whitlock stormed toward them.

Maddox turned toward the man and braced himself for whatever this conversation would hold.

TWENTY-ONE

TARYN'S EYES widened as she saw Phil charging across the lawn.

She hurried outside to try and act as intermediary between him and Detective Conners.

"What is going on here?" Phil demanded, stopping in front of the detective. "Is it my father? Is he okay?"

Taryn stopped near them, gulping in a few breaths.

Her gaze met Maddox's, and he cast her a concerned look.

"Excuse me." Detective Conners narrowed his gaze as if perturbed. "But who are you?"

"I'm Phil, Mr. Whitlock's son. Did something happen?"

"Your father's fine," Taryn rushed. "He's upstairs

lying down. His heart started racing when he heard the news."

"What news?" Phil placed his hands on his hips, still looking annoyed.

Taryn looked at the detective, waiting for him to share. It didn't feel like her place to do so.

"Leroy Matthews was found dead in the labyrinth," Detective Conners said.

Phil's eyes widened. "What? How could that have happened?"

"It appears to be a tragic accident," Conners explained. "That said, I have to ask, where have you been for the last two hours?"

"Me?" His voice screeched higher. "If you must know, I was at the bank. Anyone who works there can vouch for me."

At the bank? For more than two hours? Exactly what was he doing there for so long?

This man definitely raised Taryn's suspicions—in a very bad way.

"When did you last see Leroy?" Conners continued.

Phil's shoulders flew up, almost as if he were offended by the question. "I think I crossed paths with him this morning before I left. He was running the edger outside. But we didn't talk."

"I'm not accusing anyone," Conners interrupted.

"I'm simply asking questions. I'll be interviewing everyone here on the property."

"Good. Because if this wasn't an accident, I demand —on my father's behalf—to know what happened."

Taryn wanted to roll her eyes. But she didn't.

Phil was putting on such an act—pretending as if he were loyal and protective. Even his appearance here seemed suspicious.

Did he truly care about his father?

She couldn't say—it wasn't her place.

But if she had to guess, she'd say a definitive no.

The police stayed at the house for four hours.

Maddox had mostly remained outside with them as he tried to keep an eye on everything. He took mental notes of everyone's reaction to Leroy's death.

Danielle and Eleanor had seemed sad.

Phil had seemed outraged.

Mr. Whitlock's heart had acted up.

Gerald remained stoic and professional.

Perhaps it was the fact he'd seen Alana and Shawn talking that interested him the most—especially since the two had been whispering.

He had the impression they didn't even know each other before meeting yesterday. So, what had they been discussing? And who exactly was the man talking to late last night about investments?

Maddox didn't know, but he would keep an eye on those two.

Right now, he escaped back to his room for a few minutes.

As soon as he stepped inside, his phone rang.

It was Colton.

Maddox answered, anxious to hear what he had to say. He'd sent his leader a picture of the symbol he'd found in the greenhouse.

"I think you may be onto something," Colton started.

Maddox leaned back in the plush chair near his window. "What's that?"

"We did some digging. That symbol you sent us is associated with a group known as The System. Have you ever heard of them?"

"The System?" He squinted as he searched his thoughts. "I can't say I have."

"They're an interesting organization, about four thousand strong. Some information about them is online, but not much. I think they're trying to stay off anyone's radar right now. In fact, if you hadn't found that symbol, I would have never explored the option that they could be associated with what's going on."

Maddox folded his leg over his knee. "What kind of group are they? Like a cult?"

"No, more like a militia that wants to change the course of our country by making it more socialist. They believe people abuse their freedoms so those very freedoms should be taken away for the sake of all mankind."

His mind raced . . . a militia? Hadn't Gerald been involved with some kind of group like that back when he was in college?

The man shot to the top of Maddox's suspect list.

He shared the information with Colton.

"I'm trying to dig up some information on this group," Colton continued. "But it's too early to say if or how they're involved. In the meantime, if you discover anything else, let us know."

"Will do. Same here."

"And Maddox?" Concern stretched through Colton's voice. "Until we know what's going on, stay alert."

"I will, boss." Maddox stared outside at the labyrinth. "I will."

CHAPTER
TWENTY-TWO

IT HAD BEEN A LONG DAY, and all Taryn wanted was to unwind with one of her favorite shows in the staff living room. Gerald had finally left. But, of course, Alana remained. Shawn had also decided to stay one more night, which wasn't uncommon. According to the staff, he stayed here often.

However, managing everyone had left Taryn exhausted.

Though she had a small television in her room, Taryn found sitting in bed and watching TV wasn't enjoyable—especially if she wanted popcorn.

She hated having crumbs in her bed, which made relaxing in the living room area ideal.

But, first, she'd change into some sweats and a T-shirt.

Taryn stepped into her room and flicked the light switch.

Nothing happened.

Dread pooled in her gut.

Not another power outage. No, it couldn't be. The light in the hallway worked.

Maybe her bulb had just burned out.

Trying to keep a level head, Taryn found the flashlight on her phone and turned it on. Then she stepped into her room, trying to put on a brave front—not that anyone was watching.

She wanted to be strong for herself.

As she crossed the floor toward the lamp beside her bed, something lunged from the darkness.

A person.

A *man*.

Before she could comprehend what was happening, he shoved her toward the wall.

Taryn stumbled to the floor.

Her head collided with the nightstand, and pain shot through her.

What was happening?

Who was this guy?

What did he want?

Fear choked her, growing with every question.

Maddox had just settled on the couch in the staff living room, ready to work on some crocheting, when he heard a crash.

He jumped to his feet.

That sounded close.

He darted into the hallway and glanced around.

No one was in sight.

But a door a little farther down was open.

Was that Taryn's room?

He dashed toward the space, worry pulsing through him.

Without invitation, he barreled into the dark room.

Taryn lay on the floor with her eyes closed as what appeared to be a trickle of blood dripped from her forehead.

"Taryn . . ." He raced toward her and knelt beside her.

As he touched her arm, she let out a moan.

Relief filled him.

She was alive.

But a knot had already begun forming on her head.

His heart pounded harder.

What had happened?

Taryn blinked several times before moaning again.

Then, at once, fear seemed to capture her.

Her gaze darted around, and she withdrew, pulling her arms and legs toward her chest as she scooted backward.

"Where is he?" Her voice trembled.

"Where is who?" Maddox narrowed his eyes as he waited for her to continue.

"The man who pushed me down."

Maddox's muscles went rigid. "There was a man in your room?"

"The light wouldn't turn on. He was hiding. He shoved me and then . . . I must've blacked out for a moment."

Anger burned through Maddox. He glanced up and saw the open window.

That must have been how the guy got away.

"Did he strike you?" He turned back to Taryn.

"No . . . I hit my head on the nightstand."

Maddox gritted his teeth and crossed the room to look out the window. He wanted to go after the man, but the guy had already disappeared.

Right now, he needed to take care of Taryn. She was his first priority.

As he helped her to her feet, his mind wouldn't stop racing.

Just how far would someone go to get whatever it was they wanted?

And the even bigger question: what exactly was it they wanted?

TARYN'S HEAD was spinning as Maddox helped her to her feet and directed her to sit on the edge of her bed.

As she lowered herself there, she touched her head. She drew her hand back and saw the blood staining her fingers.

Another wave of lightheadedness washed over her.

The next moment, Maddox appeared with a washcloth. After flipping on a lamp in the corner, he sat beside her and gently pressed the cloth into her wound.

"It's going to be okay." His voice sounded reassuring and kind.

But nothing felt like it would be okay right now. Too much had gone wrong.

Now someone had been in her bedroom . . .

Why? Had this person been looking for something?

All she had in here were her clothes and toiletries—nothing that anyone would consider of value.

"Taryn?" Maddox stared at her. "Stay with me, okay?"

She blinked several times, trying to pull her thoughts together. "I'm . . . sorry. I'm just flustered."

"You don't have to worry. I'm here."

Her breath caught at his words.

What would that be like? To not have to worry because someone was watching her back? Protecting her?

In all her years, Taryn had never known that feeling.

But she'd craved it so badly.

Badly enough that she'd run into the arms of Grissom Smith, thinking that's what he offered. She'd been sorely mistaken. And she could never make that mistake again.

Never.

Maddox pulled the cloth away and studied her wound. "The good news is that I don't think you need stitches."

"That is good news."

"A couple of butterfly bandages should do the trick. Do you have a first aid kit?"

"There's one under the sink."

"I'll be right back." He slipped into the bathroom and returned a moment later with a plastic box. He rifled through the contents before finding what he needed.

Gently, he dabbed some ointment on her forehead before covering her cut with the bandages.

"There. All better. If you wear your bangs down, no one will even notice."

Taryn felt a quiver start inside her. She wanted to cry.

And she hardly ever cried.

But having someone lurking in the shadows of her own bedroom made her feel so vulnerable . . .

Especially considering everything else that had happened.

Everything like Leroy.

"Taryn?" Maddox's voice sounded low and warm as he leaned closer.

Her gaze fluttered to his. When she saw the concern in his gaze, a tear slipped from her eyes.

"Taryn . . ." The next instant, Maddox pulled her into his arms.

He didn't say anything. There was nothing to say.

Instead, he held her against his chest.

Taryn sagged against him as she let the tears fall.

Had God sent this man into her life just when she'd needed him?

Or was Maddox's presence here too good to be true?

———

Maddox wished he could take away Taryn's pain and confusion.

He couldn't do that.

But holding her seemed like the next best option.

He refused to let go until she was ready to pull away.

Probably five minutes passed before she finally eased back.

As her face came into view, Maddox saw that her eyes were red and moist.

A wet splotch adorned his T-shirt now.

He didn't care.

Using the edge of her sleeve, Taryn wiped her eyes, a hollow look in her gaze.

"I'm sorry," she nearly whispered. "I don't usually cry on people."

"No apologies necessary."

"I just feel so overwhelmed . . ." Her voice cracked. "Like things are out of my control."

"You're doing fine," he assured her.

"The police think Leroy died because of an accident. But you and I both know that's not true. Something is going on here. But I don't know how to prove anything."

Maddox considered telling her who he really was. This seemed like the perfect opportunity.

But how would things change if he did?

He felt he could trust her. He felt certain she was innocent of all, a victim just like Leroy.

But he couldn't blow this investigation. If their hunch was correct, someone was planning something with life-altering repercussions.

The stakes were too high.

Still, indecision pressed on him.

There *had* to be a way to fix this . . .

"You could leave." Maddox craned his neck lower so their gazes could connect. "If you don't feel safe—"

"I refuse to abandon Mr. Whitlock." She sniffled again, grabbing a tissue from her nightstand this time.

"Maybe he'll go with you."

She shook her head adamantly, as if that wasn't even a consideration. "Mr. Whitlock said this is where he wants to die. He's not going anywhere. He's a lot of things, and stubborn is one of them."

Maddox let out a long, pent-up breath as he considered other options. The problem was—there really weren't any other viable alternatives. "If you're staying here, then the only thing we can do is watch out for each other."

Taryn's gaze met his. "How so?"

"You let me know if you see anything suspicious, and I'll keep an eye on you as well. Make sure nothing happens."

More moisture glistened in her gaze. "You'd do that for me?"

Something about the surprise in her voice made his heart patter out of control. "Of course, I would."

As their gazes locked, Maddox felt warmth rush through his blood.

Had no one offered to look after her before?

Taryn looked so beautiful. So vulnerable, yet so captivating.

He hadn't come here looking for romance. He wasn't looking for romance *period*.

Lindsey hadn't been able to handle the changes Maddox had undergone while deployed. When he'd gotten back to the States—a broken semblance of the person he'd once been—she'd decided she didn't love him anymore.

Her rejection had only compounded the PTSD Maddox had already been dealing with.

At that point, he was done trying.

But something about Taryn made him want to give love another shot.

His throat went dry as his gaze went to her lips.

What would it be like to kiss Taryn? To lean close and enjoy the scent of lilac in her hair? To feel her soft skin beneath his fingertips?

He really wanted to find out.

But did Taryn want the same?

TARYN WANTED TO KISS MADDOX.

The thought surprised her just as much as it might surprise anyone.

But she did.

Especially when the man looked at her like he did now.

He just seemed so . . . safe.

Safe in a good way—not the boring kind of safe that involved never taking risks.

Love was *always* a risk.

Taryn had dated someone with an explosive temper before, and she'd vowed to never do that again. Dating Grissom had been one of the worst decisions of her life.

She didn't need someone who would rock her world. She needed someone who'd be her rock.

Someone like Maddox.

Steady. Solid. Dependable.

Was it possible that her feelings for the man had grown this quickly? It didn't seem likely—more like something that only happened in the movies. Yet Taryn couldn't deny her attraction despite her reservations about the man.

She leaned ever so slightly toward him.

Just as quickly as it had appeared, the swirling desire in Maddox's eyes vanished.

He jerked away from her and rose to his feet, clearing his throat as he did. "I should probably let you get some rest."

Taryn quickly shoved a hair behind her ear as disappointment—and a touch of embarrassment—rushed through her.

Had she read him wrong?

Or had he changed his mind about her? Could he see through her façade into all her broken places?

Probably.

Taryn's mom had always told her no one would ever love her. Looking back, her mother had probably just been projecting her own feelings of no self-worth onto Taryn. But memories of those conversations still stung.

What if her mom had been right?

Taryn pulled herself from those thoughts.

She just needed some normalcy right now.

No thoughts of romance—from either failed past relationships or dreams of future possibilities.

She wanted to unwind.

"I'm going to head into the living room to watch some TV," she said. "I don't think I'll be sleeping right now after everything that happened."

"Would you like some company?"

Surprise rushed through her. Taryn didn't want to be alone right now. The thought of hanging out with Maddox was very tempting—too tempting to pass up.

She smiled and nodded. "I'd love some."

Why had he pulled away from Taryn so abruptly? Maddox asked himself.

He knew the truth.

He couldn't allow himself to get too close. Emotions could compromise his investigation.

And, ultimately, allowing his logic to be clouded by feelings could put Taryn in harm's way. He didn't want that—not at all.

But he *had* wanted, more than anything, to kiss the woman tonight.

Maybe some of the walls around his heart were finally coming down after all—brick by brick.

He walked with Taryn down the hallway toward the staff living room.

Anger still burned through his blood at the thought of someone shoving Taryn to the floor.

Who had been in her room? And why?

Maddox would save those questions for later.

Whoever was behind these acts was smart. Almost too smart.

He watched as Taryn hesitated in the doorway. Her gaze wandered the room before she stepped inside. No doubt she was looking for trouble also.

But her eyes stopped on the yarn and crochet hook on the couch. "What's that?"

"The yarn? It's nothing."

Taryn turned toward him. "Wait. Is it yours? Do you knit?"

He shrugged. "Crochet, actually. And, yes, I might crochet a little here and there."

She squinted with curiosity. "Really?"

Hearing people's reactions always brought Maddox a certain level of amusement.

He shrugged again. "It's a long story."

"I want to hear it. I just want to pop some popcorn first. If I make a bag, will you help me eat it?"

"Sure."

As Taryn went to the little kitchen set up in the corner and started the popcorn, Maddox sat down on the couch and began working on his beanie again.

A couple of minutes later, the microwave hummed, and the smell of butter filled the room. Taryn lowered herself into the seat across from him.

Her gaze sparkled as she observed him. "So . . . crocheting?"

"Sure, why not?" Maddox said the question as if his hobby weren't a big deal or anything abnormal. "It helps me manage stress."

"Manage stress? You seem pretty low-key to me." She leaned back, still studying him with open curiosity. "How long have you been crocheting?"

"Ever since I got out of the military. I had PTSD, and I found this helped me cope." He pressed his lips together. He hadn't intended on sharing *that*.

He never talked about his PTSD—unless it was with his therapist or closest friends.

The popcorn made gentle popping sounds in the distance, and his stomach rumbled as he again smelled the butter floating through the air.

He was hungrier than he thought.

"PTSD?" Taryn's shoulders seemed to soften. "I'd say there are far worse things you could do to relax."

"That's what I like to think too." Maddox continued using his blue yarn to form rows.

As the microwave beeped, she rose and grabbed the bag then poured the popcorn into a bowl.

Approaching him again, Taryn set the bowl on the table between them and turned the TV on at a low volume. "Help yourself."

"Thanks."

Maddox's gaze went to the TV as a breaking news story flashed across the screen. His interest sparked.

"Can you turn that up?" he asked.

A reporter holding a microphone stood outside the North Carolina State Capitol building. "At approximately 5:30 this afternoon, State Senator Erwin Gately was walking to his car when shots were fired. At least one of those bullets hit the senator. Authorities arrived at the scene moments later and secured the area. There's no current update on the senator's condition."

The reporter then began to interview a witness who'd seen it happen.

"That's crazy." Taryn pulled her knees to her chest, her gaze fixed on the screen. "I feel like the whole world has gone mad sometimes."

"I get that. I pray the senator is okay." Maddox began to crochet faster. "In the meantime, I say we don't need to watch any more of this. It's too depressing."

"Yes, it is." She turned the volume down and popped another fluffy kernel in her mouth.

Maddox's thoughts turned over what he'd just heard.

An attempt on a senator's life? That was some serious stuff.

Before he had time to think about it any longer, a shadow filled the doorway.

Maddox braced himself for whatever might happen next.

CHAPTER
TWENTY-FIVE

"TARYN." Phil stepped into the room. "Good. I was looking for you."

Taryn's heart raced at the sight of the man. Where had he come from? He never came to the staff quarters—and he hardly ever came looking for her.

She sat up straight. "Can I help you with something?"

"I can't log onto my father's wi-fi. Can you help?"

She tried not to sigh or roll her eyes. "Right now?"

She already worked entirely more than she was required. While she didn't mind helping Mr. Whitlock, she did mind helping Phil.

Phil seemed to read her hesitation, and his entire demeanor softened. "You were the only one I figured knew the answer. You're so efficient at keeping everything straight. You're really good for my father —in case I haven't told you that."

He'd never said anything even *remotely* close to that. "Thank you."

"I know you're probably still shaken up about Leroy." He lowered his voice, almost as if trying to sound understanding. "I was really sorry to hear what happened."

"I think we all were." She glanced over at Maddox and saw he'd started crocheting again—this time, even faster than before.

Interesting.

And was he scowling? Was that because he didn't like Phil?

If so, Taryn didn't blame him. Phil wasn't a particularly likable guy.

"So, about that password?" Phil held up his dad's iPad.

"You don't have your own iPad?"

"Mine broke, and my father said I could use his. Is that a problem?"

"No, of course not." Taryn hoped he was telling the truth. She took the device from him and pressed her finger onto the pad. The screen came on.

"Wait . . . your fingerprint activated that?" Phil questioned.

"Your father put my hand and thumbprint on a few devices around here that have biometric security." She shrugged, not thinking it was a big deal.

"Yours? Why yours?" Barely contained indignation simmered beneath his voice.

Taryn shrugged again as she typed in the wi-fi password. "You'd have to ask him that question."

"I will."

Taryn handed the device back to him, determined not to take his bait. "There you go."

His expression softened. "This is just perfect. Thank you."

"No problem." This man was about as temperamental as her old Ford Fiesta. He made her head want to spin. No, more than that—he made her want to scream at times.

He started to step away but paused. "Taryn, I know this seems random, but is there any chance I could take you to dinner sometime?"

Maddox let out a soft grunt beside her and continued crocheting.

Taryn held back a groan of her own. Dating Phil was the last thing she wanted. She needed to shut him down. Fast.

"I'm not sure it's a good idea that I date my boss's son."

Phil stared at her a moment before nodding. "I guess you're right. But I just had to try, right?"

"Have a good night, Phil."

"You too." He nodded at her before glancing at Maddox.

As he stepped from the room, Taryn let out the breath she held.

Why did that man put her on edge?

Maddox tried to remain calm.

But his crochet stitches came faster and faster as outrage built inside him.

The only reason Phil had asked Taryn out was because he wanted to use her for something.

Maddox felt certain of it.

Not that Taryn wasn't attractive enough to ask out. But Maddox saw through this guy.

The fact that the fingerprints and handprints allowed her access to Mr. Whitlock's devices? It probably wasn't something she should have shared.

But now that Maddox knew that . . . he needed to store away that information as well.

Did it give her more motive?

He wasn't sure.

But it did give her more opportunity.

Maddox drew in a deep breath and slowly released the air from his lungs.

Right now, he just needed to relax—and pace himself before he had to undo all his stitches.

"He's a piece of work," Taryn muttered.

Her analysis brought Maddox a surprising measure of delight. "He is."

She let out another long breath as if she was still annoyed.

Maddox tried to tap into his conversational skills and change the subject. "So, how long did you say you've been here?"

This was a great opportunity to learn more about Taryn. He only hated that he had to pretend to be someone he wasn't.

"Six months." Taryn popped a piece of popcorn into her mouth.

"Mind me asking how someone gets a job like yours? Do you have a background in project management or as a nurse?" Maddox already knew the answer, but he asked anyway. He wanted to hear Taryn's take on things.

Hesitation gripped her expression, and he figured she wouldn't answer. But he waited, just in case.

Finally, Taryn released a long breath. "I was actually hiking—"

"You like to hike?"

"I love it, and this area with its mountains is perfect. Plus, it's generally free, so that makes it even better. It helped me work out my own problems after a bad breakup recently—kind of like you and crocheting, I guess."

Maddox stored that information away. He liked seeing different sides of Taryn—maybe too much.

"Anyway, I was hiking when I found Mr. Whitlock on the ground beside the trail. It seemed like he'd had a heart attack. He was alone and couldn't call for help. So, I called 911 and waited with him until they arrived."

Maddox's eyebrows shot up. That wasn't the story he'd expected.

"And he stayed in touch with you after that?" he asked.

Taryn shrugged, her expression pensive. "When I stumbled upon him, he just seemed so alone. So, I went to the hospital to wait until a family member or a friend could get there. I wanted to make sure Mr. Whitlock had someone there to watch out for him. It sounded so awful to think about waking up from a trauma like that only to be alone."

"Did you know who he was when all that happened?"

"No, I had no idea. I've never exactly been one to keep up on the social scene around town. I was too busy working to pay the bills." She frowned. "Anyway, I was there when he came out of surgery and when he got the news that he had congestive heart failure. I prayed with him and told him everything would be okay."

Maddox kept listening, his rapt attention on her as he eagerly waited to hear the rest of her story.

"It didn't take long for people to start showing up. A lot of people. I realized Mr. Whitlock must be someone important. Before I left, he asked for my name and phone number. I told him, not thinking anything would come from it. But less than a week later, I got a call from him. He asked if I'd come work for him."

"Just out of the blue?"

Taryn nodded. "Totally out of the blue. I told him I wasn't qualified. He said I was a natural caregiver and that he could teach me what I didn't know."

"So, you put in your two weeks' notice at your other job and moved in here?"

A sad smile spread over her lips. "It wasn't exactly like that. I'd lost my job and, in the process, the apartment where I was living. It's a long story. But I was in a low place, and Mr. Whitlock's job offer was an answer to prayer."

"Sounds like it." Maddox leaned back, trying not to watch Taryn. But, in some ways, it was hard to take his eyes off her.

Could this woman really be a killer who'd come here to take advantage of a dying old man?

Or was she just a victim in all this?

That's what Maddox needed to figure out.

TWENTY-SIX

THE NEXT MORNING, Taryn still felt shaken as she sorted through Mr. Whitlock's medications, making sure none of them needed to be refilled.

Part of why she felt shaken was because of the encounter in her bedroom. She still had no idea who'd been in there or what he'd been doing.

The other part of her tremors was because of Maddox. She hadn't expected to feel something for him so quickly or so deeply.

She'd thought about him all night. Thought about how he crocheted. How he looked tough but had such a tender side also.

He got both her thoughts and her blood racing— and that seemed like the perfect combination.

But, right now, the best thing Taryn could do was to focus on her job.

She placed another RX bottle into the bin and checked it off the list in front of her.

Maddox officially worked under her, and she needed to remain logical, in spite of everything going on here.

All these so-called accidents.

Accidents she had no proof were anything but mishaps.

The man who'd been in her room had left no traces behind either.

There was absolutely nothing Taryn could show the police that would definitively point to the fact someone was up to no good.

Unless she showed them those threats sent to Mr. Whitlock.

She frowned and placed another checkmark on her list.

Yet Mr. Whitlock was the only one who hadn't been on the receiving end of any of the incidents.

None of this made sense. She sighed in frustration and leaned back in the chair where she was seated.

She needed to concentrate so she wouldn't miss anything. Medications were nothing to be played with. Yet she couldn't seem to shake her preoccupation.

Taryn had already grabbed a quick breakfast this morning. Chef seemed anxious today, as did Eleanor. Everyone at the house was on edge after Leroy's death—especially since they were still dealing with Gary's death also.

She'd briefly crossed paths with Maddox, but he was still working on updating security measures at the house. He stopped for long enough to tell her that he checked the security footage from last night, but he hadn't seen anything.

Last night, he'd been kind enough to walk her back to her room to check things out before saying good night.

Part of her had wanted to tilt her head up. Had wanted to know what it would be like to feel him kiss her. To touch his soft beard with her fingertips.

Instead, they'd exchanged cordial nods before heading their own ways.

She frowned as she remembered her disappointment.

As the doorbell rang and pulled her from her thoughts, she let out a deep breath.

Who was it now?

Since Taryn was close, she headed toward the door and pulled it open. A dark-haired man wearing a suit and carrying a briefcase stood on the other side.

She'd never seen him before.

But his bright smile was nearly disarming.

"Good afternoon. I'm sorry to stop by unannounced like this, but I was hoping to meet with Mr. Whitlock."

Taryn narrowed her eyes. "And you are?"

"My name is Brandon Hale. I'm a businessman with a proposition for Mr. Whitlock. I tried emailing and calling, but I never got a response. Someone told me he was here at this estate, so I decided to give this one last shot."

The man sounded friendly enough, but Taryn knew to be careful. "Mr. Whitlock doesn't like unscheduled meetings."

Brandon shrugged. "It's like I said. I tried my best, but I'm not even sure if my emails or voice mails were received."

She stared at him another moment, soaking in his clean-cut look. Was this man who he claimed to be?

It was hard to trust anyone given everything that had happened lately.

With a sigh, she ushered him inside and closed the door. "Stay here while I go talk to Mr. Whitlock. I can't make any promises."

"Of course." He offered a nod and a quick thanks.

Taryn hurried upstairs to find Mr. Whitlock.

She prayed that allowing this man into the house didn't stir up any more danger. They already had more than enough.

Maddox wasn't happy.

He'd gotten back to his room last night and found his cell phone—smashed. He'd left it charging on his nightstand, and then when he'd heard the crash in Taryn's room, the device had been forgotten.

Until he'd gotten back after spending time with Taryn.

Someone had gone into his room while he was out, even though he'd locked the door.

Did someone suspect him? Did someone know who he really was?

Either way, he'd need to remain even more on guard until he knew who'd destroyed his phone.

He'd already searched Eleanor's, Danielle's, and Chef's bedrooms this morning while doing his security checks on the house.

They were clean, with no sign of the missing tech.

He still needed to search Taryn's space, but for some reason he felt hesitant to do so. No, first, he would try to look through Phil's and Shawn's rooms —just in case.

As Maddox passed through the living room, heading to the front porch so he could install more security lights, he paused when he spotted someone standing near the door.

His eyes widened when he saw his colleague there.

He glanced around to make sure no one was

nearby before approaching Brandon Hale. Maddox almost hadn't recognized the man in a suit and tie.

Maddox lowered his voice. "What are you doing here?"

Brandon rubbed some lint from his sleeve. "I'm trying to arrange a meeting with Mr. Whitlock to discuss some business deals."

"Business deals? I thought I was the one who's supposed to find out the information here." Maddox bristled, something he didn't usually do around his teammates.

"I know. You're doing a fine job. But, given everything that's going on, it's clear that this needs to be a team effort. We're running out of time, so we decided to try a different tactic. I tried to call and give you a heads-up, but it went straight to voice mail."

"Someone smashed my phone last night, and I need to replace it."

"Good to know. We were getting worried. I have some updates for you. But I know we can't talk now. Just one thing." Brandon leaned closer and lowered his voice. "We're still looking into The System. But we found a post on the dark web that mentioned some GPS coordinates. The location is only ten minutes from this estate."

"What?"

Brandon nodded. "I'm going to fish for information about that property. We also sent a drone up. We saw some vehicles parked on this property, but there's no road leading there."

Maddox remembered those lights he'd seen behind the stables. Could that tie in with this?

"I'll send you more information as soon as we learn anything else."

As soon as those words left Brandon's mouth, Maddox heard footsteps in the distance. He grabbed the toolbox at his feet and stepped away before anyone could see him talking to Brandon.

Instead, he headed across the room on his original path.

But he paused on the other side of the doorway as he heard Taryn's voice.

"Mr. Whitlock says you have five minutes," she said. "He'll meet you in his office."

"Perfect. I really appreciate this."

Maddox heard the two of them walking away.

But his curiosity remained.

What else had Brandon discovered about this operation?

Maddox would love nothing more than to sit down with his colleague and talk face-to-face about everything.

But that couldn't happen right now.

CHAPTER
TWENTY-SEVEN

"TARYN, I would like for you to stay with us." Mr. Whitlock turned toward her as he slowly lowered himself into his leather chair.

Taryn paused at the office door, unsure she'd heard him correctly. "Me? Are you sure?"

Mr. Whitlock nodded and rubbed his leg as if his edema made him uncomfortable. "It will be good for you to get a feel for what goes on with my business."

She wasn't sure exactly what Mr. Whitlock meant by that, but she didn't ask any questions. Especially not right now.

Instead, she listened as Mr. Whitlock directed Mr. Hale to sit in the seat across from him.

Mr. Whitlock, who normally seemed so frail, suddenly seemed like the consummate businessman again as he pulled out a leather-bound notebook and picked up his pen, looking ready to take notes. "What can I help you with, Mr. Hale?"

"I'm looking to develop some property, and I was hoping you might be interested in selling some of your land. I can make you a good offer."

Mr. Whitlock's eyes narrowed as he sat back in his seat. "Money no longer entices me."

"I can understand that. But I also understand this land is just sitting unused. I thought you might want to see some good come from it."

Mr. Whitlock raised a shaggy eyebrow. "Some good? Which piece of property are you talking about?"

"It's about ten minutes from here. Near Mt. Caleb."

Mr. Whitlock let out an almost scoffing breath. "That old piece of land? What could you possibly want to do with that? It's in the middle of nowhere."

"I'm one of the board members with Eagle's Wings, a nonprofit that helps veterans. As you know, Mt. Caleb was the site of an historic Civil War battle, and since our charity focuses on veterans, the land seems like the perfect fit for our mission. We're hoping to start a retreat where people can go and get away from it all. We feel like this property would be ideal."

Mr. Whitlock closed the notebook without writing

anything down. "I'm sorry. But my land is not for sale."

Mr. Hale frowned and shifted in his seat. "If you don't mind me asking, do you have other plans for it?"

"I like green space. That's why I bought up so much land. I did so much developing, and I feel like it's my duty to give back to this community by preserving some forest land."

"But we would just be creating a camp—"

"I said no." Mr. Whitlock's voice hardened. "The land isn't for sale. That's the end of this discussion. Now, Taryn, if you would show our visitor out. I'm sorry he wasted his time by coming out here."

Taryn nodded, surprised at how quickly Mr. Whitlock had slipped back into businessman mode. His opinion had been unchanging and confident.

She glanced at Mr. Hale and motioned him toward the door. "I'll show you out."

The two of them began walking side-by-side back toward the front of the house.

"That man's quite the legend, you know," Mr. Hale said.

"That's what I've heard. Once he makes a decision, he doesn't sway from it, now, does he?"

"No, he doesn't. That's for sure."

They paused by the door, and Mr. Hale nodded at her. "I'm sorry to disrupt your day. You have to understand that I needed to try, at least. To give it everything I had."

"I understand. Now, I hope you have a great day." Taryn opened the door for him, and he stepped out.

But as he departed, she couldn't help but wonder if there was more to that whole offer than he'd let on. Was this somehow connected with the other strange occurrences here?

Could that man be the one who'd sent those threats to Mr. Whitlock? Did land have something to do with what was going on around here?

One thing was for certain: there were too many unknowns for Taryn's comfort right now.

Entirely too many.

As Maddox headed toward the west wing to fix a leaky faucet, he paused outside one of the rooms.

A voice rang out from the other side.

Shawn's voice.

He was still here.

And he was still talking to someone about investments.

He raised his hand to knock at the door. Before he could, Shawn pulled the door open and stared at him.

"Can I help you?" A knot of confusion formed on his brow.

"I'm checking on the window latches," Maddox told him. "It's an official order on my to-do list."

The knot remained on Shawn's forehead as he opened his door wider. "Come in. I can wait."

Disappointment bit at Maddox.

He wouldn't be able to search the man's room.

But maybe he could talk to him.

"So, you're a finance guy, huh?" Maddox asked as he walked toward the window.

"That's right."

"I thought I heard you outside the other day talking to someone about it. You take it very seriously."

"You heard that?" Shawn raised his eyebrows. "One of my clients is in Australia on a business trip right now, and he wanted to transfer some of his assets."

Maddox stored that information away. He supposed it made sense, and Shawn didn't seem to stumble over his words.

But he couldn't completely rule the man out.

Not yet.

He checked the other window.

He'd have to come back later if he wanted to look through any of Shawn's things.

"Looks good." He tested the window before stepping toward the door. "By the way, how long will you be staying here?"

"I plan on leaving this evening."

"Have a safe trip back."

"Will do."

Maddox felt Shawn's gaze on him as he left the room.

His thoughts raced through everything he'd already learned in his time here at the estate.

What had happened in that labyrinth the day before?

Leroy had a squeaky-clean record—not even a parking ticket.

So, why had someone killed him? Maddox might be able to understand trying to scare people away, but the fact Leroy was dead took this whole investigation to another level. Had the man seen something he shouldn't have?

If what Brandon said was true then time was running out, and Maddox needed to find answers now more than ever.

He needed to know what was in that safe in Mr. Whitlock's office. Was it the missing tech? Finding out needed to be his next step.

But if he was caught . . . then this whole operation would be over. Mr. Whitlock would fire him. Maybe even prosecute him.

Maybe Maddox would even be blamed for everything that had been happening here.

He frowned.

He had some work to finish up. But as soon as he had some time off, he knew exactly what he wanted to do.

TWENTY-EIGHT

AFTER LUNCH, Taryn slipped into the library to look through some books.

She'd just finished reading *The Great Gatsby* to Mr. Whitlock, and he'd told her she could pick the next book.

Reading was such a nice escape from all the craziness surrounding her.

She was about to climb down the rolling ladder when she heard someone behind her and twirled around.

She felt herself beginning to tumble when Maddox caught her.

The breath whooshed from her lungs.

Especially when she looked up and saw Maddox's face mere inches from hers.

"I didn't mean to scare you." Maddox set her back on her feet.

She smoothed her blouse as she tried to compose herself. "I should have been more on guard. Is everything okay?"

"Everything is fine." He shifted in front of her, almost as if self-conscious. "Look, I'm done with my to-do list for today, so I was wondering if I could have the rest of the afternoon off?"

She raised her eyebrows, wondering exactly what he was so anxious to do. Then she nodded. The staff here couldn't be expected to work twenty-four/seven.

"Of course." She gripped the novel she held close to her chest. "As long as everything is done that needs to be done."

"Perfect. Thanks." He nodded to the book she practically hugged. "Good read."

"You've read *Anna Karenina*?"

"Of course. It's a classic."

This man never failed to surprise her.

He started to step away when her curiosity got the best of her, and she called to him. "Do you mind if I ask what you're planning on doing?"

Maddox shifted again before shrugging. "I thought I'd take a walk and explore the woods around here. I've always loved the mountains and so much of this property seems untouched. How many acres did you say Mr. Whitlock owned around here? Two hundred forty or something?"

"Yes, and that's just the land that's considered his estate property. He's bought much of the property in the surrounding area as well." At once, she remembered the conversation Mr. Whitlock had with Mr. Hale.

Why had Mr. Hale been so interested in Mr. Whitlock's property? Was there something there of value?

Maybe she needed to check the land out also.

Maddox nodded slowly. "I heard Danielle talking to someone and saying there was a waterfall, so I thought it might be fun to look for it."

"Really?" Now *that* sounded interesting.

Maddox paused. "Any chance you want to go with me?"

Her cheeks warmed at the invitation. She knew she should say no.

But she didn't want to.

However, it wasn't that simple.

"I'm not sure if I could get away," she finally said.

It was the truth. She didn't schedule very much time off for herself. When the nurse was here, Taryn usually tried to do things for herself—things like check her email or just simply relax for a few minutes.

Maddox slowly nodded. "I understand."

"But let me see what I can do. Can you give me ten minutes?"

A grin stretched across his face. "Absolutely. Come find me then. I'll be on the back patio."

Taryn didn't know why she wanted to go with him so badly. Was it to spend more time with Maddox? Or was it because she needed some breathing room from this place?

She was beginning to feel suffocated lately. Or like she was in over her head. Or maybe a little bit of both.

She hurried toward Mr. Whitlock's room to see what he might say.

***

Maddox knew he probably shouldn't have offered to let Taryn go with him. But another part of him wanted to continue getting to know her better . . . so he could figure out if she was guilty or not.

Of course.

At least, that's the reason he told himself.

If he were honest, he'd admit he'd already concluded Taryn was innocent. Whenever Maddox looked into her eyes, he felt as if he saw the truth there.

He was pleasantly surprised when she appeared

ten minutes later in hiking boots, jeans, and a sweatshirt.

"I'm ready," she announced.

"Mr. Whitlock is okay with this?"

Taryn paused beside him. "His nurse just arrived. She's going to be here with him for the next four hours. So, the timing actually worked out great."

"Perfect. I already packed some water and snacks, just in case, so I'm ready to go."

Maddox knew where he wanted to head to first—toward the back of the property to see if he could figure out any information on those lights he'd seen moving back there.

He would just explore, and he wouldn't do anything that could get Taryn hurt.

That was the last thing he wanted.

They started toward the back of the property, sunshine hitting their shoulders until they reached the canopy of trees.

"Do you hike a lot?" Taryn asked as they stepped into the woods a few minutes later.

"I love a good hike," Maddox said. "It's a great way to sort out my thoughts."

"Kind of like me in the labyrinth," Taryn said.

"Yes, I suppose that's correct."

She nodded farther into the woods. "So, there's really a waterfall back here?"

Maddox *had* heard something about a waterfall,

but there was no guarantee they were going to find it today. He would need to play this cool.

"I thought it would be fun to look for it," he finally said. "Plus, it's a beautiful day, and some fresh air will probably do us both some good, right?"

"For sure."

They walked a few paces in silence. Maddox needed to figure out a way to bring up Taryn's association with Grissom, but he hadn't exactly been a smooth talker. He was just going to have to dive right in.

"Can I ask you a question?" he started.

"Sure. I may or may not answer." She shrugged as she continued forward, looking in her element out here in nature.

He chuckled. "That's fair. Are you . . . single?"

Great. Now it sounded like Maddox was hitting on her. His wording could have been better, but it was too late to change that now.

"I am." Her voice sounded relaxed, like she hadn't been put off by his bluntness. "Have been for the past year and a half."

"What happened, if you don't mind me asking?" Maddox stepped over a downed tree as they traversed deeper into the mountainous woods.

She let out a long breath. "I don't mind. It's probably good for me to talk about it. I've bottled it away for so long. For about a year, I dated this guy named Grissom Smith."

"Grissom? Now there's an interesting name."

"Yeah." She practically snorted. "I was applying for a job at a drugstore—after my mom died—when he heard the manager telling me they didn't have any openings. I nearly started crying. I only had another few weeks where I could live at my mom's old place. Then I would be out on the streets."

Maddox's heart pounded in his ears as he listened to her story. He waited for her to continue.

"Anyway, as I was there, this guy came up and said he had an opening at his restaurant, and it came with housing. He said the job was mine if I wanted it, and I could start right then. So, I did. It seemed like an answer to my prayers. And, at first, it was."

"What happened?"

As Taryn hesitated, Maddox held his breath.

Was this the moment he'd discover the truth?

And what if it was a truth he didn't like? What if Taryn really was a part of this somehow?

He didn't think his heart could handle the disappointment if that were the case.

MEMORIES PUMMELED TARYN. Memories she'd rather forget.

But there was also something refreshing about not having secrets—about not having anything to hide.

Besides, Maddox was a great listener. He grunted a lot to let her know he heard her. Normally, the act might sound neanderthal, but somehow with Maddox it seemed strangely appealing.

As was his crocheting.

Both made him unique and fascinating.

She drew in a deep breath before continuing. "We started dating, and I began to suspect Grissom was involved with some shady stuff. Drugs, mostly. I knew I didn't want to be associated in any way with what he was doing."

"So, what did you do?" Maddox glanced over at Taryn as they continued to navigate the forest.

"I told him I would find a new job and that we were through. When I did, he kicked me out of the apartment where I'd been staying—the apartment he owned and rented to me."

"Ouch."

"Definitely." She shrugged at the memories. "Thankfully, I had a couple of friends I could stay with. But I knew I couldn't live at their place with them forever. Meanwhile, Grissom was going around town, trying to ruin my reputation so no one would hire me. He actually told people that I'd stolen from him."

Maddox's eyes narrowed. "That's not cool."

Taryn let out a long breath as memories pummeled her. "Thankfully, it was around that time I met Mr. Whitlock and things turned around."

"Sounds like good timing." Maddox reached for her hand and helped her over an especially rocky area.

"It was." As their fingers touched, fire shot through her.

Fire?

Taryn was in trouble. A lot of trouble.

She really had to keep her thoughts focused here before her feelings derailed her.

No matter how tempting Maddox might be, there

were more reasons to keep her distance than there were to get close.

As a noise sounded in the distance, Maddox's arm jutted out. He pushed Taryn back as the noise became louder.

Was that . . . a car?

How was that even possible?

Taryn froze.

No roads were supposed to cut through this property.

She hadn't done any research on this land, but she felt for certain the only road close to Mr. Whitlock's home was the one out front. She and Maddox had walked in the opposite direction of that route.

Her heart pounded in her ears as she waited to find out what was happening.

Maddox remained out of sight as they waited, watching.

The path in front of them had expanded, transforming into a narrow dirt road.

And someone was coming.

His muscles pulled taut across his back.

A moment later, a truck went past, kicking up dirt behind it.

The vehicle looked and sounded old. Two men

were inside, and a gun rack was attached inside the back window.

Were hunters using this property without permission?

Maddox didn't think it was that simple.

Once the truck had gone past, Maddox took Taryn's hand and led her toward the path the vehicle had taken.

It was just as he thought—a small dirt road, only big enough for one vehicle to pass by. It appeared almost new with tall tufts of grass growing down the middle of it.

How did someone even access this area?

Those lights he'd seen at the back of the property . . . they somehow connected with this road. He was certain of it.

"Does Mr. Whitlock know about this?" Maddox muttered.

"I have no idea." Taryn frowned. "This isn't what I expected to find at all. I have so many questions."

So did Maddox.

"I wonder where this leads," Taryn continued. "And who those people were inside the truck."

Maddox remained quiet, a bad feeling churning in his gut.

"We should find out," Taryn announced.

Her words caused concern to spring to life inside him. "I'm not sure that's a good idea."

Taryn turned toward him, determination in her gaze. "If something's happening on Mr. Whitlock's property, then he deserves to know about it. That man who came today? He was asking about some of this property also. That can't be a coincidence."

Maddox's pulse pounded harder. "Was he?"

"Yes, he wanted to buy it for some reason. He gave some excuse about its historical significance. But now it's becoming clear there's more to it than that."

He needed to redirect her thoughts—and quickly. She was getting too close to the truth.

"Most likely those guys are just hunting illegally," he said. "They had rifles in the back of their truck."

"Yeah, I noticed that too. But what if there's more to it than that? All these tire tracks look fresh, and the road looks as if it's been used quite a bit."

Maddox wanted more than anything to follow that truck also. But he couldn't do anything to endanger Taryn. He wouldn't forgive himself if she got hurt because of him.

He also needed to maintain his cover.

And he needed to buy a little time.

"Let's walk down it just a short distance." Maddox nodded toward the road. "But we need to stay to the edge just in case anyone else comes by. Until we know what these people are doing, we should be extra careful."

"Of course. Believe me, the last thing I want to do is . . ." Taryn rubbed her throat. ". . . is to end up like Leroy."

That was the last thing Maddox wanted as well. "Then let's move. We don't have much time."

TARYN'S MIND continued to race.

What was going on here?

Whatever it was, Mr. Whitlock deserved to know about it.

He deserved to know about a lot of things.

But that didn't mean Taryn wanted to tell him.

Instead, she felt it was her job to absorb things for him. To take the brunt of what was happening. To make sure no one took advantage of a dying man.

Maddox paused and reached into his pocket before tossing something on the road.

She squinted as she tried to figure out what he'd just done.

Nails, she realized. Maddox had thrown nails in the road.

She glanced up at him, not bothering to hide the questions in her eyes.

He shrugged. "If someone else comes by, maybe this will slow them down or make them think twice about using property that doesn't belong to them."

His explanation made sense. Mostly.

"I just happened to have the nails left from some work I was doing earlier," Maddox continued.

Okay, so he hadn't planned on this.

That was good to know, she supposed.

But as she glanced into his pocket, she saw something else there.

Something blue and fuzzy.

"Do you have yarn with you?" she asked.

He shrugged as if it wasn't a big deal. "You never know when it might come in handy."

Wait . . . did Maddox crochet all the time?

The more she discovered about him, the more interesting he seemed.

They hiked another quarter mile, but all Taryn saw were trees, boulders, and the road. No other cars. No buildings. No voices.

Maddox paused and glanced at his watch. "I hate to say this, but we may need to come back another day."

A frown tugged at Taryn's lips. But she knew he was right. She needed to get back to Mr. Whitlock before his nurse left. "I was really hoping for some answers."

"So was I. But maybe it's for the best. We have no idea what's going on here."

Taryn swallowed her disappointment as they turned around and walked through the woods again, trying to stay out of sight.

But as they got closer to the spot where they'd seen that truck pass, voices carried through the air.

Maddox grabbed Taryn's arm and tucked her behind a tree.

He peered out before muttering, "It looks like those nails I left worked. There's an SUV on the road —with a flat tire."

She didn't know whether to be impressed or frightened.

Taryn peered around the tree also.

Three men stood outside a black SUV staring at their flat tire.

Did these men have anything to do with what was happening at Mr. Whitlock's estate?

If it wasn't for Maddox beside her, Taryn would be terrified. But he kept a firm hand on her back, his touch grounding her.

Even though he just worked maintenance, he somehow seemed capable. Like he could take care of himself. Like he could take care of those he cared about also.

Without ever saying it, Taryn felt like one of those people.

One of the ones he'd let into his inner circle.

She put those thoughts on hold as a conversation drifted their way.

"Who dropped nails out here?" one of the men asked.

"Maybe they fell out of Duncan's truck."

"Well, he needs to be more careful. We don't have any time to waste. Let's get this tire changed so we can get to the meeting."

The meeting? What meeting?

Taryn's curiosity grew.

She and Maddox watched as the men began to jack up the vehicle to change the tire.

None of these guys appeared to be hunters. Sure, they wore flannel and jeans. But most hunters Taryn knew wore camouflage.

Something was definitely going on here.

"What's the next step?" one of the men asked. "Have you heard?"

"We need to find the safe."

"Why?"

"That's where we think the blueprints are. We can't do anything without them."

"Is there a plan for how we'll get in?"

"Not yet. But hopefully we'll come up with something at the meeting."

"I thought we were going to talk about the Great Awakening."

"We are . . ."

The Great Awakening? What was that?

And they'd mentioned a safe. Were they talking about Mr. Whitlock's safe?

They had to be. It was the only thing that made sense.

Exactly what was inside that metal box? And what were these guys planning?

Maddox and Taryn remained at their spot for twenty more minutes—until the men changed the tire and continued down the road. Only then was it safe to leave.

The guys hadn't said anything else of interest.

But Maddox's mind raced as he and Taryn headed back to the estate.

Were these guys with The System? Were they the ones using this property?

But for what purposes?

Why, of all places, would they choose land owned by Mr. Whitlock? Sure, the area was private and secluded. But there were plenty of pieces of property like that.

And what kind of blueprints were they after?

What safe had they referenced? It only made sense that it was Mr. Whitlock's.

Perhaps the biggest question was: what was the Great Awakening?

The questions raced through his mind.

"Can I tell you something?" Taryn's voice pulled him from his thoughts.

"Of course." His pulse spiked when he heard the hesitation in her voice—hesitation that made whatever she was about to say sound important.

She rubbed her hands on her jeans as if nervous. "Mr. Whitlock has been receiving threats."

Maddox's shoulders tightened at her words. "Threats?"

Taryn nodded. "I haven't told him. But for the past few weeks, he's been getting letters in the mail. There's no return address—and just a typed sheet of paper inside the envelope."

"What do these threats say?"

"That if he doesn't pay up, there will be consequences. That people he cares about will be in danger if he doesn't comply."

Surprise rushed through Maddox. "Why didn't you tell him? Because of his heart?"

Taryn nodded. "I still don't know if I'm doing the right thing or not. I just want to protect him."

Maddox frowned at the new detail. "How many has he gotten?"

"Five."

The bad feeling in Maddox's gut only grew. "Can I see them when we get back?"

"Of course."

His mind continued to race. *Was* Mr. Whitlock somehow involved in this plot?

He had no idea.

Maddox had never felt as relieved as he did when they finally reached the estate again. Not that it was necessarily safer here. But at least he had a better idea of what to expect.

Still, there was something he needed to talk to Taryn about. He'd been thinking about it all day. Had been weighing his options. Considering the pros and cons.

He knew what he needed to do—and now he couldn't second-guess himself.

If he was going to find answers, then he needed to be honest with Taryn. She could be a great asset to this investigation, and he felt certain he could trust her.

But before they emerged from the woods, Maddox touched Taryn's arm. She turned toward him, her eyes widened with surprise.

She was a smart lady. Certainly, she'd started to put some things together.

Maddox swallowed hard as he tried to find the right words to start. "Taryn . . . you probably shouldn't tell anybody what we just overheard."

She tilted her head. "But don't you think that Mr. Whitlock needs to know—"

"He *does* need to know. However, I'm not sure who we can trust right now."

Her eyes narrowed, a wrinkle forming on her brow. "You mean, you don't think we can trust Mr. Whitlock?"

He hesitated only a moment before diving in. "I mean . . . something's clearly going on. Those men we saw . . . I have a feeling they're involved with some people who are bad news. And I have a feeling that someone who works for Mr. Whitlock is helping these guys. It only makes sense."

Realization rolled over her features. "You think one of Mr. Whitlock's staff is working with these guys on this Great Awakening thing?"

He nodded. "I do. A staff member . . . or a family member or associate."

"I don't know." Taryn stepped back, her hand going to her temple. "I just feel like Mr. Whitlock should know all this. I know I haven't told him about those threats yet. But this . . . it seems like something he might want to handle."

Maddox gently grabbed her arm. He'd been wanting to tell her the truth. Knowing that he should. Maybe this was the time.

Especially since it sounded like he needed to get into Mr. Whitlock's safe.

And, if his hunch was correct, Taryn's handprint just might be the key to unlocking it.

He swallowed hard, praying he was making the right decision. "There's something I need to tell you."

Her eyes widened as she looked up at him, trust emanating in her gaze. "What's going on, Maddox?"

"There's more to me than you might think." Now that he'd started, he knew there was no going back.

AS TARYN STOOD at the edge of the woods, she waited to hear what Maddox had to say.

Her heart pounded in her ears as she anticipated the worst.

Clearly, whatever was on his mind was important.

Maddox stepped closer, a thin layer of sweat across his forehead. "I'm not just a maintenance guy."

"What do you mean? Who are you then?" Instinctively, Taryn took a step back.

What if she was being too trusting right now?

Something was going on here—something that had gotten worse since Maddox had arrived.

She had to be smart—to be ready to act. Ready to run if necessary.

Maddox started to reach for her, but he dropped his arm as if he'd second-guessed himself.

Instead, he drew in a deep breath before raking a hand through his hair. "The truth is I work for an organization called Blackout."

Taryn took another step back as fear rippled through her. "What's Blackout? Are you the reason so much has been happening at the estate lately?"

His eyes lit with alarm. "No. Not at all. In fact, I work to take down people who think they're above the law."

Taryn crossed her arms, still unsure what to think. She knew, however, that it was essential she remain on guard. "Keep going."

"As I mentioned before, I was a Navy SEAL. When I got out of the military, some of my friends and I joined a private security group called Blackout. People hire us for protection or to help them investigate. It depends on what they need."

She narrowed her eyes as she tried to figure out where Maddox was going with this. "So, Mr. Whitlock hired you?"

Maddox's cheek twitched. "No, he didn't. A woman named Finley Cooper did. She's the CEO of Embolden Tech."

"I've heard of the company—I think. But why would this woman hire you to come here?" Questions pinged in her head.

"Some proprietary technology the company developed has disappeared. Because of a past incident, she now places trackers in each of the boxes. The tracker for these particular products showed that, instead of being delivered to the buyer, they were brought to this area, where the shipment disappeared and the tracker was disabled."

Taryn still wasn't following. "Why would proprietary technology disappear here in the middle of nowhere?"

"That's what we're trying to figure out." Maddox paused. "It gets worse. The delivery driver died as well. His body was found about an hour from here, left in a ditch."

Taryn sucked in a quick breath. Someone else had died?

She tried to stop the quiver that raked through her, but she couldn't.

What Maddox was telling her . . . it only proved that something dangerous was going on.

She raised her chin, knowing she still needed more information. "What kind of proprietary technology is this exactly? Are you talking weapons?"

"No, it's nothing like that. It's listening devices and security cameras that are nearly undetectable. If technology like that gets into the wrong hands, someone could use it for some less-than-honorable purposes."

"You think Mr. Whitlock is involved?" Was that what all of this was leading up to?

"We're not sure. That's what we're trying to figure out." Maddox shifted again. "Taryn, have you ever heard of a group known as The System?"

"No." The name didn't even sound vaguely familiar.

"My team and I are just learning more about them, but they're some kind of underground militia group that wants to change the United States as we know it. We believe they may be setting up some kind of compound on Mr. Whitlock's property."

"What?" Had Taryn even heard him correctly? His words seemed surreal. Yet Maddox wasn't the dramatic type . . .

"We're still uncovering things."

"We?"

"Me and my team. The man who came to the house yesterday? Brandon Hale? He works with Blackout. They sent up a drone and saw some cars on the property. That was one reason I wanted to hike out here today."

"Not because of waterfalls?"

Maddox shook his head. "Not because of waterfalls. I'm sorry."

Taryn's mind continued to race. "Why come to the estate under false pretenses?"

"I needed a way to get inside so I could figure out

what was going on. When I saw the job opening for the maintenance worker, I thought it might be the best way. I didn't want to deceive you. But, of course, I didn't know you then either."

Her gaze locked with his as she searched for the truth. "Did you think that *I* could be a suspect?"

"Everyone was on the table." His voice sounded unwavering even though his gaze almost looked apologetic.

Taryn shook her head, pinching the skin between her eyes. "I just don't know what to think about this."

"I know it's going to take a while to comprehend. It's a lot."

"Why are you telling me everything now?"

"I need you to trust me. I need you to know that something dangerous is going on here. And I need your help."

"My help?"

Maddox nodded before launching into his proposal.

All Taryn could think was: what if all this was just another big deception? What if she couldn't trust Maddox, just like she couldn't trust most of the other people who'd ever been in her life?

Maddox hated to leave Taryn alone. But he had to get a new phone if he wanted to talk to Brandon.

After making sure Taryn was secure inside the house, Maddox headed to the closest store, which was still twenty minutes away. As he drove, his mind raced through everything he'd learned.

He still wasn't sure if he should have shared the truth with Taryn or not. At least, she hadn't pushed him away, and she seemed open to what he was doing.

By the time he found a new phone, purchased it, and had it set up, an hour had passed. As soon as his phone was operational, he texted Brandon. Thankfully, his colleague was available to meet—which was exactly what they did thirty minutes later.

Maddox grabbed a drink and a package of salted peanuts from a gas station before wandering to a picnic table in the grass beside the station. No one else was here, which made it the perfect place to meet Brandon.

His colleague arrived right on time.

Maddox gave Brandon an update on what he'd learned today.

"Are you sure you can trust Taryn?" Brandon narrowed his gaze skeptically. "That she's not in on this?"

Maddox's answer was unwavering. "My gut tells me I can trust her. Besides, we need her help."

Brandon started to nod, but the action morphed into a tense shrug. "If she tells Mr. Whitlock . . ."

"I know. But I really don't think he's in on this. I think someone is using him. That someone else is pulling the strings. But I need to get inside that safe in his office."

"How do you propose to do that?"

"Mr. Whitlock has used Taryn's handprint and fingerprint in the house to access several things. I think she can open the safe using the biometric lock."

Brandon nodded slowly. "Not a bad idea. Just be careful."

"I will be." The last thing he wanted was to put Taryn in danger. He'd do whatever it took to keep her safe.

"There are two other things I thought you should know," Brandon continued.

Maddox took another sip of his Cheerwine soda and waited to hear what Brandon had to say. "Go on."

"First of all, Mr. Whitlock called today and hired Blackout to provide security at his estate. We're sending Titus out."

"What?" Why hadn't Maddox heard about this yet? Questions pounded through his head.

Brandon nodded. "Apparently, Taryn recommended the agency."

She hadn't said anything else to Mr. Whitlock, had she?

Maddox didn't think she would do that. He prayed that was the case.

"Secondly, we were able to make out a license plate on one of the vehicles on the property," Brandon continued. "We ran it, to see who the plates belonged to. It's a man named Duncan Cartwright."

"Who is Duncan Cartwright?" One of the men on the side of the road had said the name Duncan, but Maddox didn't know who that was.

Brandon leaned closer. "Here's where things get strange. Duncan actually works for Donovan Sullivan."

Maddox sucked in a breath. Donovan Sullivan was another man with more money than he knew what to do with. He was recently involved in a human trafficking operation. Not only that, but he had ties to some missing caustic substances.

His jaw tightened.

Just what were these people doing up on that property?

CHAPTER
THIRTY-TWO

BACK AT THE HOUSE, as Taryn sat with Mr. Whitlock, she couldn't stop thinking about what Maddox had told her. Her mind turned their conversation over and over. It almost seemed surreal.

It shouldn't surprise her that the man wasn't just a maintenance worker. He clearly had a lot of skills in many areas. His ability to keep a cool head in the middle of a crisis should have been another indicator.

Taryn thought he was telling the truth when he told her about Blackout. She thought she could trust him. In fact, she'd even looked up some information on the organization and they appeared legit. Of course, none of the employees' pictures were on the site, so she couldn't definitely prove Maddox worked for them.

Seeing their site had given her an idea that she'd run past Mr. Whitlock. She wished she had time to talk to Maddox about it first, but she hadn't. Now she was anxious to see his reaction, however.

But what if all that was just a sham?

She wanted to trust her gut. But she'd been so wrong about Grissom . . . Why would she think she'd be right about Maddox?

Maybe it was because of the way he looked at her. His eyes just seemed so sincere, so concerned.

"Taryn, I think I'm going to have a nap," Mr. Whitlock said as he stifled a yawn.

She rose from where she'd been seated beside him —preoccupied unfortunately.

"I'll give you some privacy then," she said. "But can I ask you a question first? Maybe even two?"

"Go ahead."

She nibbled on her lip a moment, contemplating the outcome of what she was doing. She was clearly fishing for information.

But time was of the essence here. She could ask questions *and* keep her promise to Maddox.

Taryn shifted, hoping she looked casual. "You started to tell me something the other day. It sounded important, but we were cut off."

He shrugged. "I'm sorry, Taryn. Whatever it was, I can't recall right now. If it comes back to me, I'll let you know."

She tried to hide her disappointment. "I understand. And also . . . the man who stopped by here earlier today . . . Mr. Hale. I'm curious. Why do you think he wants that land so badly?"

Mr. Whitlock shrugged. "I have no idea. But he's the second person who brought up that property in the past few months. Do you think there's something special about it?"

Her breath caught. "Who else asked about it?"

"Strangely enough, it was Leroy. He said he knew someone who wanted to buy it."

As Maddox headed back to the estate, he glanced in his rearview mirror. It was getting dark outside. But headlights were behind him as he wound down the curvy mountain road.

Who else would be heading this way?

Other than Mr. Whitlock's estate, there wasn't much out here.

As the headlights got closer, the tension between Maddox's shoulder blades tightened.

Was someone following him?

Did someone know who he really was?

He had a feeling this person would be trouble.

Even worse, there was nowhere for him to pull

off. No shoulder beside the road. No driveways. No shopping centers.

Only miles and miles of secluded mountain road.

Maddox pressed the accelerator harder, watching to see what the driver behind him would do.

The other driver accelerated also.

This was going to get dicey.

He gripped the steering wheel more tightly as he sped down the road.

This guy wasn't going to give up, was he?

The next instant, the other driver nudged him.

Maddox's SUV jolted forward.

Oh no. That wasn't going to work.

As he saw a bend in the road just up ahead, he knew what he had to do.

He pressed the accelerator harder, his headlights illuminating the road in front of him.

Just as he reached the bend, he jerked the wheel, barely making the turn. His vehicle edged danger-ously close to the guardrail.

Maddox held his breath as he waited for his SUV to right itself.

As he did, he glanced behind him.

The driver tailing him hadn't been able to see the bend coming. He'd been driving too close to Maddox to see anything but Maddox's SUV.

The other vehicle careened through the guardrail —before disappearing off the side of the mountain.

MADDOX DARTED from his SUV and ran to the edge of the road. As he did, he called 911. The operator promised someone would be right out.

A man climbed from the car, staggering as he grabbed hold of the rocky cliff.

A few trees held up his vehicle, preventing it from toppling any farther.

Maddox had to make a decision—and fast.

Without contemplating it anymore, he reached his hand down. "Let me help you."

He wanted to see this guy's face.

But he wasn't sure what would happen after that.

Things could turn ugly.

The driver glanced up at him, the nighttime concealing his features.

After a moment of hesitation, the man reached up.

Maddox grabbed his arm. Straining his muscles, he began to pull.

A few tugs later, the man's torso reached the ground above. He clawed the rocky terrain before collapsing on the side of the road.

Maddox didn't give him any time to recover.

He jumped to his feet and pulled the man up by his collar. "Why were you following me?"

Maddox's eyes widened as the man's features came into view.

This couldn't be . . . but it was.

Dinner was late, and everyone had gathered in the dining room.

Taryn glanced around the table at everyone who'd joined them for some beef tenderloin tonight. Mr. Whitlock, of course, sat at the head of the table. Danielle had also joined them as well as Eleanor and Phil.

Taryn wasn't sure where Alana had disappeared to, but she was on the property somewhere. Her car was still outside, but Taryn hadn't seen her.

And Maddox wasn't back yet either.

She prayed he was okay.

Just then, the doorbell rang. Could that be Maddox?

He wouldn't ring the bell . . . would he?

When Taryn opened the door, a man in his mid to late twenties with honey-blond hair strode into the room. The guy clearly worked out, based on the bulging muscles peeking out from beneath his black T-shirt. But his serious expression made her cautious.

"You must be Titus," Taryn muttered. "You got here quickly."

"I didn't want to waste any time."

She extended her arm. "I'm Taryn. Mr. Whitlock's assistant."

He shook her hand. "Nice to meet you."

Backup had arrived.

Having someone else here she could trust brought her an even greater sense of comfort.

They needed as many people as they could get on this now.

She was just so thankful that Mr. Whitlock had listened to her when she suggested hiring security.

"You're just in time for dinner," Taryn said. "Let me introduce you to everyone."

Taryn led him into the dining room and paused near Mr. Whitlock.

"Everyone, this is Titus," Taryn said. "He'll be offering additional security here at the house. Mr. Whitlock agreed that we needed to up our security measures here considering everything that's happened around here lately."

Murmurs went around the table.

Finally, Titus was seated.

Taryn hadn't had the opportunity to share this update with Maddox.

But, right now, all she could think about was that she hoped he was okay.

THIRTY-FOUR

"GRISSOM SMITH," Maddox muttered, his muscles bristling.

The man—despite his accident—still managed to sneer and jerk back. "Maddox King."

Maddox bristled even more. "How do you know who I am?"

"I've been watching you."

"Watching me? Or watching Taryn?"

The man scowled. "I was just keeping an eye on her. Nothing wrong with that."

"It's been you I've seen on the property, hasn't it?"

"Maybe on occasion I like to go check on her." His words slurred, and his breath smelled like beer. He had definitely been drinking. "It's no big deal."

"It is a big deal—especially since you're scaring her."

"I don't want to *scare* her. I want to *help* her."

"That's why you fired her? Kicked her out of the apartment she was renting?"

"She was supposed to run back to me."

"And you can't stand the fact she didn't." Maddox's jaw hardened. "But that still doesn't explain why you were following me tonight."

"I just wanted to see who you were. I saw the two of you talking the other day. I didn't like the way she was looking at you."

"You're lucky to be alive right now, you know."

"I didn't do anything illegal . . ." the man growled.

"How about drinking and driving?"

Just as Maddox said the words, sirens sounded behind them.

First responders were here.

This guy might be a menace, but Maddox doubted he was involved in everything going on at the estate. However, he'd feel better once he was behind bars.

Maddox got back to the estate an hour later. He felt disheveled, but he tried to clean himself up before stepping inside the dining room.

He was happy to see Titus was there.

He'd gotten a text about it, one he'd read as soon as he pulled into the driveway.

His colleague's presence would make things a little easier here at the estate.

Chef had saved a plate for him, and Maddox tried to enjoy his meal, but it was nearly impossible. Not with everything he had going on in his mind.

As everyone else enjoyed some dessert, Maddox turned his attention back to the people at the table.

Was someone who was eating with him right now a killer? He didn't want to think they were . . . but it was a good possibility.

At least, Titus was here so there would be a second set of eyes watching everything going on.

Just as he was about to take another bite of his meal, a scream cut into the air.

Maddox and Titus jumped to their feet and started toward the back door.

Someone outside was in trouble.

MADDOX TORE OUTSIDE, followed by Titus.

The scream had come from a woman. He was certain of it.

And only one person was missing from dinner.

Alana Whitlock.

He and Titus paused on the patio and glanced around, hoping something would indicate where the scream had come from.

But everything around them appeared still.

"You go to the left, and I'll go to the right," Maddox said.

Maddox raced across the lawn, searching around the outer perimeter of the labyrinth. He'd go into the space if he had to.

But after what had happened to Leroy, he hoped

he didn't have to. There were too many unknowns in that maze.

Maddox didn't see any signs of anyone around the area.

After circling the labyrinth, Maddox paused.

He glanced at the pool in the distance.

As he did, his breath caught.

He couldn't be certain, but it almost looked like . . . someone floated facedown in the water.

He raced toward the pool just as Titus darted that way also.

Titus dove into the water before Maddox reached the pool.

Maddox waited at the edge.

Stared at the slim figure.

A woman.

Dark hair.

He didn't have to see her face to know who she was.

Alana Whitlock.

Titus swam with her to the edge of the pool, and Maddox pulled her out. He began doing CPR as the crowd from inside the house gathered around.

"I called the police," Taryn said. "They're on their way."

Maddox continued with chest compressions, hoping to see a sign of life from Alana.

Any sign of life.

A breath. A fluttering. A slight movement.

But it was too late.

Alana Whitlock was already dead.

And Maddox was fairly certain someone had killed her.

Anxiety bubbled inside Taryn as she stood near the pool watching everything play out.

Alana was dead.

How could this have happened?

Another death . . . it felt surreal.

She studied the faces of the crowd around her.

Mr. Whitlock had come outside and dropped into a chair. He looked off-balance and pale, which worried her.

Eleanor paced and fanned her face.

Chef kept her hand over her mouth and stared at the swimming pool as if dazed.

Danielle stood with her hands on her hips, looking the least grieved of everyone. No, she almost looked angry.

Phil was on his phone, speaking to someone in sharp tones about a business deal he was trying to close. His conversation seemed heartless at a time like this. Yet, at the same time, it fit the man.

Maddox and Titus talked to the police.

Everyone out here had been inside when Alana had screamed and presumably fallen or been pushed into the pool.

By all appearances, no one in this group was guilty.

But if that was true, then what had happened? Was there an intruder haunting this property? Just looking for the opportunity to make a move?

Taryn shivered. She didn't like the thought of that.

But nothing else made sense.

She paced to Mr. Whitlock and placed a hand on his shoulder. He squeezed her fingers, not saying anything.

There was nothing to say.

Another tragedy had occurred.

And they were no closer to answers than before.

MADDOX SHOWED Titus and Detective Conners to a small room where monitors were set up displaying security camera footage. Since Titus had just started on the job, Maddox explained to them both what security measures were in place around the property.

He was anxious to talk to his friend in private, but Maddox knew this wasn't the time.

Instead, he located the camera facing the pool and scrolled through the footage until he found the moment Alana came onto the screen.

"Here she is," Maddox mumbled, his eyes glued to the images playing out before him.

"She's . . . alone." Titus stared at the screen, his jaw tight.

In the images, Alana carried a wine goblet in her

hand as she walked around the pool wearing a thin, silky black robe and heels.

A wine goblet? Maddox thought he remembered seeing broken glass on the pool deck.

She stood at the edge of the water and took a sip of her drink. Then she muttered something as if talking to herself, shaking her head as if she didn't like where her internal conversation was going.

A moment later, her arm dropped to her side. The glass fell onto the pavers. Her hand went to her chest.

Then she lost her balance and screamed as she toppled into the pool.

No one else had been nearby.

"Do you think she was just drunk?" Titus rested his hands on his hips as he continued to stare at the screen. "She didn't even fight to stay above water after she fell in—almost as if she were already unconscious."

"It's a possibility." Detective Conners frowned. "Alana does have a reputation around town for drinking too much."

"How much time passed before we found her?" Titus asked.

They checked the footage.

"It was only about three minutes," Maddox confirmed.

"Which is about two minutes longer than it can

take someone to drown." Titus scrubbed a hand down his face.

"My gut says she was already gone before she hit the water." Maddox looked at Detective Conners. "You'll test the glass to see if there's anything on it?"

"Of course. We'll see what we can find. Hopefully, there will be enough trace evidence on the shards of glass that we can test to see what might have been in her drink."

Maddox frowned, wishing there was a more definitive answer.

Then Detective Conners turned to him. "This is the second death at this estate in the past two days. I don't like the pattern I'm seeing emerge here."

"Believe me, no one does." Maddox crossed his arms.

"Then it's good Mr. Whitlock brought me on to work security." Titus stepped forward. "I'm going to help keep an eye on the place."

"That's probably smart," Conners said. "While we have no evidence yet to suspect foul play, any time there's more than one death like this, it gives us a reason for pause."

Maddox drew in a deep breath, considering whether to share his suspicions.

But this wasn't the time.

First, he needed more proof.

"We'll be keeping a close watch on everything

around here," Titus said. "Believe me, the last thing we want is for anyone else to be hurt."

Detective Conners straightened, and his gaze shifted from Maddox to Titus. "If anything else happens, please let me know. In the meantime, can I have a copy of this video?"

"Of course." Wasting no time, Maddox saved the video in a file that he could give the detective.

"I'd also like to check out some other video angles of the property, just to make sure that Alana wasn't meeting someone before she came to the pool," Conners said.

"The cameras mostly focus on the pool and on the front of the house," Maddox said. "But we can keep looking, just in case."

He had a feeling, however, that whoever had killed Alana was long gone.

Maddox had no doubt her drink had been poisoned, and that was what had led to her demise.

But why had she been killed? What did she know that had made someone else feel so threatened?

As everyone lingered on the back patio, waiting for their turn to be questioned, a sense of danger and worry rippled through the air. Taryn felt it. She was sure everyone else did also.

"I just don't know if I can work here anymore." Eleanor stopped pacing as she made her announcement.

Taryn wasn't surprised at the woman's proclamation. Not at all. In fact, in different circumstances, Taryn might also want to flee.

What made her nervous was the fact that she didn't know where this conversation was going, though she did have an inkling.

"I'm not comfortable being here either." Chef joined their newly forming circle. "Not until we have some answers about what's going on. Three people are now dead."

"Everyone, just calm down," Taryn encouraged, feeling the need to take charge of this situation.

Phil stepped forward. "I've got to agree. Dad, I don't even think that you should be here. It's not safe."

"This is my property, and nobody's going to drive me away from it." Mr. Whitlock jammed his finger in the air to drive home his point.

"Maybe everyone doesn't have to leave permanently." Danielle shrugged. "Maybe it can just be temporary until we can figure out what's going on."

Mr. Whitlock narrowed his eyes. "I'm not the feeble old man you all might think I am. My heart may not be good, but my brain still works. Something is happening here, and I don't like it."

Taryn looked up as Maddox and Titus appeared at the edge of the group. They'd clearly overheard most of that conversation and could probably feel the mounting tension in the air.

Titus stepped forward, his gaze connecting with everyone's in the circle. "I want to assure you all now that I'm working here, I'll be keeping an eye on everything here at the estate."

"But will you be enough?" Eleanor wrung her hands together in front of her. "I mean, no offense, but Alana, Gary, and Leroy all died practically right under our noses. How does this even happen? What if one of us is next?"

Murmurs went around the group.

Maddox stepped closer. "Before you jump to any conclusions, the police think these deaths were all accidents."

"But none of us believe that." Eleanor's gaze shifted to each person gathered in the semi-circle. "I know I'm not the only one. I don't even know how I'm going to sleep at night in this place."

"If anyone would feel safer somewhere else, then leave." Mr. Whitlock rose to his feet to address his staff, even though he looked like a burst of wind could knock him down. "I don't want to keep anyone here if they don't feel safe. But I, for one, am not going anywhere."

Taryn quickly joined him, holding onto his elbow

so he wouldn't collapse. She didn't know what she thought about Mr. Whitlock's declaration. Part of her wanted to usher him away, to get him to safety.

But was there anywhere they would be safe?

She wasn't sure.

For now, Taryn waited to hear what everyone else would say. Waited to see who might leave.

Whoever was behind this . . . they wouldn't stop until they got what they wanted.

What if that meant Mr. Whitlock was in grave danger also?

MADDOX WATCHED the group around him, anxious to see what they'd decide. He couldn't blame any of them if they wanted to leave. He also couldn't blame Mr. Whitlock for wanting to stay.

They desperately needed answers to what was going on around here. Someone was playing a deadly game.

He and his team not only needed to figure out who, but they also needed to figure out why.

What was this person hoping to accomplish? Why would they kill Leroy and Alana in order to get what they wanted? Had Gary's heart attack not been natural? Had the three of them somehow stumbled upon evidence? Maybe they knew something someone didn't want them to know.

Questions churned inside him as he continued to wait.

"I need to sleep on it," Eleanor finally said. "I don't know what to do or where else I would go if I left."

"I'm going to go pack my things." Chef raised her chin, making it clear her decision was now made. "I get offers every week from others to be their personal chef. Maybe it's time for a career change for me."

"I'm not going anywhere." Danielle crossed her arms. "I have horses to take care of. No one's going to scare me off."

"Dad's staying here, and so am I." Phil offered an affirmative nod. "But I'll be sleeping with my door locked from now on—and with my gun by my side. I don't suggest any of us go anywhere alone from here on out, not until we have some answers."

Everyone in the group exchanged glances.

Could someone in this circle be guilty?

Even though everyone here was at the dinner table when Alana died, had someone poisoned her before then?

That was the answer that Maddox needed to find.

At ten o'clock, Mr. Whitlock was finally settled into bed.

He'd been anxious, and his overnight nurse had given him some anxiety medication. Finally, he'd drifted to sleep.

Taryn left his room, gently closing the door behind her. Titus would be monitoring this hallway tonight, which made her feel a little better.

Phil stayed two doors down from his father. She hadn't seen him since he disappeared into the west wing an hour ago. But she didn't feel any better about him being here. Her gut told her he was trouble.

Knowing she wouldn't be able to sleep tonight either, Taryn paced toward the main living room.

As she did, she almost collided with Maddox as he came around the corner. She glanced up at him, and the breath left her lungs.

She'd been hoping to run into him.

Taryn wanted to talk to him. But, as she quickly studied his face, she sensed he had something on his mind also.

Maddox glanced behind her before leaning closer.

A shiver went up her spine at his nearness.

She tried to ignore the feeling. Tried to ignore her attraction to the man.

But the task nearly felt impossible sometimes.

Maddox placed his hands on either side of her arms, and their gazes locked. "I need to tell you something, Taryn, Grissom tried to run me off the road tonight."

Her heart skipped a beat. "What?"

Maddox told her about what happened.

"Grissom did that? Is he responsible for anything else that's happened around here?" Her head spun at the thought.

"He's been watching you here. But he should be behind bars now—for driving under the influence, amongst other things."

"Maddox . . . I'm so sorry. Things could have turned out so much differently. And it would have been my fault—"

"It was in no way your fault." Maddox's voice didn't leave room for any questions. "That was all Grissom. I just wanted to let you know."

She nodded, still dazed by the news.

Taryn tried to imagine what it would be like if Maddox had died. Her life wouldn't feel as . . . positive.

It might be a ridiculous thought, but it was true.

In the short time she'd known Maddox, she'd become fascinated with the man.

"There's one other thing." Maddox paused. "I need to get into that safe. Tonight."

Alarm raced through her. "Tonight? After everything that's already happened?"

"It's even more important now than it was before. We need answers."

Taryn shivered and shook her head, suddenly second-guessing her decision to help him. "It's just that the timing . . ."

"The timing is everything." He shifted. "Taryn, I know this must be stressful for you, and I'm sorry to put you in this position. If I thought I could do this without your help, I would."

Taryn let out a long breath. She knew exactly what Maddox was saying. She only wished that she didn't have to break her trust with Mr. Whitlock like this.

Finally, she nodded. "What time?"

"Midnight. Can we meet down here then?"

She nodded again, even though her heart raced out of control. "Okay. I'll be here."

"Thank you." Maddox's voice sounded calm and reassuring. "It's going to be okay."

Taryn nodded, unsure if his statement was correct or not.

But she did know that she couldn't keep on doing what she was doing and just hope nothing bad would happen again. She had to be proactive . . . if she wanted to survive.

THIRTY-EIGHT

MADDOX KNEW one thing for sure. He could *not* be caught.

If he was, he'd be sent away from here, and they might not get the answers they needed.

He dressed in all black so he could blend in with the shadows. He also brought gloves with him in case anyone checked for prints.

He'd double-checked the security cameras around the house to make sure none were recording him going into the office. Sure, he'd gone into the room earlier. But there had been no reason for anyone to be suspicious then.

With everyone being on edge, Maddox had to be extra careful.

He needed to see what was in that safe. With the

way things had been going, it was only a matter of time before someone else got hurt.

He couldn't let that person be Taryn. He'd do whatever necessary to protect her.

At five minutes to midnight, he slipped from his room and glanced up and down the hallway.

Everything was quiet.

He strode down the hall, trying not to make any noise as he did. Usually, everyone was asleep at this time. But nothing was guaranteed.

Titus would be monitoring the rest of the house and keeping his eyes open for trouble.

Now Maddox just needed to get to the office without being spotted.

He slipped from the staff's quarters into the main living area.

But as he started toward the west wing, someone stepped in his path.

And Maddox wondered if he'd been made.

***

Maddox stared at the person.

The person holding a knife.

Chef.

His muscles tightened with alertness.

"What are you doing out here?" She stared at him with her nostrils flaring.

"I might ask you the same thing. I thought you'd left," Maddox countered as he studied her face.

Chef narrowed her eyes, almost as if angry. "I did. But I realized I forgot one of my favorite knives. I came back, and that boy let me in."

"That boy?"

She rolled her eyes. "Yes, that . . . that *security guard*."

She said the words as if they were dirty.

Her explanation should be easy enough to verify —if Maddox got that chance.

He stared at the knife again, his throat tightening at its size and nearness.

He hoped things didn't turn ugly.

"That must be one pretty special knife." Maddox nodded at it again. "Especially if you're willing to come all the way back here to get it in the middle of the night."

"This butcher knife is expensive, and I paid for it myself. Mr. Whitlock might have all the money he wants and needs, but I don't. I didn't want there to be any confusion, and the more time that passes, the more likely it is that someone becomes suspicious about me coming back here."

Maddox supposed Chef's explanation made sense. But he still felt on edge.

"Now that I've explained myself, how about

you?" Chef raised her eyebrows as she waited for his answer.

"I'm helping Titus with security tonight." Maddox hoped that explained his all-black clothing. Thankfully, he hadn't put his gloves on yet. They were still shoved in his pockets.

Chef stared at him another moment before nodding as if his answer had been deemed acceptable. "I guess that's suitable given everything that's been going on."

His lungs loosened—but just slightly. "Do you have everything that you need?"

She raised the knife again.

As she held it in front of her, Maddox's lungs froze.

He waited on edge, halfway expecting her to make a move.

Finally, she smiled. "Yes, I have everything I need. Now, would you escort me to my car? I'd prefer not to go outside by myself . . . especially after what happened two nights ago."

Maddox paused. "What happened two nights ago?"

"I looked out my window and saw Shawn talking to someone. It was heated, to say the least."

"Who was he speaking with?"

"I don't know. A man I'd never seen before. But I could have thought for sure I saw that same man lurking near the labyrinth yesterday. That, on top of everything else that's happened, has left me spooked."

Shawn . . . another person Maddox needed to investigate more.

CHAPTER
THIRTY-NINE

TARYN GLANCED at her watch again.

Where was Maddox? It was five past midnight.

Maddox didn't strike her as the late type.

Had he changed his mind?

She glanced down the dark hallway.

What would Taryn say if someone spotted her standing outside Mr. Whitlock's office right now? What kind of excuse could she possibly come up with?

Besides, she was a terrible liar.

Tension gripped her until she could hardly breathe.

She shouldn't be doing this.

If she was caught . . . not only would Mr. Whitlock be disappointed in her, but she'd be fired and back out on the streets again.

She wasn't qualified to work any other jobs—not jobs that would offer a true living wage. She'd saved up some money, but was it enough to put down a deposit on an apartment?

Too many uncertainties plagued her. She had no safety net to fall back on. No family or good friends to speak of.

Maddox . . . if things went south with him, he would still have his job. His friends. A place to live.

Taryn didn't have those luxuries.

This was a terrible idea. Maybe she should leave now before Maddox came. She could mumble some type of excuse to him in the morning and—

Before she could continue the thought, a shadow appeared at the end of the hallway.

Her hand went to her throat as she froze.

The figure came closer until a familiar face came into view.

Maddox.

He was here.

She wanted to relax, to feel reassured. But Taryn didn't know if that made her feel better or worse.

"Sorry I'm late." Maddox stepped close, his voice just above a whisper. "But I ran into Chef. She forgot something and had come back to get it."

Taryn's eyebrows flew up. "That sounds suspicious."

"That's what I thought too. But she's gone now. I walked her to her car and watched her leave myself." He nodded at the door behind Taryn, clearly single-minded right now. "Are you ready to do this?"

She shook her head. "I don't know if I am or not. I keep going back and forth."

"I'm sorry to put you in this position. I wouldn't ask unless it was important. This is bigger than me and you. It's even bigger than Mr. Whitlock and this estate. If our theories are correct, then whatever is going on could have wide-reaching implications. A lot of people could be hurt unless we find answers."

Maddox's words made sense, and his reassuring tone made Taryn want to do whatever he asked.

Still, her hands trembled as she took her keys and thrust the correct one into the lock. She had doubted she would get it inside, nonetheless be able to turn it.

But she did.

The door opened, and she motioned for Maddox to go inside first.

Taryn looked up and down the hallway one more time but saw no one.

Quietly, she closed the door again and locked it behind her.

Now came the hard part.

Maddox was thankful he and Taryn had gotten this far.

But they were nowhere close to hitting a home run.

First, they had to figure out how to get this safe open.

He walked to the bookcase and pushed the barricade of books. As they sprang back, the safe came into view.

He glanced back and saw Taryn's eyes widen as she watched.

"That's pretty incredible," she muttered.

"What will be even more incredible is us getting this open." He nodded toward the safe.

"Of course." She quickly walked toward him to get a better look.

After she examined the hand scanner, she let out a long breath as if considering what she was about to do.

She rubbed her palms on her jeans as her gaze fluttered to his. "You really think this will work?"

"I do. Just take a deep breath and remain calm."

She nodded again and inhaled. Held her breath a few seconds. Exhaled.

Then she placed her hand on the biometric scanner.

The next instant, the safe door popped open.

Maddox's heart skipped a beat.

It had worked.

TARYN STARED inside the open safe.

This was it. They'd done it. They'd broken into the locked metal box.

Now they needed to figure out what was inside that was so valuable.

What people may have lost their lives over.

It seemed unfathomable to Taryn that people would go to such extremes.

But she knew this kind of desperation was a real possibility. She knew that evil existed in this world. Evil in the forms of selfishness, greed, and power-mongering—among other things.

Her goal was to build a life as absent as possible from those things.

It was why she'd broken up with Grissom.

Yet she'd found herself here now, surrounded by danger again.

Maddox reached into the safe.

Taryn halfway expected to see money or patents or some type of priceless jewelry.

Instead, he pulled out rolled papers.

He handed her one side of one, and he began tugging at the other so they could see what was on the document.

She squinted when she saw what looked like a blueprint. "Is that the design for this estate?"

Maddox shined his flashlight onto the paper as he studied it. "No, this isn't the estate. It's the wrong shape."

"Then what else could it be?" Taryn scanned the drawing again, looking for some type of clue. "Why in the world would Mr. Whitlock have blueprints anyway?"

"Here, help me hold these papers open. I'm going to take pictures so we can study these later."

She nodded and laid the blueprints on the desk to stretch out the rolls.

There were probably six designs all together.

Taryn wanted to study them more right now, but she knew they didn't have time. Not now.

Not here.

Maddox took a picture of the last blueprint before rolling the papers back up and placing them in the safe. Quickly, he closed the door and put the book façade back in place.

Maddox turned toward her. "We'll examine these images more as soon as we get a chance. The less amount of time we're in here, the better."

That sounded like a plan to her.

Just as they stepped toward the door, a sound filled the air.

A footstep.

Right outside the office.

Taryn braced herself for what she was certain would be a fight for her life.

Maddox knew they didn't have time to hide.

Instead, he grabbed Taryn and pushed her into the corner behind the door. Then he stood in front of her, his body shielding hers.

He waited, his heart thumping in his chest.

Had someone followed them? Had someone known what they were doing?

Or was one of those guys they'd heard talking on the dirt road trying to break in here to get those blueprints also?

He wished he had eyes in the hallway outside.

But he didn't.

All he could do right now was wait and pray that

whoever lingered out there didn't try to come inside the office.

He glanced at Taryn as she stood in front of him, the wispy moonlight from outside illuminating her features.

Her breaths were shallow. A tremor captured her limbs.

But she'd been a real trooper tonight.

Being this close to her . . . it brought out a different part of him. A part of him that he thought had died.

He felt more than the need to protect her.

He wanted to know what it would be like if he leaned closer. What her skin might feel like against his lips. How soft her hair might feel under his fingertips.

But none of those things were important right now—not in comparison to getting caught.

Instead, he listened for any telltale signs out in the hallway.

Was the person they'd heard still out there?

As if to answer the question, a click sounded.

Someone was trying to pick the lock, he realized.

Taryn froze next to him.

Maddox would need to think quickly before he got them both killed.

TARYN COULDN'T BREATHE.

She wasn't sure whether to blame it on the person outside the office or on Maddox's closeness.

Maybe it was a bit of both.

Somehow, despite her fear about the person on the other side of the door, she knew Maddox would keep her safe.

There were very few people in her life she'd ever been able to say that about.

Yet she instinctively knew that about this man in front of her. A man she'd known for less than a week.

Was she losing her mind?

Or was she simply trusting her gut?

She'd have to figure that out later.

Her lungs froze as she anticipated what would happen next.

The handle turned as if someone was coming inside.

Who could it be?

Her best guess . . . Phil.

Besides, no one else had access to the office—only Mr. Whitlock and her.

Someone *could* be trying to pick the lock. Or perhaps they'd stolen one of their keys and made a copy of it.

Taryn's thoughts continued to race.

What exactly were those blueprints of? Why lock them up?

As tension pounded at her, she dug her fingers into Maddox's arm.

A whiff of his leathery cologne filled her, and she wanted to lean into him.

But she didn't.

Or did she?

Her nose was practically pressed up against his shirt right now. She nearly held on for dear life, now that she thought about it.

She tried to release her grip and step back, but she couldn't.

Nor did she want to.

A second later, the door handle went still.

On the other side of the wall, footsteps raced away.

Maddox waited, unmoving despite the sound of someone fleeing.

Though he wanted to step into the hallway and see who it had been, he couldn't risk being caught. Right now, he had to think about Taryn's safety.

He waited a good minute before moving.

He turned to Taryn and studied her face, anxious to see how she was holding up. She had so much on the line here. She'd risked everything by helping him into that safe.

The woman was admirable . . . and fascinating . . . and beautiful.

As he looked at her now, her skin looked pale, and her movements stiff. He wished he could take that away.

Instead, he whispered, "Are you okay?"

"I think so. You?"

"I'm fine. But we need to get out of here."

Taryn gripped his arm again, trepidation across her face. "What if this was a trap? What if someone's waiting out there?"

Maddox nodded and texted Titus. "I'll get Titus to come this way, just to be sure the coast is clear."

She pushed a hair behind her ear as she waited for him to do that.

A moment later, Titus texted back. He was in the hallway and confirmed the corridor was empty.

Maddox took Taryn's hand before quietly opening the door and glancing out.

He spotted Titus standing guard.

They slipped out, locking the door behind them, before joining Titus in the hallway.

"Anything?" Titus held himself upright, like a soldier on a mission.

Maddox's pulse increased as he remembered those blueprints. "Yes, but it's not what you think."

Titus twisted his head in anticipation. "Now you've got me curious."

"Let's meet in my room. We need some privacy, so no one sees us all together. Come in about ten minutes. Okay?"

Titus nodded. "Got it. I'll see you then."

Hopefully, between the three of them, they could figure out what exactly they were looking at.

FORTY-TWO

TARYN'S THOUGHTS continued to race as she paced in Maddox's room.

Right on time, Titus showed up.

Maddox had sent the images of the blueprints to his laptop, where he'd enlarged them on the screen so they could see better. He sat on the edge of his bed, Titus and Taryn on either side of him.

She squinted as she tried to get a better look at the images.

In the corner of each blueprint, where the title of the building had once been, stretched a thin white line. Someone had purposely obstructed the name of the buildings.

"This one looks familiar." Titus leaned closer and rubbed his chin. "It's almost too big to be a house.

Maybe it's more of an office building. Did Mr. Whitlock work as an architect?"

"No, but apparently his grandfather or great-grandfather was. One of them designed this house." Maddox glanced at Taryn. "Isn't that what you said?"

She nodded. "Mr. Whitlock once told me that his grandfather made his start as an architect, but he found that he liked land development and real estate better, so he moved on to do that. Mr. Whitlock really doesn't talk about it very much. I know his grandfather designed that labyrinth out there also. Wait . . ." Taryn muttered. "I think I might know what this is."

She pulled out her phone to confirm her idea.

A few minutes later, she held up a picture on her phone and placed it beside the drawing.

They matched.

"It's the North Carolina Capitol Building," she muttered. "I went there on a class field trip when I was in elementary school."

"I think you're right," Maddox muttered.

Her pulse quickened.

"The other blueprints look like they could be government buildings too. Looks like someone wants to know the layout of them." Maddox leaned back and shook his head. "I don't like the sound of this."

Maddox's mind wouldn't stop working.

Was this the information they'd been looking for? By all appearances, the answer was yes.

"What are you thinking?" Taryn's voice pulled him from his thoughts.

His gaze connected with Taryn's then Titus'. "I'm not sure you really want to know."

"Try us," Titus muttered.

Maddox let out a long breath before starting. "When we combine the fact that Embolden Tech is missing cameras as well as listening devices with the fact that someone affiliated with Donovan Sullivan was spotted near this property—"

"Wait . . . what does that guy have to do with any of this?" Taryn blinked as if confused.

"Do you know who Donovan Sullivan is?"

Taryn shook her head. "I can't say I do."

"He's a business mogul," Maddox continued. "Not long ago, we caught one of his men stealing caustic substances from a factory in Asheville. Donovan was involved in a human trafficking organization, but he ultimately pinned those crimes on a man who worked for him. However, we still believe he's involved."

Taryn nodded. "Okay. So, we have missing listening devices, missing cameras, missing caustic substances, possible human trafficking, and . . ."

"A shooting attempt on a state senator in front of

a government building," Maddox finished. "When you put that together, what do you have?"

"A domestic terrorist attack," Titus muttered.

Maddox nodded slowly. Hearing the words out loud jarred him. "That's worse than I thought."

Taryn shook her head. "So, this militia group—The System—is possibly using property Mr. Whitlock owns to plan a terrorist attack? Meanwhile, they're trying to steal blueprints to government buildings as part of this scheme?"

Maddox shrugged. "It's the only thing that makes sense to me."

"Can't they find blueprints online? I thought I heard something on the news about that recently."

"I'm sure they can find *some* form of the blueprints online," Maddox said. "But the real blueprints might contain things like hidden rooms—things obscured to the public for security reasons. If they're planning something, they might need a more detailed layout of the buildings."

Taryn glanced at Maddox then Titus. "Do you really think these guys had something to do with the senator who was shot this week?"

"I'd say there's a good chance of it." Maddox shook his head. "I didn't think about it until now. But it makes sense."

Taryn rubbed her neck as tension formed there. "I don't like the sound of any of this."

Maddox glanced over at Titus, and he knew they were both thinking the same thing.

He grabbed his phone. "I need to call Colton and tell him about our theory. Because it might be time to get the FBI involved in this—if they aren't already."

FORTY-THREE

TARYN COULDN'T BELIEVE what she was hearing. It seemed like something out of a movie or a novel.

But there was a good possibility someone was using the adjacent property to plot something destructive. Not only destructive, but something with the potential to change the course of life as millions of Americans knew it.

Was she overthinking this?

She didn't think so.

Domestic terrorist attacks like the Oklahoma City bombing or the Boston Marathon bombing changed lives forever.

Her mind continued to race through the possibilities.

"Are you okay?" Maddox's voice pulled her from

her thoughts.

She started to nod but then shrugged instead. "I don't really know. This is all . . . overwhelming, to say the least."

"Colton's going to take this information to our contacts with the FBI and the ATF. I'm hoping, based on what we've discovered, that they will be able to act."

"Certainly, they're already keeping their eyes on these guys, right?" Did the FBI have a pulse on these types of things? Or had this group managed to stay off-grid with an unnatural expertise?

"I'm sure they're listening to any chatter surrounding the group," Titus said. "But they need credible evidence in order to act."

"Do you think that's what we have right now?" Taryn looked up at them with hopeful eyes.

Maddox pressed his lips together before shrugging. "I wish I could say yes for sure. But I can't. What we have right now is circumstantial. We have theories, but we don't have any direct proof of what they are planning."

Taryn shivered and rubbed her arms before staring into the distance. "This sounds serious."

"It could be very serious." Maddox's voice sounded dead serious too. "Tonight, I think we should get our rest. In the morning, we can regroup."

She nodded, knowing that made sense. What else

could they do right now? Nothing.

As she rose to head to her room, Maddox followed behind her.

"I'd feel better if I walked you to your room, especially considering everything that's going on." Maddox glanced back at Titus. "Can you stick around for a few minutes? There are a few more things I'd like to go over with you."

Titus nodded.

Maddox checked the hallway to make sure no one was there before the two of them stepped out.

There was so much Taryn wanted to say to Maddox. But she couldn't force any of the words to leave her mouth.

She'd already been burned by love once—and burned badly, at that.

She didn't think that Maddox was anything like Grissom. But she had a hard time trusting her instincts after her previous bad choices.

Maddox paused beside her door and turned to her, shoving his hands into his pockets and almost looking nervous himself. "Thank you for your help tonight."

"Of course. I'm glad I could do something."

"I know the risk you took, and I appreciate it."

Taryn swallowed hard, part of her wanting to reach up and run her fingers across his beard, through the hair at the nape of his neck.

But she didn't.

Even if there was a chance the two of them might both like each other, as soon as this was all over Maddox would leave and move on to his next assignment.

And what would Taryn be doing?

She might not have a job at the end of this. She could be back out on the streets. She'd been saving away her paychecks. But she didn't have nearly enough saved to feel secure.

What would this new development do to her plans?

She didn't like not knowing.

"If you don't mind, I'd like to check your room." Maddox nodded at the door behind her.

"Of course." Taryn tried to snap from her thoughts.

Maddox was all business—of course.

She hoped her growing feelings for the man didn't turn her life upside down. She had to be stronger than that.

Maddox took the key from her hand, unlocked the door, and then opened it. She stepped inside behind him.

But she froze when she saw the shadow in the corner.

No, not a shadow.

A man.

He sat on the edge of her bed as if he'd been waiting for Taryn to return.

———

Maddox bristled as the figure came into view.

He started to reach for the Glock at his waistband when he heard the intruder's gun click.

"I wouldn't do that if I were you," a deep voice said.

Maddox froze, unafraid to act if it came down to it. But he wouldn't grab his gun now. Not yet.

Instead, he remained on guard.

The man arose from the bed and stepped toward them.

As he did, his face came into view.

"Phil?" Taryn practically gasped.

"Yes, it's me. Hope you don't mind the intrusion." The man stepped closer.

"What are you doing in here?" Maddox demanded.

"I could ask you the same thing." Phil looked Maddox up and down. "What are the two of you up to?"

Maddox's spine stiffened. "We're hanging out. Last I knew, when I read my contract, that wasn't against the rules."

"That's not what I mean." Phil scowled. "I know

the two of you are up to something. Are you the ones causing all this trouble around the house? It didn't start until you came." Phil glared at Maddox.

Maddox raised his hands in innocence. "I don't know what you're talking about. If you think I did something to Leroy or Alana, you're wrong. In fact, I was working here in the house when Leroy went missing, and I was eating with everyone when Alana screamed."

"Something's going on around here." The gun shook in Phil's hands. "And I need to find out what."

"Maybe you could put the gun down, and we can talk like rational people." Maddox nodded at Phil's weapon, afraid the man might accidentally pull the trigger.

Phil's nostrils flared. "No way. I've considered everyone who works here, and the two of you are my best suspects."

"Simply because of when we started working here?" Taryn's voice squeaked higher.

Phil's nostrils flared again. "No. Because I don't want you here. You put on that sweet and innocent act. But I can see through you. You're conniving, and you arranged to work for my father because you want his fortune after he dies."

"I didn't even know who your father was when I met him."

He let out a harsh chuckle. "I find *that* hard to

believe. Everyone around here knows who my father is."

"I was too busy going to school and taking care of my mother to keep up with the area's social scene. Sorry to let you down."

"Again, I'm not going to fall for your Little Miss Innocent act. I think you know exactly what you're doing. I'm not going to let you get in my way." The statement ended with a growl.

"What does that mean?" Maddox growled back.

"I know my father wants to meet with Gerald about revising his will. I am *not* going to let you get anything when he dies."

"That's not your decision," Maddox said.

"Besides, I don't want anything," Taryn rushed. "That's not why I came to work here. I was in a bad place in my life, and your father took me in. I'm forever grateful he allowed me to get back on my feet."

"I'm sure you are," Phil muttered.

Maddox continued to stare at the man's gun. He could easily use his skills and take it from him. Considering the danger in front of him, he had no choice.

This confrontation had gone on for too long.

It needed to end.

Now.

CHAPTER
FORTY-FOUR

TARYN'S LUNGS FELT FROZEN.

She couldn't believe the accusations Phil was hurling at her.

Yet she shouldn't be surprised.

Everyone liked to assume ulterior motives were involved when it came to money.

"Have you ever considered that maybe it's *your* appearance here that's suspicious?" Maddox's voice pulled Taryn from her shock.

Her lungs tightened even more when she heard Maddox turn the accusation around on Phil. He had a valid argument.

Phil let out a harsh chuckle and stared at them both as if they'd lost their minds. "You're crazy. You don't know what you're talking about."

"I know I heard some of the staff here saying that

you didn't bother to come around until your father was given his latest diagnosis. Most people here are actually looking at you. You have the most to gain from your father's death. I'm sure almost everything will go to you."

Phil narrowed his gaze. "Even if that was true, why would I kill Leroy or Alana? Because, just to be clear, I do *not* think their deaths were accidents as the police say."

"Maybe Leroy and Alana discovered what you were doing." Maddox stepped closer, something close to a challenge in his gaze. "Maybe you're planning to get rid of your father early before he can change his will."

Taryn's eyes widened. What if Maddox was onto something? What if all these incidents had nothing to do with the adjacent property and whatever schemes might be taking place there?

"You're out of your mind." Phil's nostrils flared. "You're not going to turn this around on me."

Maddox stepped closer, his muscles bristled with irritation. "You snuck into Taryn's room, and now you're holding a gun to us. You're the one who looks guilty here."

"I'm not guilty!" But Phil's voice trembled as he said the words. "I just want answers."

"So do we," Taryn said softly. "None of us like what's happening here. Despite what you might think, I care about your father. I don't want to see anyone take advantage of him. And I don't want his money. I wouldn't even know what to do with it. All I want is shelter and a place to live and . . ."

She almost said, "someone to love her." But she realized how desperate and needy that might sound.

Besides, she'd done fine on her own all these years.

Kind of.

Truthfully, there was nothing more Taryn would love than to have someone to share her life with. But this wasn't the time to hash out her dreams for the future.

Instead, she glanced at Phil again. "Will you lower the gun? Please?"

He stared at her another moment before finally dropping his weapon to his side. "I guess you're right. Maybe I shouldn't have come in here. I just thought I heard someone in the house, and then I saw you two walking down here. I thought I could find out some answers."

"We wouldn't hurt your father." Maddox's voice left no room for doubt. "And, please, put your gun on the table."

Phil did as Maddox asked before crossing his arms and turning back toward him. "What were the two of you doing out together at this hour?"

Taryn's throat tightened again. How would they explain that?

The next instant, Maddox's arm snaked around her waist, and he pulled her closer. "We were spending some time together . . . alone."

Her cheeks flushed at the intimate tone of his voice. Before Phil could see her blush, Taryn placed her hand on Maddox's chest and leaned closer. His excuse sounded believable—but they were going to need to sell it.

"I didn't know Maddox when I hired him," Taryn explained. "But we had an instant connection. I assure you, this won't interfere with my job."

Phil stared at them another moment as if trying to decide whether or not he bought their story.

Taryn prayed that he did.

Maddox stared at Phil, waiting for his reaction.

If the man didn't buy his excuse and demanded another explanation, things might get sticky again. Touting a fake relationship seemed like the safest option. But would he believe it?

Finally, Phil nodded—almost with disappointment. "I should have figured. At least, we now have all this out in the open."

Maddox continued to hold Taryn, not daring to

let go. Besides, having her close felt nice. A little too nice.

He'd have time to dissect those thoughts later.

Phil grabbed his gun before stepping past them and heading toward the door. "I'm sorry I broke into your room. With everything that's happened . . . I'm on edge. I just wanted answers."

Maddox nodded, not wanting to give this man an excuse to stay in Taryn's room for longer than necessary. "I understand."

He kept his eye on the gun, making sure Phil didn't try to pull any more stunts.

A moment later, Phil left, closing the door behind him.

Maddox released his breath.

As soon as he was gone, Maddox dropped his arm from around Taryn. But he instantly missed the warmth. Missed the sweet smell of flowers saturating her hair.

He swallowed those emotions as he turned toward her. "That was close."

Taryn raked a hand through her thick hair. "I know. If Phil found out what we were really doing . . . we'd both be out of here. He'd convince his father we were up to no good."

"I'm not so sure Phil has that much pull with his father. I don't think his dad trusts him."

"Do you think Phil has something to do with all that's going on?"

Maddox let out a breath before rubbing a hand over his beard. "I don't know. He seemed sincere. If he was really behind this, I think he would have pushed more."

"So maybe we can rule him out?"

"For now."

They stared at each other a moment, something silent passing between them. This experience . . . it had bonded them, hadn't it? But it was more than that.

His feelings for this woman had grown quickly. Too quickly.

The sheer speed of it made him want to put up his walls even higher.

His heart couldn't handle another repeat of Lindsey.

Maddox finally cleared his throat. "I'm sorry I made up that excuse about you and I dating. The reasoning just made the most sense."

Taryn shrugged stiffly. "Yeah, of course. Total sense."

He stared at her another moment before finally nodding toward the door. "I should go."

Taryn licked her lips before quickly averting her gaze. "Of course. Thank you for being here tonight."

Maddox slowly walked toward the door, almost

reluctant to leave. But when he reached it, he turned to her, and their gazes locked again.

He wanted nothing more than to kiss her.

The thought was crazy. Insane.

But that still didn't change the facts.

Maddox wanted to know what her lips would feel like against his.

But that was a bad, bad idea.

He shoved away the impulse and stepped back, knowing Titus was waiting for him. He shouldn't waste any more time. They had things to discuss.

"I'll talk to you in the morning?" he told Taryn instead.

Taryn shoved a hair behind her ear and nodded, a hint of disappointment in her gaze. "Sounds good. I'll see you then."

But tension gripped Maddox as he stepped from her room.

He wasn't supposed to develop feelings for anyone on this assignment. But he had.

Still, he'd always thought he was better off alone.

Just him and his crocheting projects.

But what if he'd been lying to himself all this time?

CHAPTER
FORTY-FIVE

THE NEXT MORNING, Taryn grabbed some coffee, feeling as if she hadn't gotten any sleep all night.

Probably because she hadn't. She'd had too much on her mind.

The rest of the night had been quiet, which had been a relief.

But when Taryn thought about what today might have in store, a new rush of anxiety flooded through her.

She gripped her cup and paced across the floor to the window overlooking the backyard. She stared at what appeared to be the start of a bright, sunny day.

She'd yet to see Maddox this morning, but she expected him to pop out of his room at any time now. He usually began working promptly at nine.

Taryn had already checked on Mr. Whitlock, who seemed to be having an especially bad morning. He appeared groggy and almost lethargic. After taking his medicine and eating a small breakfast, he'd settled down to take a nap. His nurse would be here soon to check on him.

Taryn wanted to ask her employer questions. Wanted to find out more about his grandfather's job as an architect.

But now wasn't the time to ask him. Maybe later when he felt more alert.

She'd need to figure out a way to find out more information without raising any suspicions as well.

Footsteps sounded, and she glanced at the doorway.

Maddox stepped into the room.

Warmth filled her cheeks at the sight of him.

Why was she letting that man have this effect on her? She should know better.

Either way, her feelings were there. Taryn simply had to figure out what to do about them.

He's not Grissom. He's nothing like that man.

Yet Taryn couldn't seem to trust herself.

Maddox paused beside her. "How are you today?"

She let out a long breath. "I could have used more sleep, but otherwise I'm fine."

"Good. Everything look good around here?" His

voice contained a subtle undertone, an implication that danger could be lurking close by.

Taryn repressed the shiver that tried to capture her limbs. "Best I can tell."

He slowly nodded as he followed her gaze outside.

Taryn straightened as she spotted something out of place in the distance.

A moment later, a horse galloped across the lawn.

Taryn sucked in a breath.

What was one of Mr. Whitlock's horses doing out here so close to the house? They always stayed in the pasture in the back.

That's when Taryn realized the truth . . . something was wrong.

* * *

As soon as Maddox saw the horse, he turned to Taryn. "Go get Titus. He'll help you with the horse. In the meantime, I'm going to check on Danielle."

Before she could answer, he darted outside.

His legs burned as he ran across the lawn, but he didn't slow until he reached the pasture.

Maddox paused and glanced around, looking for a clue as to what had happened. Several horses grazed nearby, the morning sunlight illuminating their coats.

Where was Danielle? If she knew a horse had gotten out, she would have taken off after it. Maddox felt certain about that.

Unless something was wrong.

Wasting no more time, he sprinted to the stables.

As soon as he stepped inside, he spotted a figure laying on the ground.

Danielle.

His chest tightened.

Not another casualty.

Maddox rushed toward her, knelt at her side, and put his finger to her throat.

She still had a pulse.

His shoulders softened—but just barely. Danielle wasn't out of the woods yet.

Quickly, he called 911. She needed to be checked for a concussion.

As Maddox put his phone away, Danielle began to stir.

Her eyes fluttered open, and she muttered, "Cricket . . ."

That must be the horse.

"Titus and Taryn are going after her," Maddox rushed. "Are you okay?"

As Danielle pushed herself upright, Maddox placed his hand on her back to steady her. Her eyes looked dazed, and he hoped that paramedics would be here soon.

She clearly needed to be checked out for a concussion.

"I don't know," she muttered. "I was getting Cricket out when she got spooked. I tried to grab her. Before I could, she took off and knocked me down."

What she told him sounded like an accident.

But what had really happened?

Maddox quickly glanced around the stable, looking for a sign of what could have scared the horse.

That's when he saw a rubber snake in the corner.

He had no doubt someone had placed the critter there on purpose, hoping for an incident like this to happen.

CHAPTER
FORTY-SIX

TARYN AND TITUS walked back to the stables with Cricket. They'd been able to catch the horse before she reached the road stretching in front of the estate.

The horse still seemed agitated, but at least she trotted beside them. Titus had seemed like a natural with the animal as he'd grabbed Cricket's halter and murmured in her ear.

Taryn had to admit that the man was fascinating, with his quiet demeanor, his muscular frame, and his serious eyes. She wondered what exactly was going on inside his head, what kind of baggage from the past he carried.

"What do you think happened?" Taryn fought the anxiety trying to build inside her.

Titus frowned. "Good question. I don't know

Danielle that well, but she doesn't seem like the type who'd let one of her horses go."

"She's not. She loves these animals as if they were her own."

"How long has she worked here?"

"She was here before I was hired. So, if I remember correctly, she's been here a couple of years, at least."

They reached the stables, and Taryn spotted Danielle sitting on the ground with Maddox beside her. Maddox rose to his feet as they stepped inside.

Danielle tried to stand also. Instead, she wobbled, nearly toppling back over. Maddox grabbed her elbow and helped her steady herself.

"Oh, Cricket . . ." Danielle stepped toward the horse and rubbed the mare's face. "I'm so sorry about that."

"What happened?" Taryn's thoughts raced as she tried to put together the pieces.

Maddox explained the fake snake that had now been removed from the area.

As soon as she heard the explanation, Taryn knew the truth.

Someone had placed that snake in the stable on purpose, hoping Danielle would get hurt.

Again, someone was trying to eliminate everyone here at the house by knocking them off one by one and making each incident appear as an accident.

There had to be better ways than killing people.

She glanced at her watch. Now that the situation here was under control, she needed to go check on Mr. Whitlock.

Did her boss hold some answers?

"Another accident?" Mr. Whitlock paused with a cup of lemonade in hand as he sat in his favorite chair near his bedroom window. Concern stretched across his features.

At least, his color was better—or it had been this morning before this conversation.

"Thankfully, Danielle is okay. The horse just saw a snake and . . ." Taryn shrugged as she sat in the chair across from him.

Mr. Whitlock narrowed his eyes. "Why do I feel like there's something you're not telling me?"

Taryn stared at him, unsure where he was going with this. But alarms went off in her head. Did he know she'd been snooping? That she'd been in his safe? That Maddox wasn't who he claimed to be?

"I'm not," she started." It's just that—"

"You don't have to protect me." Mr. Whitlock locked his gaze on hers. "I know I might appear to be a fragile old man. But I'm stronger than you think I am. What's going on, Taryn?"

She drew in a deep breath, knowing she couldn't put this conversation off any longer. He deserved to know—maybe not everything all at once. But she could share a few details and ease him into the truth about what was happening here.

She only prayed his heart would remain steady as she gave him the update.

"There have been some strange things happening here at the estate," she started.

"I haven't been foolish enough to think that the deaths here have been accidents. Whenever money and power are involved, greed also surfaces. I know what my impending death means. I know there are people who would love nothing more than to have my wealth."

Taryn's heart pounded in her ears. She'd expected him to know that.

But hearing the admission spoken aloud made her heart ache for the man. How hard it must be to never be certain if people liked you for who you were or if it was because of what you could offer them.

She'd never had that problem because she hadn't grown up with money. Still to this day, the most expensive possession she owned was her car, but she'd paid less than a thousand dollars for it. The vehicle regularly broke down, and Taryn expected at any time it would completely quit on her.

"It's funny as you near the end of your life what you think about." Mr. Whitlock stared outside.

"What do you mean?" Taryn prodded.

His gaze remained focused on the labyrinth beyond the patio. "I mean, I used to be so certain that I needed to prepare for the worst. Perhaps I got that from my family. Despite my father's success, he was always a tad paranoid. Anyway, I would listen to the news and know that one day something bad would happen."

"Something bad?" Mr. Whitlock's words sounded ominous.

"It seems like history always repeats itself. Famine, wars, political shifts, ideological changes." He leaned toward her. "I'm going to tell you something about myself that not many people know."

Taryn's breath caught as she waited for him to continue.

"I'm what most people would call a prepper."

Her eyebrows shot up. "You are? But you have so much. I'm surprised you feel like you need to prepare even."

"It's true. I have food and supplies stored up for me. Like I said, the trait was probably passed down to me from my parents and grandparents. They survived the Great Depression and saw many of their friends lose everything."

"But weren't they wealthy also? Your grandfather was an architect, correct? He designed this house."

"He designed many things." Mr. Whitlock's eyes sparkled. "But wealth doesn't always equal a sense of security. Haven't the incidents around here proven that? As well as my declining health?"

"I can't argue with that. So, you have food and supplies stored up here at the estate?" If so, why hadn't Taryn ever seen them?

"No, not at the estate." His eyes twinkled. "But somewhere safe where I can go if I ever need to shelter in place."

She started to ask him more questions when someone knocked at the door.

She looked up and saw the nurse had arrived.

They would have to talk about this more later.

But Taryn was anxious to hear what else he had to say.

AFTER SPEAKING WITH COLTON, Maddox put his phone away. As he strode into the living room, he spotted Taryn coming down the stairs from Mr. Whitlock's room.

A frown tugged at her lips, making his mind instantly go to worst-case scenarios.

"Everything okay?" he rushed.

"It's fine. The nurse just arrived, and I'm tired, I suppose." She stared at him for a moment, questions in her gaze. "What's wrong? Did something else happen with Danielle?"

He shook his head, realizing they were both on edge after everything that had happened. "No, the paramedics checked her out. Said she would be okay. I just got off the phone with Colton."

"And?"

"Blackout sent another drone over the property." He stepped closer and lowered his voice. "There were six cars parked in the area but no building."

"Where were the people who came in the cars?"

"That's the weird part. They all walked into the woods and disappeared."

"That is weird." Taryn paused, a wrinkle forming on her brow. "What did your guys tell the FBI?"

"They let them know what was going on, but the feds still need more evidence before they can take any action. They're going to keep an eye on things until they have concrete proof."

"But those people could be planning something." Urgency stretched through her voice. "This can't wait."

Maddox's jaw tightened. "That's what I think too. I need to go check it out and see if I can find anything to offer them more proof."

"Let me go with you again. Please." Taryn glanced up at him, her gaze pleading.

Tension stretched across Maddox's chest at the thought of Taryn being in danger. "I don't know . . ."

"I'm on my break. The timing is perfect. And I know these woods better than you."

He frowned again as he thought through the possibilities. "Even with Titus being here, I don't really want to leave you."

"Exactly . . . Maddox, I want to figure out what's going on here just as much as anyone. If I don't, I might be the next person who 'accidentally' dies."

His gut churned at the thought of it. She certainly knew how to drive home an argument and seal the deal.

He nodded. "Can you be ready in ten minutes?"

"Absolutely. Everyone will just think I'm out spending my time in the labyrinth. That's what I usually do."

"Perfect. I'll meet you then." Maddox prayed he didn't regret his decision.

Taryn changed into her hiking boots and grabbed a backpack, filling it with some water bottles and nuts.

Part of her was thrilled Maddox had agreed she could come. Another part felt a quiver of nerves. Even though they were just going to look for evidence, that didn't mean they wouldn't run into trouble.

Still, if someone was targeting Mr. Whitlock, Taryn needed to figure out why. What exactly was going on at that compound?

If they could find definitive proof, maybe they could show Mr. Whitlock. If he knew, he could call the proper authorities and ask them to run these people off his property.

Right on time, she met Maddox near the labyrinth. Her heart skipped a beat when she saw him wearing his cargo pants, a black shirt, and hiking boots.

Tough and manly . . . while also soft with a love of crocheting.

The combination was absolutely fascinating . . . and endearing.

Taryn didn't think her feelings for someone could grow this fast. But it was better if she kept them at bay. For now, at least.

Her emotions were so charged at the moment that she knew she couldn't trust them.

A smile tilted Maddox's lips when he saw her. "Are you ready?"

Taryn nodded as she gripped the straps of her backpack. "Ready as I'll ever be."

He nodded toward the trees in the distance. "Let's cross into the woods before anyone sees us. I don't want people asking a lot of questions."

He was right. The fewer people who knew about this, the better.

As they started between the trees, Taryn shared with Maddox what Mr. Whitlock had told her about being a prepper. He looked just as surprised as she was.

"He seems like the type who'd rely on his money to get him through the hard times."

Taryn nodded. "That's what I thought too. But I guess you can have all the money in the world and still have the same fears as everyday normal people. At least, I think most preppers are normal people."

Maddox smiled. "I think so. I guess some people live their lives thinking about their futures by saving for retirement, paying off debt, and lining up insurance. Other people live for the moment and take life as it comes. There's not really anything wrong with either of those. It's just a different approach to life, I suppose."

"What type of person are you?" Taryn glanced at him as she pushed a low-hanging branch out of the way.

He grunted. "Good question. I think I'm somewhere in the middle. I like a reasonable amount of planning for the future. But I've seen a lot of people lose their lives. For that reason, I know we're not promised tomorrow. There's a delicate balance in it all."

"That makes sense."

"How about you?" He stole a glance at her as he tromped in front, leading the way.

"Unfortunately, I've lived from paycheck to paycheck for my entire life. Saving up and planning for the future really hasn't been an option for me."

"I understand. I didn't come from a lot of money either. I still don't have a lot, but I also don't need a lot. I don't know what I'd do if I had all the money Mr. Whitlock does. That kind of wealth might make me feel a little crazy."

"That's what I think too. That's why it stunned me when Phil talked about me being here just to get Mr. Whitlock's money. That thought never even crossed my mind."

Maddox was quiet for a moment.

Taryn cast him another glance. "You thought that about me when you first came here too, didn't you?"

He shrugged and continued through the woods.

But he wasn't going to get out of answering that easily.

"You thought that I came here just to try to get his money?" she asked again, unwilling to drop the question.

"In my defense, I didn't know you before I came. But anytime you have a younger, attractive woman—"

"You think I'm attractive?" Taryn didn't normally tease, but she couldn't resist the quip.

Maddox may have blushed, which was almost as adorable as his crocheting.

"I think you know the answer to that question." Maddox let out a trademark grunt before shrugging, looking anxious to change the subject. "Anyway, whenever you have a younger woman suddenly paired with a rich older gentleman, that's usually the first conclusion most people jump to."

"I guess I can see that. But Mr. Whitlock is like a father figure to me."

"Now that I've been around you, I can see that."

But Taryn couldn't stop thinking about how she had been one of Maddox's suspects. She wasn't sure how she felt about that. Then again, she'd dated Grissom. Not only was he up to trouble, but he'd worked hard to tarnish her reputation.

Still, for some reason, the thought of Maddox suspecting her stung.

"Taryn . . . I'm not who you think I am."

"We've been over that . . ." She had no idea where he was going with this. Maddox had already admitted to his true identity.

"No, I mean . . ." He rubbed his beard as his steps slowed. "I'm not as noble as you might think."

"What do you mean?" Part of her didn't want to know. She didn't want her image of Maddox to be tarnished.

"While my SEAL team and I were on a mission, we had a support team member with us. He was driving our boat and guarding it at the scene. Another team member yelled, so I went to go help him. While I did, Stephen was ambushed. He . . . he died before I got back to him."

"I'm so sorry." Her heart panged with compassion. "But why would that change my opinion about you or make you seem less than honorable?"

"He was . . . he was young. Dating the girl of his dreams. Planning his future. And, with that one act, everything was taken away. He used to wear beanies all the time . . . it's one of the reasons I started crocheting—in his honor."

"I like that."

"Stephen reminded me a little of me, to be honest," Maddox continued. "Me before I became a SEAL. Before I witnessed everything I did."

"I understand how difficult and tragic that must have been, but it still wasn't your fault."

Maddox helped her up another rocky embankment, but his gaze remained heavy. "When I returned, I was a different person. Lindsey noticed."

"Lindsey?" Taryn's curiosity spiked. She'd wondered about his dating history. If he'd been married before. If he'd ever had his heart broken.

"We'd been dating for two years. But she couldn't handle the changes she saw in me after that mission. She said I was too broken to be fixed."

"That's terrible." Taryn couldn't imagine doing that to someone she loved.

"That's when I reached the end of my rope and felt like I was totally lost. Thankfully, I had some good friends who came alongside me." Maddox helped Taryn up a large boulder.

As she reached the top, she nearly tumbled forward.

Maddox's chest stopped her—as did his arms when they seemed to instinctively go to her waist.

Taryn's breath caught as she glanced up.

Their faces were mere inches apart.

Maddox wanted to kiss her.

She could see the desire in his eyes. Could tell by his enlarged pupils. His stiff breaths.

Was she willing to give love another chance?

She thought she knew the answer.

A resounding yes.

She licked her lips, wondering what it would be like to feel his mouth against hers.

Should she reach up? Meet him halfway?

Abruptly, Maddox stepped back, the moment seeming to burst.

"I'm sorry . . ." Maddox muttered. "But . . . I can't. I just can't."

"You can't?" Taryn felt her shoulders droop, unable to deny her disappointment.

"I'm just . . . I'm not the guy you want, Taryn. Believe me."

A surge of outrage rose in her. "You don't get to make that call."

He shrugged, almost apologetically. "In this case . . . I do. I'm sorry, Taryn."

Taryn's heart pounded with disappointment as Maddox continued down the trail, the conversation done.

What had just happened?

MADDOX'S THOUGHTS raced as he started back through the woods.

Why had he just done that? He'd seen the affection in Taryn's eyes. Seen her desire.

Yet he'd pushed her away.

He knew what had happened.

He'd felt a moment of hope . . . and then reality had torpedoed him.

He couldn't bear any more heartache. He'd already experienced enough that he'd almost been permanently derailed.

Even though he wanted to open his heart to Taryn, his past urged him to remain distant.

But if remaining distant was the right thing, why did it feel so wrong right now?

He didn't know.

He needed time—because making another mistake wasn't an option.

Would Taryn understand that?

Maddox needed to change the subject until he could sort out his feelings a little more.

Talking about this case seemed like a much safer subject.

"So . . . who do you think is most likely behind this at the house? If you had to choose?"

Taryn frowned, not bothering to hide her disappointment.

But she pulled herself together. She twisted her head as if she didn't want to throw anyone under the bus. "I don't know. It's hard to say. I don't want to think about anyone I know doing this. Yet, at the same time if I'm honest I haven't been able to stop wondering."

"What conclusions have you come to?"

She let out a breath and pushed a hair out of her eyes. "I'm assuming it's a man."

"Why is that?"

"I don't really have any good reasons," Taryn said. "But I suppose when I was chased through the maze it sounded like a man's steps behind me. A woman would have sounded lighter. I know that's probably not much to go on, but it makes sense in my mind."

"No, that makes sense to me. Leroy is out because

we know someone got to him. There's Phil to consider. But he wasn't here when you were in the labyrinth, nor were Shawn and Gerald."

Taryn let out a sigh as she climbed up another boulder. "I don't want to think of any of them as being this calculated. Even though they weren't here, they're the types who'd hire someone else to do their dirty work."

"Chef told me she saw Shawn arguing with someone outside a couple of nights ago. She couldn't tell who it was."

"Shawn? I know he and Phil don't see eye to eye on many things. If I had to guess, that's who Shawn was arguing with."

"I suppose that makes sense." Maddox took her hand and helped her down. "That's something else we need to consider. Whoever is behind this may have the means to have hired Dagger."

"Dagger?" Taryn glanced up, not bothering to hide the confusion in her gaze.

Maddox shrugged as if realizing he hadn't explained. "They're another private security agency. Except, unlike Blackout, they seem to be everywhere trouble is involved. In fact, they're usually the ones causing the trouble."

She frowned. "That's unfortunate. Have you seen any of their agents around here?"

"No, but I've halfway expected to. They seem to pop up in each of our investigations lately."

"That can't be good."

Before they could talk about it anymore, the sound of a vehicle coming toward them caught their attention.

Just as last time they'd been out here, Maddox grabbed Taryn's arm and pulled her back behind a tree so they wouldn't be spotted. Then they waited to see who was coming down the road now.

Taryn held her breath as she waited to see who it might be.

A car—a rather nice one at that—started past. She craned her neck as she struggled to see who was inside. The tinted windows were too dark.

As the vehicle passed, Maddox snapped a picture of the license plate and texted it to someone.

"I'm going to see if Colton can run the plate so we can get an idea who might be driving," Maddox explained.

"Smart thinking."

"If my calculations are correct, the compound is about another mile up the road. We'll stay to the side. But if we move quickly enough, we should be able to get there and get back to the estate before anyone asks any questions."

They continued through the woods. As they did, Taryn waited to hear more vehicles.

But the road was quiet.

When they were probably a quarter mile away, Maddox's shoulders seemed to tense as if he anticipated possibly running into trouble.

As a group of parked vehicles came into view, he paused and put his finger over his mouth.

Taryn peered around him. There weren't only vehicles there, but two armed guards also stood nearby.

These people meant serious business.

Just as Taryn spotted the guards, one paced in their direction.

Maddox quickly pulled Taryn down behind some bushes.

Taryn's heart thudded into her chest.

What would those men do with them if they were caught?

Just as the question went through her mind, a footstep crackled the underbrush nearby.

That man was coming right in their direction.

As he walked, something jangled in his pocket.

Her breath caught.

This was the guy who'd chased her through the labyrinth, wasn't it?

CHAPTER
FORTY-NINE

MADDOX DIDN'T THINK that man had spotted them. That guard had simply started his rounds, making sure no one was close.

But Maddox and Taryn couldn't be discovered. From what Maddox knew about this group, they'd kill anyone who got in their way.

And they would definitely see Maddox and Taryn as adversaries.

He should have never brought Taryn here. Yet he hadn't wanted to leave her at the estate either.

Now it seemed clear that Taryn may have been safer at the house than with him.

His gun was holstered at his side. He didn't want to use it, but he would if necessary.

The footsteps sounded closer.

If the man rounded the tree beside them, he'd spot them.

But it was too late for Maddox and Taryn to run.

Instead, Maddox made himself as small as possible and waited.

A moment later, the footsteps stopped.

Did the man see them?

Maddox didn't know.

He glanced at Taryn and saw her eyes were squeezed shut and her head buried in her legs.

The minutes seemed to stretch into hours, even though he knew that wasn't the case.

He continued to wait.

Finally, the footsteps retreated.

Maddox and Taryn remained where they were. They couldn't move until they knew the coast was clear.

Finally, enough time passed.

But before they stood to head back, Maddox's phone buzzed.

He glanced at the screen and saw that Colton had gotten a hit on that license plate Maddox had sent him.

His lungs tightened when he saw the name.

Taryn was counting down the seconds until they could leave.

Her heart thudded in her ears, and her lungs felt tight.

But, by all appearances, that guard was long gone. She knew Maddox was simply being cautious, and she was thankful for that.

Still, she felt as if she might lose her mind if she stayed here a moment longer.

Finally, Maddox stood. "Let's go."

She placed her hand into his outstretched one. Maddox's strong fingers gripped hers.

Remaining silent, he led her through the woods.

They both stooped, remaining low so no one would spot them.

It wasn't until they were probably a half mile away that Maddox finally spoke. "That was close."

"A little too close." Taryn straightened her back as they walked deeper into the woods, where they were less likely to be spotted. "You mentioned something about Dagger. Is that who that man was? A Dagger agent?"

"I'm not sure. But if I had to guess? Yes, I think so."

She frowned as the stakes climbed even higher.

"I had no idea it was such a high-security operation up there." Maddox held a branch out of the way for her to pass. "I can't believe no one else knows about this."

"It's private property," Taryn reminded him. "People aren't supposed to go onto it. Why would someone choose to set up camp there of all places? Even if they want these blueprints, there's no reason for them to pick this specific property. Certainly, there are many other places they could meet."

"That's a good question. I'm not sure. I know Colton said something about the fact it's located on Mt. Caleb and that it was a Civil War battle site."

"And how are they getting there? We've never followed this road back to where it starts."

"I saw some lights at the back of the property one evening. It's back behind the pastures. There must be a road back there—one that's gone unnoticed because most of us don't head out that way."

"That makes sense, I suppose." Taryn frowned.

"What bothers me the most is that we still don't know where these people are going once they get out of their vehicles. There are no buildings on the property. So where are they heading?"

"Good question," Taryn muttered.

"There's one more thing." Maddox raised his phone. "I got a text from Colton telling me who the car belongs to."

"Who?" Taryn glanced up at him, sensing by the tone of his voice that it would be a big reveal.

"A woman named Lacey Sanders."

"I've never heard of her." Taryn shrugged.

"I hadn't either. But Colton said she works as an aide at the North Carolina State Capitol."

Taryn blinked as she processed his words. "But that doesn't make sense. If they already have someone who works inside the capitol building, then why would these people need the blueprints?"

Maddox nodded slowly as if he'd already had that thought. "Exactly. That leads me to my next question. What if those blueprints aren't the ones these guys are looking for?"

Taryn let his words swirl around in her head.

He was right.

What if the two of them had been totally offtrack?

MADDOX TURNED everything over in his mind as he and Taryn walked back through the woods.

He kept his ear attuned to the noises around him. The last thing he wanted was for someone to sneak up on them. Next time, they might not be so lucky.

Taryn had made a good point earlier. Why would these people need the blueprints to federal buildings if they already had someone working for them on the inside? It didn't make any sense.

Was this in some way connected with the shots fired at Senator Gately? Was The System responsible for the act?

Whatever was going on, he didn't like it.

"You're worried, aren't you?" Taryn's voice cut through his thoughts.

"A little," he admitted. "I just want to know what

they're planning. The stakes are high. Bigger than Mr. Whitlock and what's happening at his estate."

"I know. That worries me too. But how do we find answers?"

He rubbed his jaw as he fought a frown. "I feel like this is more than we can handle on our own. The FBI needs to get involved. We just need to provide them with enough evidence to prove to them that something is going on first."

"Maybe I should talk to Mr. Whitlock," Taryn said. "And tell him everything."

Maddox stole a quick glance at her. "Do you think that's a good idea?"

She shrugged, her eyes misting as if the thought made her emotional. "I've been trying to protect him. I don't want him to have a medical issue because of the stress of the situation. But I also think he'd want to know. He's a good man, and he wouldn't be okay with someone using property he owns for nefarious purposes. You don't think he's involved with this somehow, do you?"

Maddox pressed his lips together, unsure what to say. All he wanted was to protect Taryn . . . but this seemed like a no-win situation.

Finally, he settled with the truth. "I don't think he is. But, at this point, it's hard to know who to trust."

"I just can't see him knowingly being involved with something like this. Besides, if he *were* involved, then why would someone be targeting him? Why would they send him threatening letters?"

Maddox rubbed his beard, unable to argue. "All good points. I agree. But I don't want you to do anything you're not comfortable with."

"At this point, I don't feel like I have any other choice." Taryn paused as the edge of the woods came into view and Mr. Whitlock's estate beyond that. "I'm going to talk to him."

Maddox nodded. But he felt terrible for putting her in this position. He only hoped this conversation didn't ruin his whole mission.

Taryn knew she needed to wait until the nurse left before she talked to Mr. Whitlock.

She glanced at her watch.

She probably had another ten minutes until they could speak in private.

In the meantime, she and Maddox made themselves sandwiches in the staff living area. They needed to eat if they wanted energy to navigate the rest of this day. Titus joined them, and, with the door shut, Maddox gave him a brief update.

"If we're not looking for blueprints to a federal building, then what blueprints are we looking for?"

Titus leaned against the kitchen counter, a perplexed look in his gaze.

"That's what we're asking ourselves," Maddox said.

"What if it's the blueprints for an operation of some sort?" Titus shrugged as if contemplating his words. "What if we were off base this whole time?"

"I thought about that." Maddox took another bite of his sandwich and swallowed before saying, "However, given the fact that Mr. Whitlock's grandfather was an architect, it seems unlikely. But it still could be a possibility."

Maddox's phone buzzed, and he glanced at it. "We have more pictures from that drone. Let me load them on my computer so we can look at them better."

He grabbed his computer from his room before joining them in the staff living room again.

A moment later, he had the photos up on his screen, and the three of them leaned together to see the images. Cars were there, the pictures showing them from a bird's-eye view.

But some photos were closer. They showed details of the cars. The grounds. The people heading into the woods.

Titus sucked in a breath as another image filled the screen.

"What is it?" Maddox asked.

He pointed to a woman on the screen. "That's Presley."

"Who is Presley?" Maddox searched his memories for a mention of that name, but he came up blank.

Titus ran a hand over his face. "She's my brother's girlfriend."

CHAPTER
FIFTY-ONE

MADDOX WASN'T sure he'd heard Titus correctly. "You're saying that your brother's girlfriend is a part of The System?"

Titus leaned back and ran his hand through his hair. "Looks that way from this picture. Then again, I haven't talked to either of them in two years. I don't know what they've been up to."

Maddox glanced back at the screen. "Is your brother in any of these photos?"

"I haven't seen him yet." Titus' eyes remained glued to the screen. "But I can't imagine him being involved with something like this."

"Do you think you could try to reach out to either of them?" Maddox continued.

Titus shook his head, his reaction swift and strong. "No. They won't talk to me."

He sounded certain, without any trace of doubt in his voice.

Clearly, there was a story there. Maddox didn't have time to pursue it right now. He knew that Taryn was gearing up to go talk to Mr. Whitlock. They needed to get that out of the way before diving into Titus' possible inside connection with The System.

Taryn's phone buzzed, and she glanced down at the screen and frowned.

"What is it?" Maddox leaned closer.

"It's a breaking news update. I usually ignore them. But this one contains a sketch of the man suspected of shooting Senator Gately . . ." She showed him the screen. "Is it just me, or does he look a lot like one of those men who was guarding the compound?"

As Maddox studied the picture, the air left his lungs.

The sketch looked exactly like one of those guys.

Was The System trying to assassinate members of the US Senate? This was even more serious than Maddox had assumed.

He and Titus exchanged a look before Maddox texted the information to Colton. He needed to know this ASAP.

Before they could talk about it anymore, Titus' phone rang. He put it to his ear and muttered a few things before turning toward them. "Danielle said another one of the horses got out. I need to go help her."

"Call me if you need a hand."

He nodded. "Will do."

After Titus disappeared, Taryn stood. Her eyes appeared glazed with hesitation.

"I need to get upstairs," she announced.

Maddox also rose. "I'd like to go with you if you're okay with that."

She stared at him a moment, and he thought for sure she'd say no.

Finally, she nodded. "Okay. But let me take the lead. Please."

Taryn couldn't ignore the rumble of nerves rushing through her as she walked up the stairs.

Maddox placed his hand on her back in a gentle reassurance.

She wasn't sure if it helped or not. In one way, his touch made her feel better about her upcoming conversation with Mr. Whitlock. But in another way, it sent a round of explosive fireworks through her.

She definitely had feelings for this man. Maybe once this was all over—assuming they both survived —she'd try to figure out what to do about those feelings. Try to figure out if Maddox was like every other guy she'd dated or if he was truly different like her gut told her he was.

They passed the nurse on the way up the stairs, and she nodded, giving them a brief update.

As they reached Mr. Whitlock's room, Taryn spotted Gerald inside with him. The two men were deep in a conversation—a conversation that ended as soon as Gerald spotted them. The man quickly excused himself and slipped from the room.

Could Gerald be the one involved in this? That seemed like a real possibility. He knew all about Mr. Whitlock's business.

Before he disappeared down the hall, Taryn called to him. "Do you have a minute?"

He squinted. "I suppose."

She closed the door so Mr. Whitlock wouldn't hear. "I need to ask you something."

Gerald shifted and glanced between her and Maddox. "What's going on?"

"Are you affiliated with an organization called The System?" She watched his face for any sign of recognition.

"The System? No. I've never heard of them. Why?"

"We know you used to be an activist . . ." Maddox said.

His brow furrowed. "You're looking into me?"

"We are trying to figure out what's going on here," Maddox told him.

"You're searching in the wrong direction. Yes, I used to be an activist. But as soon as I heard about some of the extreme measures certain people in my group wanted to sink to, I wanted out. I believe in arguing in the courtroom, not through violence."

She believed him. He'd made a very convincing argument for himself.

Taryn stepped out of his way and nodded. "Thank you."

He paused before moving forward. "Taryn, if these people are the ones behind what's happening here, I suggest you stay far away from them."

She stared at him another minute before nodding. "I'm trying."

When he was gone, Taryn and Maddox stepped into Mr. Whitlock's room.

She sucked in a deep breath as she tried to figure out exactly how to broach the subject. There was no good way to do it, she realized. It was almost as if she just needed to rip off the Band-Aid.

But she prayed this conversation wasn't all one big mistake.

CHAPTER
FIFTY-TWO

MADDOX SENSED Taryn's nerves and wished he could reassure her. But he knew the stakes. He knew how fragile Mr. Whitlock's heart was and the risk of this conversation.

However, he couldn't have this talk for her.

Taryn needed to tell Mr. Whitlock about what was going on—her first-hand experience. Mr. Whitlock trusted and respected her enough to listen.

"I can tell you have something on your mind." Mr. Whitlock nodded toward the chair across from his bed where he lay. "What is it?"

Taryn pulled the chair closer to his bed while Maddox stood near the door. She took Mr. Whitlock's hand in hers and leaned closer, obvious tension across her face. "Mr. Whitlock . . . I've struggled with how much I should tell you."

His expression remained unchanged. "I know there's something going on here at the estate. Like I told you earlier, my heart may be failing, but my mind is still good."

"I just don't want to cause you any stress." Taryn pressed her lips together as more tension spread through her gaze.

"My days are numbered already. I'm not counting on making it much longer. So go ahead and tell me."

Taryn drew in a shaky breath. Then she launched into everything, not holding back any details—except for Maddox's real identity. At this point, she didn't need to keep that secret either, but Maddox didn't interrupt.

Maddox watched Mr. Whitlock's expression as Taryn spoke. The man seemed even-keeled, not too surprised but not unaffected either.

"I knew two accidental deaths couldn't be a coincidence." Mr. Whitlock's gaze turned to Maddox. "And who are you really?"

Maddox kept his chin up, almost feeling like he was addressing a commanding officer. "I also work with Blackout, the organization that Titus is with."

Mr. Whitlock nodded slowly, no surprise in his gaze. "You came to investigate me?"

"We suspected something was happening on your property, and we've been trying to get to the bottom of it."

Mr. Whitlock continued to study him. "Who hired you?"

"Finley Cooper with Embolden Tech. Some of her products were lost in this vicinity. When we started asking questions, we realized that something was awry."

"Finley, huh? I knew her father. He was a good man. I can see where she would be concerned."

Maddox stepped closer and kept his voice low. "Do you have any idea who might be using your land? Who might have set up camp there?"

"No one else knows what's there."

Maddox's eyebrows shot up. "What's there?"

What did Mr. Whitlock mean by that?

Maddox waited to hear his explanation.

***

Taryn held Mr. Whitlock's hand as she waited for him to explain. She prayed that this conversation wouldn't get his heart rate up.

"As I told Taryn, that area of Mt. Caleb is popular because the mountains around it practically make the property a fortress. That's why my grandfather decided to construct a building there."

"I didn't realize there was a building on the property." Taryn had seen the area herself. There were no structures. So, what was Mr. Whitlock talking about?

"That's because it's not visible to the human eye."

"Then it must be underground. It's a bunker . . . isn't it?" Taryn muttered with a shake of her head.

Mr. Whitlock snapped his fingers and pointed at her. "I knew you were a smart one."

Maddox shifted, his hands going to his hips as curiosity stretched across his gaze. "What kind of bunker are we talking about?"

"A safe place in the shape of the labyrinth—only underground. And in the center? There's a vault where I keep my most valuable possessions."

Taryn's thoughts raced. What else could Mr. Whitlock have stored there?

"I keep other blueprints my grandfather had in his possession there." He frowned. "Blueprints that any number of terrorist groups would kill to have."

She sucked in a breath at the implications of his statement.

"Blueprints to what?" Maddox asked.

"The White House."

Taryn's stomach dropped. Was that what these people were really after?

They wanted to do something at the White House?

"How do you have blueprints to the White House?" she asked.

"Easy. My great-grandfather helped build it. He passed on those blueprints to his son, who was also an architect. As I've told you, my family goes back generations on this land."

"You're talking about the actual White House? In Washington, DC?" Taryn shook her head, almost in disbelief.

"Indeed, I am. The blueprints show everything—even rooms the public isn't supposed to know about."

"In the wrong hands, someone might use that to their advantage . . ." Maddox muttered.

"Do you think someone has discovered the bunker?" Worry stained Mr. Whitlock's gaze.

Taryn swallowed hard. "It looks like they have."

"At least, they can't get to those blueprints in the vault. They can only get in with the right handprint." The worry in Mr. Whitlock's gaze deepened.

"Your father installed that technology?" Taryn tried to piece together all she was learning.

"No, Embolden Tech did it about six years ago—before Finley took over the company. I hired her father to do so."

"Abe . . ." Maddox muttered before rubbing a hand over his beard.

"Who's Abe?" Taryn stared at him in confusion.

Maddox's gaze remained dark. "He's the man who shipped those products that went missing from Embolden. He must be with The System. But working at Embolden, he might have found out about the handprint that was installed in the bunker."

Taryn's gaze met his. "Maddox . . . that attempt on Senator Gately's life . . . mixed with blueprints to federal buildings, listening devices, bombs . . . I think our earlier theory was correct."

"The System is gearing up for a domestic terrorist attack." Maddox rubbed his beard again—as he always did when he was deep in thought. "The Great Awakening."

Taryn turned back to her employer, feeling a new sense of urgency. Were the threats made toward Mr. Whitlock somehow connected with the terrorist attack? Was there something else he wasn't telling them?

"Mr. Whitlock, I'm sorry to tell you like this, but you've been getting some threats in the mail in the past few weeks. I didn't want to tell you and stress you out."

He shrugged. "I've been getting threats for the past several months, actually. Someone knows I have those blueprints, and they're desperate to do anything to get them. They say they'll ruin my son's life by exposing his secrets if I don't tell them the information they want."

"How do they plan on ruining Phil's life?" Maddox stepped closer.

"He's made some bad business deals. If his reputation is ruined, his entire career will be in shambles. That's why he's always coming around. He needs my money to fix his problems before anyone finds out."

"Sounds like it's too late for that," Taryn muttered. "Someone already knows about Phil's secrets."

"I love my son . . . but I can't cover for his mistakes. If that ends up costing him his job or his reputation, then so be it. Those are hard lessons to learn, but they're also necessary." Mr. Whitlock frowned. "Besides, I can't give in to these threats. Too much is at stake."

Maddox and Taryn exchanged another glance.

Knowing what they did now, they didn't have any time to waste.

They had to stop these people.

Whatever happened, members of The System couldn't get their hands on those blueprints.

MADDOX'S THOUGHTS RACED. "Whose handprint will open the vault in the bunker? Yours?"

"Mine . . . and someone else that I recently had programmed as a backup plan."

Taryn sucked in a breath. "It's mine, isn't it?"

Mr. Whitlock smiled and patted her hand. "You have one of the purest hearts of anyone I know. I knew I could trust you. Gerald would have told you about it after I died—he would've told you to keep it safe."

"So, either your handprint or Taryn's are the only way for someone to get inside the vault?" Maddox's muscles tensed.

"Yes, the only way," Mr. Whitlock confirmed.

"Then we'd better hope no one finds out whose handprint is needed." Maddox glanced at Taryn.

"Only a few people know, and I trust them implicitly," Mr. Whitlock assured him.

Maddox didn't want to take that chance.

He needed to call Colton and tell him about this discovery. But he had something else to ask Mr. Whitlock first.

"Mr. Whitlock, I need to get the FBI involved. The stakes are getting too high. Are you okay with that?"

Mr. Whitlock nodded slowly, his eyes drooping as if he were becoming tired. "Of course. Especially if these people are planning something like you said."

More pieces clicked together in Maddox's mind. He'd already ruled out some members of the staff and household here.

But there were a couple of suspects who were becoming more and more viable.

Maddox grabbed his phone, ready to make the call.

Before he could, a shadow appeared in the doorway.

A shadow holding a gun.

Taryn gasped at the figure who stepped into the room.

"Danielle?" Taryn couldn't believe her eyes.

Was *Danielle* behind this?

Danielle's eyes narrowed as she stepped closer, still gripping her gun. "I knew you two were up to something."

"One of the horses didn't get out again, did it?" Everything suddenly seemed so clear.

"I needed to get Titus out of the way." She frowned. "Then I needed to figure out what you two were up to. I see you've already discovered everything."

"Why don't you put the gun down?" Maddox's hand was poised as if he wanted to grab his own gun but knew it was a bad idea.

"Why don't *you* put *your* gun on the floor and kick it toward me? If you don't, I *will* shoot Taryn. Don't test me." Danielle's eyes narrowed as she transformed into a different person—a hardened, calculated one.

"Danielle . . ." Mr. Whitlock muttered, betrayal cracking his voice.

"I'm sorry." Danielle shrugged. "But I don't have any other choice right now."

Taryn's pulse quickened as she realized what was at stake here. "You don't have to do this."

"Sure, I do. Do you realize how far I've come? I'm not going to let anyone put an end to my plans when I'm this close."

"No one needs to be hurt," Maddox said. "I'm

sure you just overheard our conversation. Now, you can get into the bunker and get what you want."

"I'm not stupid." Danielle scowled. "I know who you are, Maddox King. I've known since the day you came here that you're a former Navy SEAL."

"So, you're the one who's been behind all of this?" How had Taryn not seen this all along? Danielle had slipped right under the radar. "You killed Gary, Leroy, and Alana? But why?"

"Gary followed me one day, all the way to the compound, where he confronted me. That was a fatal mistake. I did some research and then mixed up some of his medications to ensure he met his unfortunate demise. Leroy was actually on our side, but he had a crisis of conscience and wanted to come clean to Mr. Whitlock. I couldn't let him do that."

"And Alana . . . ?" Maddox asked.

"Alana overheard me talking to a few of my compadres and threatened to tell Mr. Whitlock. I couldn't let that happen either. I placated her and told her I'd find a way to get her more money from Mr. Whitlock. Then I fixed her a special cocktail. She just happened to be by the pool and . . ." Danielle shrugged nonchalantly. "The rest is history."

"Danielle . . ." Mr. Whitlock said again, angst staining his gaze.

"Sorry. But we have bigger plans here—bigger than you finishing out your last days in peace. You have no idea how much is at stake." She smirked. "I suppose I should thank you. We couldn't have done this without you."

As she said the words, Mr. Whitlock grasped his heart.

Taryn started toward him when Danielle clucked her tongue. "Don't move."

"He needs his medicine." Taryn's voice cracked as she stared at Mr. Whitlock's pained expression.

"He's not going to get that medicine. Not until I get what I want."

Taryn rose to full height, hardly able to breathe as she watched Mr. Whitlock struggling. "What is it that you want?"

"I want you to use your handprint to get into a vault located in that bunker."

"But—"

"No buts about it. If you want Mr. Whitlock to live, that's what you're going to do." Danielle pulled something from her pocket and tossed it to Taryn.

Zip ties.

"Now tie up Maddox," Danielle ordered. "One wrong move, and I'll shoot him. Don't test me."

FIFTY-FOUR

"IT'S OKAY." Maddox sensed Taryn's anxiety in her trembling voice and shallow breaths. "Just do what Danielle says."

With shaking hands, Taryn approached him with the zip ties. Under Danielle's supervision, Taryn pressed Maddox's wrists together in front of him and then tightened the binding around them.

"Tie him to the bed." Danielle motioned with her gun.

Taryn took another zip tie and looped it between his wrists, attaching the second loop to the metal rail along Mr. Whitlock's bed.

"I'm sorry," she whispered as she leaned close to Maddox's ear.

"It's not your fault," he assured her.

"Tie Mr. Whitlock up too," Danielle ordered.

Taryn did the same with one of Mr. Whitlock's wrinkled, vein-riddled hands, taking care not to zip it too tight.

"You know he can't go anywhere." Taryn cast an apologetic glance at Mr. Whitlock, as anger flooded through her. "I don't know why you're making me do this to him." Her voice cracked again. "He needs me to give him his medication."

"If you're a good girl, you'll have time to help him later. But, right now, I need you more than he does."

Taryn scowled at the woman.

Maddox watched closely, wishing Taryn didn't have to go through this. But they had little choice right now. Once Danielle and Taryn were out of the room, Maddox would work on removing these binds so he could help Mr. Whitlock.

But for the time being, he needed to act compliant.

"You're going outside with me." Danielle shoved the gun at Taryn. "It's getting dark, and everyone else is preoccupied right now. But we still need to move fast, especially if you want to continue to help Mr. Whitlock."

"You're a monster," Taryn muttered.

"I've been called worse."

Before they walked out of the door, Maddox called to Taryn.

She glanced back at him, questions in her gaze.

"Be careful." His heart seemed to clog his throat.

Taryn nodded and stared at him with an unreadable emotion in her gaze.

Maddox was fairly certain the emotion was affection.

He cared about Taryn too. He'd been trying to keep her at arm's length this whole time, but now it was clear that if anything happened to her, he'd regret not having expressed his feelings earlier. He shouldn't have let Lindsey hold him back.

Because now . . . what if he never got the chance?

No, he couldn't think like that.

He prayed he'd have that opportunity.

He prayed God would keep Taryn safe.

And he prayed he'd be able to get out of these zip ties and somehow help both Mr. Whitlock and Taryn.

Taryn's muscles bristled.

She was keenly aware of the gun pressing into her side. Keenly aware of how tightly Danielle held onto her arm.

Could she take this woman down?

Considering Danielle had a gun and Taryn didn't, Taryn knew she couldn't risk it.

Instead, she needed a Plan B.

She sighed as her thoughts raced.

Would Danielle force her to walk to the compound?

That would take too much time. When Taryn got back to the estate—if she made it back—who knew what kind of state Mr. Whitlock would be in?

Tears pressed on her eyes at the thought.

Was this all her fault? Had Taryn brought trouble with her?

No. She knew the truth.

Danielle would have struck whether Taryn was here or not.

In fact, maybe Taryn's presence was a blessing. Maybe she was placed at this estate for a purpose, and she could somehow make this whole situation right.

She prayed that was the case.

"I have a UTV out behind the stables," Danielle barked. "Now that my little secret's out in the open, we can take that. It will be faster."

"Where's Titus?" Taryn rushed.

"I took care of him. No need to worry."

Took care of him? Taryn swallowed hard.

Was he okay?

They went down the stairs, each step down

causing more tension to spread through Taryn. One wrong move, and Danielle could pull that trigger.

Taryn could die.

She didn't have much to show for her life. But for the first time in a long time, Taryn felt hope about the future.

Not because of Mr. Whitlock.

Not even because of Maddox.

But because somewhere along the line, Taryn had begun to believe in herself. She was more than her past. More than her parents' mistakes or the ugly words her mom had thrown at her.

Taryn was capable. Mr. Whitlock had allowed her to see that.

And Maddox . . . at this moment Taryn had no doubt he was one of the good guys. He was nothing like Grissom. She'd been a fool to even wonder if he was.

If she got out of this alive . . . maybe the two of them would have the opportunity to explore what could be something beautiful between them.

Danielle jabbed the gun into Taryn's ribcage again before growling, "Keep moving."

Taryn tried to move forward, careful not to walk too quickly or too slowly. Instead, she forced herself to keep in step with Danielle.

Danielle opened the back door and glanced around before shoving Taryn out. "I'm going to let go of your arm. But if you try to run, I *will* pull this trigger."

Taryn heard the promise in Danielle's voice.

She meant those words.

But Taryn needed to quickly think of a way to get out of this situation and how to help Mr. Whitlock.

FIFTY-FIVE

AS SOON AS Danielle and Taryn were out the bedroom door, Maddox raised his knee toward his wrists. Normally, he'd use momentum to break through zip ties. But the additional loop around the bed railing made things more complicated.

Mr. Whitlock moaned again, spurring Maddox to work faster.

With a grunt, he forced his wrists apart.

The zip ties cut into his skin, but he didn't care.

On the third try, the plastic snapped.

His hands were free.

Mr. Whitlock writhed on the hospital bed.

Maddox rushed closer. "It's going to be okay."

He quickly glanced at the table beside him at the medications there.

He didn't know which one Mr. Whitlock was supposed to take.

But, at this point, Mr. Whitlock needed *something*. A wrong choice almost seemed better than nothing.

Because nothing might mean certain death.

Maddox scanned each bottle, briefly reading their descriptions. Finally, he looked at Mr. Whitlock. "Do you know which one you need to take?"

Mr. Whitlock only stared at him, his eyes glazed as death came nearer.

Maddox grabbed the closest bottle and held it up. "Do you know if it's this one?"

Mr. Whitlock stared.

Maddox picked up another bottle. "Or maybe this one?"

As he said the words, someone appeared in the room.

A nurse.

Her eyes widened. "What's going on?"

Maddox didn't have time to explain everything.

"He needs your help, and I need to go. I'm sorry. Please take care of him."

With one more last glance at the man, Maddox tore through the doorway. He rushed onto the balcony and glanced out.

Danielle led Taryn toward the back of the property, a gun at her back.

Maddox tore his gaze away and ran down the stairs.

As he did, he called 911. After ending the call with them, he dialed Colton. His team leader needed to know what was going on.

The minutes felt like hours as Maddox imagined what might be happening with Taryn.

He needed to get out there and help her.

As he reached the back door, he paused. Taryn and Danielle were now near the labyrinth.

If he burst outside, Danielle would certainly see him.

Instead, he ran through the house to the garage. He would exit out the side entrance and then circle around.

He needed to take Danielle by surprise. Otherwise, she might keep her promise and pull that trigger, sending a bullet through Taryn.

Maddox couldn't live with himself if that happened.

"So, did you leave that painted rock in the labyrinth on purpose?" Taryn asked as she and Danielle walked across the lawn. "Or was that a coincidence?"

"I painted them as part of an online game. But then I had the idea to leave one in your path, hoping to trip you up. I thought if you were hurt, you might have to leave. Then I realized you could be valuable, so I should keep you around."

"Because of my handprint?" Taryn asked.

"If the shoe fits . . ."

Taryn glanced toward the labyrinth and spotted a figure laying on the ground beside it.

She sucked in a breath.

Was that . . . Titus?

Was he alive?

Please, Lord. Let him be okay . . .

Taryn slowed to see if his chest was rising and falling.

"Keep moving," Danielle growled as she shoved Taryn forward. "Don't worry about pretty boy over there."

Taryn pulled her gaze from Titus, trying to focus on her own survival right now. She couldn't help anyone else if she was dead.

"You tried a little bit of everything to get your way, didn't you?" Taryn said to Danielle. "But I know you couldn't have done all those things. You had to have some help with some of the shenanigans you pulled."

"I may have hired some guys."

"Dagger, you mean?" Taryn stole a glance at Danielle.

Her eyes widened with surprise. "How do you . .

. ? Never mind. It's not important. All that's important is that we get the information we need. It seems fortuitous that we can use you to obtain that."

"I'm sure you've exhausted every other possibility."

Her eyes narrowed. "Just keep walking. That's all you need to concentrate on now. Soon, this will all be over."

At her words, realization fell over Taryn.

Danielle had no intention of letting Taryn walk away from this alive.

Mr. Whitlock either. Probably not Maddox or Titus, for that matter.

After Taryn helped these people get what they wanted, they would kill her and go back to take out the others.

Just as the thought rushed through Taryn's mind, she heard a yell.

Then someone tackled Danielle to the ground.

FIFTY-SIX

MADDOX SAW his opportunity to make a move, and he jumped on it.

Literally.

He'd run as fast as he could around the labyrinth, desperate to cut Danielle and Taryn off.

Then he'd lingered behind some hedges. When Danielle seemed distracted by their conversation, he realized this was the perfect opportunity to act.

His body collided with Danielle's, and they landed on the ground.

"How did you . . . ?" Danielle turned and glared up at him, surprisingly strong for her size.

But she was no match for a trained Navy SEAL.

As long as he could get the guns from her—her gun and his gun that she'd taken from him.

He glanced at Taryn and shouted, "Run!"

Taryn stared at him with a wide-eyed gaze. She seemed frozen, unsure whether to help him or listen to him.

"Mr. Whitlock is okay," he told her. "Get to safety."

With those words, Taryn turned and ran into the labyrinth.

Maddox realized exactly what she was doing.

A person could run around in that maze-like structure and never get caught if they knew their way around.

Taryn just might be that person.

Maddox slammed Danielle's hand on the ground until the gun skittered from her grasp.

But before he could get the second gun, a shadow fell over him. Something hard hit Maddox's head, and everything went black.

***

Taryn ducked between the hedges of the labyrinth.

The structure seemed like the safest place to hide.

But was it?

She was about to find out.

She took the various pathways as she kept running, knowing if she stopped someone might catch up with her.

What was going on out there?

She'd heard a grunt.

Had that been Maddox? Or Danielle?

She couldn't be sure.

She only hoped help arrived soon.

"Come out, come out, wherever you are," a singsong voice said.

Danielle.

How had Danielle gotten away from Maddox? It didn't seem possible.

But that's what it sounded like.

Maddox . . . His image filled her mind.

Taryn prayed he was okay.

Her steps slowed with uncertainty as worry seemed to weigh her down.

Should she keep running? Or should she go back and help Maddox?

"If you don't come out, I'm going to kill your boyfriend!" Danielle shouted.

Taryn paused and sucked in shallow breaths.

What should she do? She couldn't let Maddox suffer—not if she had the power to help him.

Besides, it wasn't like she could stay in here all night. Eventually, when she came out, Danielle would find her.

Unless the police got here first.

Had Maddox called the cops?

Even if he had, they were probably fifteen minutes away at least.

A lot could happen in fifteen minutes.

"I'm giving you to the count of ten, and then I'm going to shoot him." Danielle's voice sounded threatening as it stretched through the air. "Do you hear me?"

"And I'm going to help her," a new voice said. A deeper one.

Wait . . . Danielle had someone helping her?

Taryn thought she'd heard that voice before.

But where? And who was it?

Taryn paused and clutched her throat as anxiety made it hard to breathe.

She had no choice but to surrender.

Not for her own sake, but for Maddox's.

MADDOX BLINKED, trying to ignore the throbbing in his head as he pulled himself to his feet.

He spotted the labyrinth beside him and prayed Taryn didn't take the bait and leave the labyrinth. She was safer in there. But knowing her, she wouldn't be able to stay.

Not since Danielle had threatened him.

He gasped in another ragged breath as his head pounded. "Don't do it!"

As soon as the words left his lips, something hit his jaw.

Phil had slapped his gun across Maddox's face.

Yes, Phil.

He *was* involved—only he'd had an accomplice, which had complicated things by making him seem like he had an alibi.

Maddox shouldn't be surprised.

"I should have killed you when I had the chance." Phil sneered at him.

Maddox rose to his full height, determined not to let this guy win. "Then why didn't you?"

"Because as soon as I realized how much my dad trusted Taryn, I knew I had to keep her around. I knew she'd be useful to me. I was afraid if you died that Taryn would run."

As soon as he said her name, Taryn appeared from one of the exits of the labyrinth, her hands in the air. "Please, don't hurt him."

Maddox's heart sank.

No . . .

Now, she was in danger too. There was little he could do about it.

Still holding the gun, Danielle joined Phil. He quickly kissed Danielle's forehead as she stood beside him.

Wait . . . the two of them were together?

Maddox hadn't seen that one coming.

"I'm sorry, Maddox," Taryn muttered. "I couldn't let them hurt you."

Danielle turned her steely gaze back onto them. "We're all going to get on the UTV, and Taryn is going to drive. We both have guns, and if anyone makes a move, then you'll both die. Understand?"

Taryn shook her head as she stared at Phil. "How

can you live with yourself knowing that your father could be inside the house dying right now?"

Phil shrugged, not a hint of emotion on his face. "He's going to die soon anyway."

His apathy made Maddox sick to his stomach.

As Phil shoved them forward, Maddox's mind raced to figure out what to do.

Taryn's mind raced as she drove the UTV through the woods.

How could all of this be happening? It seemed surreal.

But it was all too real.

Soon enough, Taryn turned on the path leading up to Mt. Caleb. As soon as she reached the road, she noticed the other cars leaving the area.

Danielle and Phil must have told everyone there to flee. Now members of The System were escaping before the FBI arrived and arrested them.

How long would it take the authorities to get here?

It seemed as if it was already too late.

Taryn held back a frown. She hoped these people didn't get away with this.

They wouldn't—not if she had any say in the matter.

"How did you two even get involved with this group?" Taryn gripped the steering wheel as the rocky road bounced them.

"It's all about connections," Danielle said. "One of Phil's friends founded the organization. When we met, he told me about what they were trying to do. I was onboard 100 percent. This country needs to change, and it's going to take something catastrophic for that to happen."

"Like what?" Taryn's voice trembled as she asked the question.

"Wouldn't you like to know?" Danielle smirked. "Now, enough talking. Head over there."

Danielle directed Taryn onto the property, near a clearing where other vehicles had parked, and told her to cut the engine.

"Now we go inside," Phil said. "Make a move, and I think you know what the consequences will be."

With a gun to their backs, Phil pushed them into the woods.

They'd walked less than twenty feet, when an opening in the mountain appeared.

Two steel doors stood wide open.

Doors leading into a cave-like bunker that had been cut into the mountainside.

Taryn stared at it in awe for a minute. But she didn't have time to ponder the space for long.

Danielle shoved them forward. "Move!"

Taryn wanted to reach out to Maddox. Wanted to take his hand. Wanted to hear his assurance that everything would be okay.

But that wouldn't be happening.

She continued inside the bunker. As she did, the air turned cooler. Dim lights buzzed overhead.

No doubt, part of the reason Mr. Whitlock's electric bill had been so high.

People flooded out, taking supplies with them— evidence of what they'd been doing.

The pit in Taryn's stomach continued to grow.

She knew exactly what they needed her for.

And she wasn't sure how she could stop it.

Even if they killed her, they could still use her handprint.

Dear Lord . . . what should I do?

MORE THAN ANYTHING, Maddox wanted to reach out to Taryn. To comfort her. To protect her.

But none of those things could happen right now.

Danielle and Phil shoved them into a tunnel—a tunnel laid out just like the labyrinth.

That's where The System had gotten their symbol, wasn't it?

Maddox grunted.

"What are you doing?" Phil growled, his grip tightening on Maddox's arm.

"Nothing," Maddox muttered. "Just following your directions."

"Whatever you're thinking about, stop."

Maddox didn't say anything.

"Lead us to the center." Danielle shoved Taryn forward. "You'll get us there sooner than we will."

Taryn glanced back at Maddox, fear stretching through her gaze. But, instead of putting up a fight, she nodded and wound her way through the labyrinth. It was the best thing she could do right now.

However, Maddox couldn't let them get into that vault.

But he would need to plan his moves carefully.

"You put on a good act for us in my room," Taryn said through clenched teeth. "I actually believed you when you sounded concerned."

Phil shrugged, a proud gleam in his gaze. "I can pull it out of myself when I need to. When something is important to you, you do whatever's necessary to carry through."

When something's important to you . . . Maddox didn't want to believe Phil might actually have some wisdom in him, but he had to agree—people should fight for what was important.

Just like Maddox should fight for Taryn.

They needed to survive this situation first, however.

Several minutes later, they reached the center of the space.

Taryn hesitated as she stared at the scanner beside the metal door in front of her.

"Put your hand on it!" Danielle barked.

Taryn glance back at Maddox again.

"Don't look at him!" Phil held his gun out farther. "Just do what we say, and no one will be hurt."

"Like Gary, Leroy, and Alana weren't hurt?" Taryn's voice wavered.

"Just behave," Phil said. "I thought I could turn you to our side, but then I realized you were a good girl. A disgustingly good girl. That's why we're having to do this the hard way."

Taryn's entire body trembled as she turned toward the door.

Phil was right—Taryn *was* one of the good ones.

Clarity captured Maddox.

They needed to get out of this alive—and he needed the chance to tell Taryn how he really felt. He needed to realize that not everyone was like Lindsey. Not everyone flaked out at the first sign of trouble or imperfection.

Taryn was worth the risk.

Would Maddox have the opportunity to tell her that?

None of that would matter if these people got those blueprints and carried through with their dastardly deeds.

He didn't have any more time to waste.

Maddox sprang into action. He swung his leg and knocked Phil's gun from his hand.

He then ducked and used his elbow to punch Danielle in the gut.

Taken by surprise, her gun flew to the ground also.

"Run!" he told Taryn. "And whatever happens, don't let them find you."

She stared at him a moment, her eyes wide.

Then she took off in a sprint.

Taryn's heart raced.

The last thing she wanted was to leave Maddox.

But she knew the stakes.

She had no choice but to flee.

But she prayed he would be okay.

She heard sounds behind her. Grunts. Groans. Grumbling.

She wanted to stop. To help.

But she couldn't.

Instead, she wound her way around the labyrinth.

This one matched the one outside Mr. Whitlock's house. As long as she didn't let her stress get the best of her, she should be able to find her way around the space.

Otherwise, she could circle for hours in here without being caught.

That was probably what Maddox had been banking on.

"I'm going to find you!" Phil's voice echoed through the passageway.

Taryn kept running, trying to keep her thoughts focused on the pattern around her.

They couldn't get her. Couldn't get her handprint. The results would be too devastating.

She dodged another wall.

In different circumstances, she might pause with wonder in the design of this place.

But not right now.

She paused and pressed herself against the cold stone wall as she listened for footsteps.

They were there but faint.

Her heart pounded in her ears.

As she started to continue, someone stepped out in front of her.

Her breath caught.

It was a man she'd never seen before.

He had a gun in his hands.

Aimed directly at her.

TARYN WASN'T sure what to do.

But she couldn't let this guy get her.

Instead, she took off in a run.

He fired his gun, but the bullet missed.

The curves of the labyrinth would protect her right now.

But she didn't have much time.

A crash sounded and then another grunt.

She paused—but only for a second. Was that Maddox?

She had no idea.

All Taryn knew was that she couldn't trap herself in one of the labyrinth's dead ends.

She'd never get out if that happened.

Instead, she kept running.

And running.

And running.

Until she hit what felt like a brick wall.

Not a brick wall.

A person.

She stifled a scream as she realized she'd been caught.

And now those guys would get those blueprints.

Maddox grasped Taryn's arms. "It's okay. It's me."

She looked up at him and seemed to process his words before melting in his arms. Her limbs seemed to turn into jelly.

"Maddox . . ."

He pressed a kiss on the top of her head. "It's okay, sweetie. I'm here."

"Those men . . ." she murmured into his chest.

"Colton texted me. The FBI is here. They've raided the outside of the compound, and several agents are inside making arrests."

"Phil?"

"I tied him and Danielle up—using that yarn I had in my pocket. I told you it came in handy." He fought a grin, knowing that now was no time to make jokes. "I also got that other man—the Dagger agent. You're safe now."

She buried her head further in his chest. "Oh, Maddox . . ."

As more footsteps invaded the space, he held her closer. "Everything is okay now."

"I'm so glad." Suddenly, she stiffened and glanced up. "What about Titus? Mr. Whitlock?"

"Colton mentioned them also. Titus is fine. And the overnight nurse arrived before I left Mr. Whitlock. She's taking care of him."

"Thank God." Taryn melted against him again. "I was certain I was going to die . . ."

Grief clutched Maddox's heart. He'd been afraid of that also. But he'd known he would sacrifice his own life if it meant protecting Taryn. In the brief amount of time he'd known her, she'd come to mean the world to him.

He cleared his throat. "Taryn . . ."

She glanced up at him, her eyes red-rimmed and lined with moisture. "Yes?"

"I . . . you . . ." The words had trouble forming.

Before he could say anything else, she reached on her tiptoes and planted a kiss on his lips. "I care about you too."

Warmth filled his chest cavity. Taryn had expressed exactly what he wanted to say—and it felt amazing to hear those words come from her lips.

He rubbed her arms. "I'm sorry I pulled away

from you, Taryn. The past can really mess with our present sometimes."

"You just needed time. We all do sometimes."

Her understanding touched him. Taryn was exactly the kind of woman he needed in his life—someone loyal and understanding. Who could see past his rough edges to who he really was.

Staring down at her, he pushed a hair away from her face. This time, *he* leaned toward *Taryn*.

He cupped her face in his hands and drew her closer. Her eyes widened as she stared up at him in anticipation.

His lips pressed against hers. The softness of her mouth allured him—and made him curious for more.

He hoped this was the first of many kisses they'd share—that somehow, they could find a way for their futures to tie together as easily as one of his crochet patterns.

But, right now, Maddox heard footsteps coming closer. No doubt the FBI would want to talk to them.

They'd have to save any more kisses until they wrapped this up.

EPILOGUE

"SO, you grab the yarn with your pointer finger and pull it through the slip knot on the hook." Maddox helped guide the yarn in Taryn's hands as he instructed her on how to crochet. "You're doing it. You're making a chain."

Crocheting was one of the many activities the two of them had been doing together since Taryn moved to Lantern Beach two weeks ago.

She was now one of the new administrative assistants for Blackout. Her skills were coming in handy already—and she loved being close to Maddox. Based on the look in his eyes, he loved it also.

Her only regret was Mr. Whitlock.

A frown tugged at her lips as she continued making her chain.

He'd survived the ordeal at the house, but he'd

passed peacefully into eternity three days later. Taryn had been at his side. Five days later, they'd had a beautiful funeral for him where hundreds of people had come to pay their respects.

Mr. Whitlock had left Taryn a good portion of his estate—something Taryn had never expected and that she didn't know quite what to do with. She and Gerald were working on a plan for the property. Their first step had been hiring two people to take care of the horses and act as security.

Because of the house's age, they'd been approached about making the place a museum of sorts—much like the Biltmore. Taryn thought it was a great idea.

She certainly didn't want to live at the estate, not after all the death and destruction she'd seen there.

Eight members of The System—including Danielle and Phil—had been arrested, but they were all mum and refused to speak about any plans the group had or who else was a member. Presley—Titus' brother's girlfriend—hadn't been found or implicated.

Not yet.

All except two of Embolden Tech's missing cameras and listening devices had been recovered. The blueprints had been taken by the feds to ensure nothing like that ever happened again.

At least, that was the good news.

The investigation into The System was still ongoing. Mr. Whitlock's dying wish was that Taryn and Maddox get to the bottom of what was going on. He didn't want his legacy to be anything less than honorable, and he feared The System's presence on his land might ruin his otherwise stellar reputation.

Taryn knew Maddox would have to leave again soon. Blackout seemed invested in seeing this investigation through to the end. She'd heard something about Titus using his connection with Presley to find out more information.

She'd worry about that another day.

But today . . . today was a day of rest from all the craziness around them.

She and Maddox had explored Lantern Beach, eaten some fresh seafood, and now they were back at his apartment, watching the sunset out the window, and . . . crocheting.

Taryn didn't care what they did—she simply enjoyed being around Maddox.

Maddox peered closer to see her stitches before crooning, "You're doing great."

She smiled as she continued making a chain. "I think I'm getting the hang of it."

"I'd say you are." He rose and offered his hand. "Take a break a minute?"

She slipped her hand into his and rose. They walked together to the window where a coral-colored sky greeted them. The waters of the Pamlico Sound glowed under the rays of the sunset, and marsh grass danced with the light breeze.

The whole thing looked like a painting that had come to life before their eyes.

Maddox wrapped his arms around her from behind and rested his chin on her shoulder. "I was thinking of making a labyrinth right out there in the marsh grasses. What do you think?"

She started to retort when she heard the tease in his voice. "Very funny."

"I thought so."

"No more labyrinths for me. Not for a while, at least." She turned to face him. "Thankfully, I have other things to occupy me."

"Like what?"

She shrugged playfully. "The beach."

He raised his eyebrows. "Anything else?"

"The lighthouse."

"And?"

She reached up and planted a quick kiss on his lips. "And you."

"I like that idea." He grinned at her, his eyes softening. "I'm glad you're here, Taryn."

"I'm glad I'm here also."

Maybe they could both feel some peace now . . . even if struggles were certain to await them in the future. But, for now, they would enjoy each other's company . . . and the sunset.

~~~

Thank you so much for reading *Maddox*. If you enjoyed this book, please consider leaving a review.

Stay tuned for *Titus*, the final book in the Lantern Beach Blackout: Danger Rising series!

Get your copy HERE!
~~~

OTHER BOOKS IN THE LANTERN BEACH SERIES:

LANTERN BEACH MYSTERIES

Hidden Currents

You can take the detective out of the investigation, but you can't take the investigator out of the detective. A notorious gang puts a bounty on Detective Cady Matthews's head after she takes down their leader, leaving her no choice but to hide until she can testify at trial. But her temporary home across the country on a remote North Carolina island isn't as peaceful as she initially thinks. Living under the new identity of Cassidy Livingston, she struggles to keep her investigative skills tucked away, especially after a body washes ashore. When local police bungle the murder investigation, she can't resist stepping in. But Cassidy is supposed to be keeping a low profile. One wrong move could lead to both her discovery and her demise. Can she bring justice to the island . . . or will the hidden currents surrounding her pull her under for good?

Flood Watch

The tide is high, and so is the danger on Lantern Beach. Still in hiding after infiltrating a dangerous gang, Cassidy Livingston just has to make it a few more months before she can testify at trial and resume her old life. But trouble keeps finding her, and Cassidy is pulled into a local investigation after a man mysteriously disappears from the island she now calls home. A recurring nightmare from her time undercover only muddies things, as does a visit from the parents of her handsome ex-Navy SEAL neighbor. When a friend's life is threatened, Cassidy must make choices that put her on the verge of blowing her cover. With a flood watch on her emotions and her life in a tangle, will Cassidy find the truth? Or will her past finally drown her?

Storm Surge

A storm is brewing hundreds of miles away, but its effects are devastating even from afar. Laid-back, loose, and light: that's Cassidy Livingston's new motto. But when a makeshift boat with a bloody cloth inside washes ashore near her oceanfront home, her detective instincts shift into gear . . . again. Seeking clues isn't the only thing on her mind—romance is heating up with next-door neighbor and former Navy SEAL Ty Chambers as well. Her heart wants the love and stability she's longed for her entire life. But her hidden identity only leads to a tidal wave of turbulence. As more answers emerge about the boat, the danger around her rises, creating a treacherous swell that threatens to reveal her past. Can Cassidy mind her own business, or will the storm surge of violence and corruption that has washed ashore on Lantern Beach leave her life in wreckage?

Dangerous Waters

Danger lurks on the horizon, leaving only two choices: find shelter or flee. Cassidy Livingston's new identity has begun to feel as comfortable as her favorite sweater. She's been tucked away on Lantern Beach for weeks, waiting to testify against a deadly gang, and is settling in to a new life she wants to last forever. When she thinks she spots someone malevolent from her past, panic swells inside her. If an enemy has found her, Cassidy won't be the only one who's a target. Everyone she's come to love will also be at risk. Dangerous waters threaten to pull her into an overpowering chasm she may never escape. Can Cassidy survive what lies ahead? Or has the tide fatally turned against her?

Perilous Riptide

Just when the current seems safer, an unseen danger emerges and threatens to destroy everything. When Cassidy Livingston finds a journal hidden deep in the recesses of her ice cream truck, her curiosity kicks into high gear. Islanders suspect that Elsa, the journal's owner, didn't die accidentally. Her final entry indicates their suspicions might be correct and that what Elsa observed on her final night may have led to her demise. Against the advice of Ty Chambers, her former Navy SEAL boyfriend, Cassidy taps into her detective skills and hunts for answers. But her search only leads to a skeletal body and trouble for both of them. As helplessness threatens to drown her, Cassidy is desperate to turn back time. Can Cassidy find what she needs to navigate the perilous situation? Or will the riptide surrounding her threaten everyone and everything Cassidy loves?

Deadly Undertow

The current's fatal pull is powerful, but so is one detective's will to live. When someone from Cassidy Livingston's past shows up on Lantern Beach and warns her of impending peril, opposing currents collide, threatening to drag her under. Running would be easy. But leaving would break her heart. Cassidy must decipher between the truth and lies, between reality and deception. Even more importantly, she must decide whom to trust and whom to fear. Her life depends on it. As danger rises and answers surface, everything Cassidy thought she knew is tested. In order to survive, Cassidy must take drastic measures and end the battle against the ruthless gang DH-7 once and for all. But if her final mission fails, the consequences will be as deadly as the raging undertow.

LANTERN BEACH ROMANTIC SUSPENSE

Tides of Deception

Change has come to Lantern Beach: a new police chief, a new season, and . . . a new romance? Austin Brooks has loved Skye Lavinia from the moment they met, but the walls she keeps around her seem impenetrable. Skye knows Austin is the best thing to ever happen to her. Yet she also knows that if he learns the truth about her past, he'd be a fool not to run. A chance encounter brings secrets bubbling to the surface, and danger soon follows. Are the life-threatening events plaguing them really accidents . . . or is someone trying to send a deadly message? With the tides on Lantern Beach come deception and lies. One question remains—who will be swept away as the water shifts? And will it bring the end for Austin and Skye, or merely the beginning?

Shadow of Intrigue

For her entire life, Lisa Garth has felt like a supporting character in the drama of life. The designation never bothered her—until now. Lantern Beach, where she's settled and runs a popular restaurant, has boarded up for the season. The slower pace leaves her with too much time alone. Braden Dillinger came to Lantern Beach to try to heal. The former Special Forces officer returned from battle with invisible scars and diminished hope. But his recovery is hampered by the fact that an unknown enemy is trying to kill him. From the moment Lisa and Braden meet, danger ignites around them, and both are drawn into a web of intrigue that turns their lives upside down. As shadows creep in, will Lisa and Braden be able to shine a light on the peril around them? Or will the encroaching darkness turn their worst nightmares into reality?

Storm of Doubt

A pastor who's lost faith in God. A romance writer who's lost faith in love. A faceless man with a deadly obsession. Nothing has felt right in Pastor Jack Wilson's world since his wife died two years ago. He hoped coming to Lantern Beach might help soothe the ragged edges of his soul. Instead, he feels more alone than ever. Novelist Juliette Grace came to the island to hide away. Though her professional life has never been better, her personal life has imploded. Her husband left her and a stalker's threats have grown more and more dangerous. When Jack saves Juliette from an attack, he sees the terror in her gaze and knows he must protect her. But when danger strikes again, will Jack be able to keep her safe? Or will the approaching storm prove too strong to withstand?

Winds of Danger

Wes O'Neill is perfectly content to hang with his friends and enjoy island life on Lantern Beach. Something begins to change inside him when Paige Henderson sweeps into his life. But the beautiful newcomer is hiding painful secrets beneath her cheerful facade. Police dispatcher Paige Henderson came to Lantern Beach riddled with guilt and uncertainties after the fallout of a bad relationship. When she meets Wes, she begins to open up to the possibility of love again. But there's something Wes isn't telling her—something that could change everything. As the winds shift, doubts seep into Paige's mind. Can Paige and Wes trust each other, even as the currents work against them? Or is trouble from the past too much to overcome?

Rains of Remorse

A stranger invades her home, leaving Rebecca

Jarvis terrified. Above all, she must protect the baby growing inside her. Since her estranged husband died suspiciously six months earlier, Rebecca has been determined to depend on no one but herself. Her chivalrous new neighbor appears to be an answer to prayer. But who is Levi Stoneman really? Rebecca wants to believe he can help her, but she can't ignore her instincts. As danger closes in, both Rebecca and Levi must figure out whom they can trust. With Rebecca's baby coming soon, there's no time to waste. Can the truth prevail . . . or will remorse overpower the best of intentions?

Torrents of Fear

The woman lingering in the crowd can't be Allison . . . can she? Because Allison was pronounced dead six years ago. Musician Carter Denver knows only one person who's capable of helping him find answers: Sadie Thompson, his estranged best friend and someone who also knew Allison. He needs to know if he's losing his mind or if Allison could have survived her car accident. Could Allison really be alive? If so, why is she trying to harm Carter and Sadie? As the two try to find answers, can Sadie keep her feelings for Carter hidden? Could he ever care for her, or is the man of her dreams still in love with the woman now causing his nightmares?

LANTERN BEACH PD

On the Lookout

When Cassidy Chambers accepted the job as police chief on Lantern Beach, she knew the island had its secrets. But a suspicious death with potentially far-reaching implications will test all her skills —and threaten to reveal her true identity. Cassidy enlists the help of her husband, former Navy SEAL Ty Chambers. As they dig for answers, both uncover parts of their pasts that are best left buried. Not everything is as it seems, and they must figure out if their John Doe is connected to the secretive group that has moved onto the island. As facts materialize, danger on the island grows. Can Cassidy and Ty discover the truth about the shadowy crimes in their cozy community? Or has darkness permanently invaded their beloved Lantern Beach?

Attempt to Locate

A fun girls' night out turns into a nightmare when armed robbers barge into the store where Cassidy and her friends are shopping. As the situation escalates and the men escape, a massive manhunt launches on Lantern Beach to apprehend the dangerous trio. In the midst of the chaos, a potential foe asks for Cassidy's help. He needs to find his sister who fled from the secretive Gilead's Cove community on the island. But the more Cassidy learns about the seemingly untouchable group, the more her unease grows. The pressure to solve both cases continues to mount. But as the gravity of the situation rises, so does the danger. Cassidy is determined to protect the island and break up the cult . . . but doing so might cost her everything.

First Degree Murder

Police Chief Cassidy Chambers longs for a break from the recent crimes plaguing Lantern Beach. She simply wants to enjoy her friends' upcoming wedding, to prepare for the busy tourist season about to slam the island, and to gather all the dirt she can on the suspicious community that's invaded the town. But trouble explodes on the island, sending residents—including Cassidy—into a squall of uneasiness. Cassidy may have more than one enemy plotting her demise, and the collateral damage seems unthinkable. As the temperature rises, so does the pressure to find answers. Someone is determined that Lantern Beach would be better off without their new police chief. And for Cassidy, one wrong move could mean certain death.

Dead on Arrival

With a highly charged local election consuming the community, Police Chief Cassidy Chambers braces herself for a challenging day of breaking up petty conflicts and tamping down high emotions. But when widespread food poisoning spreads among potential voters across the island, Cassidy smells something rotten in the air. As Cassidy examines every possibility to uncover what's going on, local enigma Anthony Gilead again comes on her radar. The man is running for mayor and his cult-like following is growing at an alarming rate. Cassidy feels certain he has a spy embedded in her inner circle. The problem is that her pool of suspects gets deeper every day. Can Cassidy get to the bottom of what's eating away at her peaceful island home? Will voters turn out despite the outbreak of illness plaguing their tranquil town? And the even bigger question: Has darkness come to stay on Lantern Beach?

Plan of Action

A missing Navy SEAL. Danger at the boiling point. The ultimate showdown. When Police Chief Cassidy Chambers' husband, Ty, disappears, her world is turned upside down. His truck is discovered with blood inside, crashed in a ditch on Lantern Beach, but he's nowhere to be found. As they launch a manhunt to find him, Cassidy discovers that someone on the island has a deadly obsession with Ty. Meanwhile, Gilead's Cove seems to be imploding. As danger heightens, federal law enforcement officials are called in. The cult's growing threat could lead to the pinnacle standoff of good versus evil. A clear plan of action is needed or the results will be devastating. Will Cassidy find Ty in time, or will she face a gut-wrenching loss? Will Anthony Gilead finally be unmasked for who he really is and be brought to justice? Hundreds of innocent lives are at stake . . . and not everyone will come out alive.

LANTERN BEACH BLACKOUT

Dark Water

Colton Locke can't forget the black op that went terribly wrong. Desperate for a new start, he moves to Lantern Beach, North Carolina, and forms Blackout, a private security firm. Despite his hero status, he can't erase the mistakes he's made. For the past year, Elise Oliver hasn't been able to shake the feeling that there's more to her husband's death than she was told. When she finds a hidden box of his personal possessions, more questions—and suspicions—arise. The only person she trusts to help her is her husband's best friend, Colton Locke. Someone wants Elise dead. Is it because she knows too much? Or is it to keep her from finding the truth? The Blackout team must uncover dark secrets hiding beneath seemingly still waters. But those very secrets might just tear the team apart.

Safe Harbor

Guilt over past mistakes haunts former Navy SEAL Dez Rodriguez. When he's asked to guard a pop star during a music festival on Lantern Beach, he's all set for what he hopes is a breezy assignment. Bree hasn't found fame to be nearly as fulfilling as she dreamed. Instead, she's more like a carefully crafted character living out a pre-scripted story. When a stalker's threats become deadly, her life—and career—are turned upside down. From the start, Bree sees her temporary bodyguard as a player, and Dez sees Bree as a spoiled rich girl. But when they're thrown together in a fight for survival, both must learn to trust. Can Dez protect Bree—and his carefully guarded heart? Or will their safe harbor ultimately become their death trap?

Ripple Effect

Griff McIntyre never expected his ex-wife and three-year-old daughter to come to Lantern Beach. After an abduction attempt, they're desperate for safety. Now Griff's not letting either of them out of his sight. Bethany knows Griff is the only one who can protect them, despite the fact that he broke her heart. But she'll do anything to keep her daughter safe—even if it means playing nicely with a man she can't stand. As peril ripples through their lives, Griff and Bethany must work together to protect their daughter. But an unseen enemy wants something from them . . . and will stop at nothing to get it. When disaster strikes, can Griff keep his family safe? Or will past mistakes bring the ultimate failure?

Rising Tide

Benjamin James knows there's a traitor within his former command. The rest of his team might even think it's him. As danger closes in, he must clear himself and stop a deadly plot by a dangerous terrorist group. All CJ Compton wanted was a new start after her career ended under suspicion. Working as the house manager for private security group Blackout seems perfect. But there's more trouble here than what she left behind. As the tide rushes in, the stakes continue to rise. If the Blackout team fails, it's not just Lantern Beach at stake—it's the whole country. Can Benjamin and CJ overcome their differences and work together to find the truth?

LANTERN BEACH BLACKOUT: THE NEW RECRUITS

Rocco

Former Navy SEAL and new Blackout recruit

Rocco Foster is on a simple in and out mission. But the operation turns complicated when an unsuspecting woman wanders into the line of fire. Peyton Ellison's life mission is to sprinkle happiness on those around her. When a cupcake delivery turns into a fight for survival, she must trust her rescuer—a handsome stranger—to keep her safe. Rocco is determined to figure out why someone is targeting Peyton. First, he must keep the intriguing woman safe and earn her trust. But threats continue to pummel them as incriminating evidence emerges and pits them against each other. With time running out, the two must set aside both their growing attraction and their doubts about each other in order to work together. But the perilous facts they discover leave them wondering what exactly the truth is . . . and if the truth can be trusted.

Axel

Women are missing. Private security firm Blackout must find them before another victim disappears. Axel Hendrix likes to live on the edge. That's why being a Navy SEAL suited him so well. But after his last mission, he cut his losses and joined Blackout instead. His team's latest case involves an undercover investigation on Lantern Beach. Olivia Rollins came to the island to escape her problems—and danger. When trouble from her past shows up in town, she impulsively blurts she's engaged to Axel, the womanizing man she's seen while waitressing. Now, she may not be the only one in danger. So could Axel. Axel knows Olivia might be his chance to find answers and that acting like her fiancé is the perfect cover for his latest assignment. But he doesn't like throwing Olivia into the middle of such a dangerous situation. Nor is he comfortable with the feelings she stirs inside him. With Olivia's life—as well as both their hearts—on the line, Axel must uncover the truth and stop an evil plan before more lives are destroyed.

Beckett

When the daughter of a federal judge is abducted, private security firm Blackout must find her. Psychologist Samantha Reynolds doesn't know why someone is targeting her. Even after a risky mission to save her, danger still lingers. She's determined to use her insights into the human mind to help decode the deadly clues being left in the wake of her rescue. Former Navy SEAL Beckett Jones needs to figure out who's responsible for the crimes hounding Sami. He's not sure why he's so protective of the woman he rescued, but he'll do anything to keep her safe—even if it means risking his heart. As the body count rises, there's no room for error. Beckett and Sami must both tear down the careful walls they've built around themselves in order to survive. If they don't figure out who's responsible, the madman will continue his death spree . . . and one of them might be next.

Gabe

When former Navy SEAL and current Blackout operative Gabe Michaels is almost killed in a hit-and-run, the aftermath completely upends his life. He's no longer safe—and he's not the only one. Dr. Autumn Spenser came to Lantern Beach to start fresh. But while treating Gabe after his accident, she senses there's more to what happened to him than meets the eye. When she digs deeper into his past, she never expects to be drawn into a deadly dilemma. Gabe has been infatuated with the pretty doctor since the day they met. Now, can he keep her from harm? Could someone out of his league ever return his feelings or will her past hurts keep them apart? As danger continues to pummel them, Gabe and Autumn are thrown together in a quest to find answers. More important than their growing attraction, they must stay alive long enough to stop the person desperate to destroy them.

LANTERN BEACH BLACKOUT: DANGER RISING

Brandon

Physically he's protecting her. But emotionally

she's never felt more exposed. The last person tech heiress Finley Cooper ever wanted to see again was Brandon Hale. Two years ago, Brandon shattered her heart. Now Finley needs protection, and, against her wishes, Brandon is assigned the job. Even worse, they must pretend to be a couple in order to find answers. Brandon, a former Navy SEAL, met Finley while on an undercover assignment in Ecuador. But he broke her trust, and now he doesn't blame Finley for hating him. As a new Blackout operative, Brandon's first assignment throws him into Finley's life 24/7. Someone wants her dead, and it's clear this person won't stop until that mission is accomplished. To keep her safe, Brandon must regain Finley's trust. Can he convince her she's more than a job to him? Or will peril permanently silence them?

Dylan

His job is to protect her. The trouble is . . . she doesn't want protection. Former Navy SEAL Dylan Granger's new assignment requires him to use both his tactical abilities and his acting skills. Hired by Katie Logan's father, his job is to protect the gutsy university professor while concealing his identity. To maintain his cover, he takes the unassuming role of her new assistant. Katie—a disgraced reporter—has stumbled upon a lead she can't ignore. Now it's clear someone is targeting her, but she refuses to back down. Her handsome new assistant is a welcome distraction from the chaos. But Dylan's skillset goes way beyond his job description, and Katie begins to suspect there's more to Dylan than he's letting on. Dylan's mission can't be disclosed—not if he wants to keep Katie safe. But as his feelings for her grow and the danger increases, keeping his secret becomes more of a challenge than he ever imagined. With innocent lives on the line, Dylan must choose between protecting Katie or savings others.

LANTERN BEACH MAYDAY

Run Aground

A dead captain on a luxury yacht leads to a tumultuous seafaring journey . . . Med student Kenzie Anderson, tired of letting others chart her future, accepts a job as second steward aboard *Almost Paradise*. But when she finds the captain dead before the charter even begins, her plans seem to capsize. Jimmy James Gamble senses something vulnerable and slightly naive about Kenzie when he finds her on the docks. Realizing danger may still be lingering close, he uses his hidden skills to earn a place on the charter. But being there causes him to risk everything —especially as more suspicious incidents occur. As they set out to sea, Kenzie and Jimmy James both wonder if they're in over their heads. They must figure out how to stop a killer before anyone onboard is hurt . . . otherwise, both their futures might just run aground.

Dead Reckoning

A yachtie fears for her life when she's the only witness to a murder . . . Kenzie Anderson knows what she saw at the harbor—a woman strangled and pushed overboard. But there's no proof of a crime . . . only her word. Jimmy James Gamble believes Kenzie, even if no one else does. As he senses the danger in the air, all he wants is to keep her away from any more trouble—especially after their last charter. Either Kenzie or the yacht they're working on seem to be a magnet for murder and mayhem. Someone is willing to kill to get what he wants—and will do so again if necessary. Can Jimmy James and Kenzie navigate these unfamiliar waters? Or will relying on dead reckoning lead them to their deaths?

Tipping Point

Awakening in a boat surrounded by nothing but water, a yachtie has no doubt someone wants her dead. Kenzie Anderson is determined not to let anyone scare her away from completing the charter season—even with the threats on her life. The only person she can trust is Captain Jimmy James Gamble, despite their tumultuous relationship. Kenzie and

Jimmy James both suspect turbulent currents rush beneath the tranquil surface aboard the luxury yacht *Almost Paradise*. Secrets seem to abound, each one increasing the tension aboard the boat. As answers rise to the surface, neither Kenzie nor Jimmy James is prepared for what they find. Have they both reached their tipping points? Their adversaries want nothing more than to make Kenzie disappear . . . forever. It may be too late for a mayday call.

COMPLETE BOOK LIST

Squeaky Clean Mysteries:

#1 Hazardous Duty

#2 Suspicious Minds

#2.5 It Came Upon a Midnight Crime (novella)

#3 Organized Grime

#4 Dirty Deeds

#5 The Scum of All Fears

#6 To Love, Honor and Perish

#7 Mucky Streak

#8 Foul Play

#9 Broom & Gloom

#10 Dust and Obey

#11 Thrill Squeaker

#11.5 Swept Away (novella)

#12 Cunning Attractions

#13 Cold Case: Clean Getaway

#14 Cold Case: Clean Sweep

#15 Cold Case: Clean Break

#16 Cleans to an End

While You Were Sweeping, A Riley Thomas Spinoff

The Sierra Files:

#1 Pounced

#2 Hunted

#3 Pranced

#4 Rattled

The Gabby St. Claire Diaries (a Tween Mystery series):

The Curtain Call Caper

The Disappearing Dog Dilemma

The Bungled Bike Burglaries

The Worst Detective Ever

#1 Ready to Fumble

#2 Reign of Error

#3 Safety in Blunders

#4 Join the Flub

#5 Blooper Freak

#6 Flaw Abiding Citizen

#7 Gaffe Out Loud

#8 Joke and Dagger

#9 Wreck the Halls

#10 Glitch and Famous

Raven Remington
Relentless

Holly Anna Paladin Mysteries:
#1 Random Acts of Murder
#2 Random Acts of Deceit
#2.5 Random Acts of Scrooge
#3 Random Acts of Malice
#4 Random Acts of Greed
#5 Random Acts of Fraud
#6 Random Acts of Outrage
#7 Random Acts of Iniquity

Lantern Beach Mysteries
#1 Hidden Currents
#2 Flood Watch
#3 Storm Surge
#4 Dangerous Waters
#5 Perilous Riptide
#6 Deadly Undertow

Lantern Beach Romantic Suspense
Tides of Deception
Shadow of Intrigue
Storm of Doubt
Winds of Danger

Gabe

Lantern Beach Mayday
Run Aground
Dead Reckoning
Tipping Point

Lantern Beach Blackout: Danger Rising
Brandon
Dylan
Maddox (coming soon)
Titus (coming soon)

Lantern Beach Christmas
Silent Night

Crime á la Mode
Dead Man's Float
Milkshake Up
Bomb Pop Threat
Banana Split Personalities

The Sidekick's Survival Guide
The Art of Eavesdropping
The Perks of Meddling
The Exercise of Interfering
The Practice of Prying
The Skill of Snooping

The Craft of Being Covert

Saltwater Cowboys

Saltwater Cowboy

Breakwater Protector

Cape Corral Keeper

Seagrass Secrets

Driftwood Danger

Unwavering Security

Beach House Mysteries

The Cottage on Ghost Lane

The Inn on Hanging Hill

The House on Dagger Point (coming soon)

School of Hard Rocks Mysteries

The Treble with Murder

Crime Strikes a Chord

Tone Death (coming soon)

Carolina Moon Series

Home Before Dark

Gone By Dark

Wait Until Dark

Light the Dark

Taken By Dark

Suburban Sleuth Mysteries:

Death of the Couch Potato's Wife

Fog Lake Suspense:
Edge of Peril
Margin of Error
Brink of Danger
Line of Duty
Legacy of Lies
Secrets of Shame
Refuge of Redemption

Cape Thomas Series:
Dubiosity
Disillusioned
Distorted

Standalone Romantic Mystery:
The Good Girl

Suspense:
Imperfect
The Wrecking

Sweet Christmas Novella:
Home to Chestnut Grove

Standalone Romantic-Suspense:
Keeping Guard

The Last Target
Race Against Time
Ricochet
Key Witness
Lifeline
High-Stakes Holiday Reunion
Desperate Measures
Hidden Agenda
Mountain Hideaway
Dark Harbor
Shadow of Suspicion
The Baby Assignment
The Cradle Conspiracy
Trained to Defend
Mountain Survival
Dangerous Mountain Rescue

Nonfiction:

Characters in the Kitchen

Changed: True Stories of Finding God through Christian Music (out of print)

The Novel in Me: The Beginner's Guide to Writing and Publishing a Novel (out of print)

ABOUT THE AUTHOR

USA Today has called Christy Barritt's books "scary, funny, passionate, and quirky."

Christy writes both mystery and romantic suspense novels that are clean with underlying messages of faith. Her books have won the Daphne du Maurier Award for Excellence in Suspense and Mystery, have been twice nominated for the Romantic Times Reviewers' Choice Award, and have finaled for both a Carol Award and Foreword Magazine's Book of the Year.

She is married to her Prince Charming, a man who thinks she's hilarious—but only when she's not trying to be. Christy is a self-proclaimed klutz, an avid music lover who's known for spontaneously bursting into song, and a road trip aficionado.

When she's not working or spending time with her family, she enjoys singing, playing the guitar, and exploring small, unsuspecting towns where people have no idea how accident-prone she is.

Find Christy online at:
    www.christybarritt.com
    www.facebook.com/christybarritt
    www.twitter.com/cbarritt

Sign up for Christy's newsletter to get information on all of her latest releases here: **www.christybarritt. com/newsletter-sign-up/**